The Grey Man
-Payback-

JL Curtis

Author's Note: This is a work of fiction. Names, characters, places, and incidents are a product of the author's imagination. Locales and public names are sometimes used for atmospheric purposes. Any resemblance to actual people, living or dead, or to businesses, companies, events, institutions, or locales is completely coincidental.

Available from Amazon.com in Kindle format or soft cover book, BN.com in Nook format. Printed by CreateSpace.

The Grey Man-Payback/ JL Curtis. -- 1st ed.
ISBN-13: 978-1500225698
ISBN-10: 150022569X

DEDICATION

Dedicated to the families those who serve in the military, Law Enforcement, Fire and EMS professions. They keep the home fires burning.

Charity suffereth long, and is kind; charity envieth not; charity vaunteth not itself, is not puffed up. Doth not behave itself unseemly, seeketh not her own, is not easily provoked, thinketh no evil. Rejoiceth not in iniquity, but rejoiceth in the truth. Beareth all things, believeth all things, hopeth all things, endureth all things.

1st Corinthians 13 verses 4-7 KJV

ACKNOWLEDGMENTS

Thanks to the usual suspects.

Special thanks to my editor Cara Lockwood.

Cover art by Tina Garceau.

Books by JL Curtis
The Grey Man- Vignettes

Table of Contents

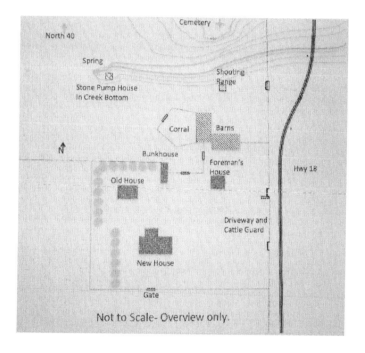

Layout of the Cronin Ranch main buildings.

Prolog

The old man drove slowly down Highway 67 toward Deputy Hart's location, wondering what he'd face at the scene. Regardless, he was out of the house and away from the *coven* as he now thought of the wedding planners. He didn't remember this much hate and discontent with Jack's wedding, but they'd been on the male side so it'd been fairly simple. Get a nice suit and show up: the total of their responsibility.

Looking out the windshield, he saw a ring of buzzards circling, so he knew he was close. Slowing down, he pulled off on the shoulder well short of Hart's cruiser. He steeled himself for whatever was to come. Knowing it was a signal seven call, he reached in the glove compartment and pulled out one of the cigars he kept there for just this reason.

He got out of the car and the odor of death assailed him; he lit the cigar immediately and was once again glad he got away with wearing the grey Dickies work shirt and pants rather than the standard uniform. Looking down to make sure his badge was secured on his belt, he hitched his gun belt, pulled out a pair of latex gloves and walked over to Deputy Hart. "What ya got Johnny?"

"Got a body, Captain Cronin, but… well there's no head and no hands."

"Ah crap. Did you call the sheriff or the Rangers?"

"Neither, I wasn't about to put that over the radio and figured he ain't going anywhere in the time it would take for you to get here."

The old man shrugged. "Okay, you call the sheriff right now on his cell, tell him to get rolling this way. Tell him to call Bucky enroute, and I'll call the Rangers."

Deputy Hart nodded. "Yes, sir. How much detail?"

The old man had his phone out and was looking at the body. "Limit the detail. Tell him I want him here."

Walking around the body, he dialed Ranger Clay Boone. "Clay, John Cronin. Got one you need to roll on. Signal seven at the first dirt road south of the sixty-seven and Old Alpine Road crossing."

Listening for a minute, he replied, "Yeah, Jose and Bucky are both going to be rolled in on this. So I'd let the major know if I were you. On and bring your full kit, we're going to need it."

He listened again, then said, "K, see you in thirty."

Turning back to Johnny Hart he asked, "You get hold of the sheriff?"

"Yes, sir. He said he'd be here in twenty."

The old man took out his wheel book and a pen. "Okay, now what caused you to come down this way?"

Hart said, "Buzzards. Don't normally see them around here, and it twern't one or two but probably ten or twelve. Saw them from sixty-seven as I came south. Decided to investigate, damn near wish I hadn't."

The old man nodded, looked at his watch and asked, "You just came on duty right? You relieved Merrill?"

"Yeah, we did a turnover and I came straight on out. He didn't say he'd seen anything unusual. I'm afraid I might have screwed the scene up. Hell, I thought it was probably a damn cow, and I drove right up."

The old man nodded and pulled out the phone again, dialing dispatch he waited. "Lisa, Captain Cronin. If you haven't already, turn Merrill around and get him headed back to the office. I need the patrol pattern and times he came by this location as best he can remember."

Nodding to himself he said, "Good girl! We're going to be here a while. Just have him complete it and go on home. If we have any questions, we'll call him."

Hanging up, he shoved the phone back in his shirt pocket and kneeled down. "Did you move the body at all?"

"No, sir. When I saw the head missing, I figured there wasn't going to be much I could do, so I called it in and waited. I set up a perimeter that extends back to the turn and left my car right where I stopped. The tape is where I've walked, best I can remember."

"Good job, Johnny, good job! Lemme see the soles of your boots."

Hart picked up each foot in turn as the old man took quick snapshots, then started backtracking toward the road along the tape. Getting back to the road, he looked for tracks and saw tire tracks extending in front of the cruiser; dropping evidence tags, he took photos of each of them. Walking further down, he could see where the tire tracks made a three point turn before heading back to Highway 67; more tags and photos followed.

As he walked back, he saw what looked like multiple tennis shoe tracks about three feet to the left of the tape. Carefully he dropped evidence tags on what looked like three or four pairs of tracks and broken vegetation.

With Hart's help he started compiling the evidence sheets and correlating them to the photos he was taking, while they waited for the rest of the folks to show up.

Hart finally said, "Captain, how do you handle this so calmly? It's all I can do to keep from throwing up, and you're acting like... Well, it's another day in the office."

The old man stopped and flipped ashes into a hole he'd dug in the dirt. "Johnny, I've been doing this for thirty years. Just because I don't appear to react doesn't mean I'm not tore up on the inside. I guess part of it is I had to learn how to deal with bodies in Vietnam, some of them friends of mine. It's a whole different level when you're stuffing pieces and parts in a damn body bag that was once the guy sitting next to you in the chow hall. And the smell here is nothing compared to a real battle. After a while your sense of smell just gets numb to it, I guess. Trust me, it don't make it any easier."

"But doesn't seeing a body without a head…"

"Yeah, it'll be another nightmare that will save itself for a night when I really need sleep," the old man continued. "The saving grace of this is we've got a chance, a slim one mind you, but a chance at actually catching the murderers and putting their asses away for a long time."

Hart nodded. "Makes sense. But with this one, well, it's obvious he wasn't killed here. No blood pooling and the lividity looks wrong. All you've got is a body and tire tracks."

The old man replied, "True, but those are clues in themselves. This is probably a cartel killing, and if we can find out why that will point us to who. That will narrow down the list of suspects, and there's usually at least one that will roll over, either through fear or self-preservation." Cocking his head, he heard cars coming hard on Highway 67. "And here comes the cavalry, so it's time to get to work. If you want to continue this conversation later we can, Okay?"

"Yes sir, I want to learn, but I wouldn't want your job," Hart replied.

Another Day at the Office

The old man, Sheriff Rodriguez, Texas Ranger Clay Boone, and Bucky Hendrix from the Laredo office of the DEA[1] were taking a break and brainstorming who might be lying in the bar ditch when the old man suddenly cussed and trotted over to his cruiser. Reaching in, he pulled out a file from his gear bag and flipped through it rapidly. He pulled one piece of paper out and hurried back to the group, "I knew something about this was bugging me. It was that damn BOLO[2] from Brewster County that came out Tuesday morning. Jose you need to make a call, I think we've found Eddie Guilfoile Junior."

Clay started cussing viciously, startling all the others. "Gahdammit, this ain't good at all, his old man is in Huntsville doing three to five for smuggling marijuana and this has all the signs of a cartel hit. I need to make some calls."

The sheriff looked at the BOLO and walked back to the body. "Yeah, red and white striped shirt, blue jeans, six-one. Let's measure what we've got and see."

The sheriff held the tape against the bottom of the left foot, which had set pretty straight, and the

---

[1] Drug Enforcement Agency
[2] Be On Look the Out

old man measured to the top of the body and said, "Yep, five-three, maybe five-four. There's a formula for that, but I can't remember it right now, so I'm just adding ten inches so that makes it six-one or two, which fits. Let's go ahead and release the body to the coroner, we can't do anymore now. I'd suggest you have Sheriff Garcia send a car out to the house and see if the head or hands are in the mailbox or on the front porch, or hell, maybe sitting in the car seat."

Bucky came over. "None of the pocket litter tests positive for anything, shoes are clean; I think this is a payback killing."

Jose hung up and said, "Hector is going to send a unit and he's going personally to see if he can get a better description of the shirt and pants. Turns out the kid was an athlete, starting tight end on the football team and point guard on the basketball team. He was pretty much the opposite of his old man."

The sheriff motioned to the ambulance crew that had been standing by. "Go ahead and bag the body, you'll be taking it to the Coroner in Brewster County since it's closer and Doc Truesdale is out of town. If it is the Guilfoile kid, then so much the better."

The crew worked quickly, loaded the stretcher, and headed for the coroner's office in Alpine.

Clay and Bucky came back to the old man's car, with Clay saying, "Looks like the Guilfoile boy's old man got in a beef with a cartel type in the Goree Unit a couple of weeks ago. That whole situation is screwed up; Goree is used for non-violent offenders to train horses, but they run all the illegals through

there on the way to deportation. Apparently the
cartel types sent an enforcer to take care of him, but
he cut the enforcer up with his own shiv. The
enforcer was known as Smiley, so Guilfoile gave
him an ear-to-ear smile, then dared any of the rest of
them to come get him. As soon as the guards came
on the yard, he dropped the knife and just stood
there. They rolled him over to the Walls unit and his
parole hearing was supposed to be today. I think
they're gonna let him out in the next day or two,
probably Monday."

Bucky nodded. "Yeah. I've heard of Fast Eddie.
He's a Cedar chopper down by Big Bend and he's
always been on the fringes of whatever illegal stuff
needs to be moved. Low-level type, just wants to
put food on the table. But he's one of those cat-
quick little shits and apparently has quite the
temper."

The old man asked, "If he's a little shit, how do
you explain a six-one kid? And they're gonna let
him *out*?"

Clay kicked at a rock. "Well, he's married to an
Irish girl named Iris that came over from the old
country and apparently she tops him by at least four
or five inches. I'm thinking her side of the genes
won. As far as letting him out, he'd had a perfect
record for the last three years, and was a trustee.
Hell, he's the one that trained Dusty, my buckskin!"

The old man shook his head. "Well, Bucky, I
think this one is going to fall into your and Clay's
bailiwick as a cartel job, and it appears we've got a
hit team working this side of the border. Normally,

that crap stays over in Arizona, but if it's coming here, there must be some indicators we're missing."

Clay said, "That's the problem, we've had no indications of anything out of the ordinary. I'm going to Huntsville on Monday to see if I can tease out who and what cartel group this guy that Guilfoile had the beef with is associated with. Bucky, can you check with EPIC[3] and see if they've got anything?"

Bucky nodded and made a note on his pad.

The old man looked at his watch and decided to head back to town for lunch rather than go home, since he figured the women were all still there, *planning.* He hit the truck stop on I-10 and grabbed a burger, then went to the office and worked on the report from the crime scene. He downloaded the pictures and formatted them into the document and thanked his stars they'd gone digital. Ten years ago, he'd have had to go to the lab, print the pictures, wait for them to dry, cut and paste them into the report; and if somebody wanted another copy, he'd have to do it all over again. By the time he had all the forms filled out, the evidence logged and the reports emailed to the various agencies, it was almost 6 PM.

He got up and groaned, rolled his shoulders and tried to get the kinks out. *John Cronin you're getting too old for this shit between the Army and now thirty years as a deputy sheriff,* he thought. Halfway succeeding, he stopped by dispatch on the way out and told them he was going home, and that he would be out of town Monday and Tuesday. Lisa noted the

---

[3] El Paso Intelligence Center

information in the log and wished him a good evening.

As he drove home he debated how much to tell Jesse; then decided what the hell, she needed to know and he was tired of her bitching about not being in the loop. He also made a mental note to get Francisco to make sure all the rear accesses to the property were locked all the time. He figured he'd better let the neighbors know too, since Highway 18 was a major cut-through from I-10 to I-20.

The old man pulled into the drive and was relieved to see the driveway was empty. His thoughts bounced wildly from subject to subject as he drove in. *Jack, I wish you and Pat could see your little girl now, and I'm sorry she got hooked up with a Marine, but he's a good kid and he loves her. This whole wedding is getting out of hand, and thankfully there isn't a coven of damn women here again. How are they going to explain that kid's death to his parents, much less with the father in prison?*

As the old man walked in the house, Rex slunk out of the office to come see him. "Yeah, Rex, it's me and you against all of them, ain't it." Rex wagged his tail and whuffed in agreement. The old man took off his hat, gun and handcuffs and hung the belt on the hat rack next to the desk. He looked at the desk and realized Jesse hadn't even been in the office all afternoon. Shaking his head, he headed for the kitchen with Rex following close behind.

Juanita, the wife of the ranch foreman, and Jesse were sitting at the table, looking at one of what seemed like a six-inch stack of books, and laughing.

He thought to himself *Juanita has become Jesse's de facto mother figure. Hard to believe she and Francisco have been here almost twenty years now. God, Jesse is a grown woman, fixin' to get married. Where have all the years gone?* As he stepped into the kitchen he took the laughter as a good sign saying, "I take it y'all made some progress today?"

Jesse looked up, "Papa, there is no such thing. At this point I think we're in a holding action, and I'm about to tell every one of the bridesmaids to wear what the hell they want! I swear, I thought we all got along, but now I'm beginning to wonder if eloping might make more sense!"

He laughed and took the cup of coffee Juanita handed him. "Well, that would certainly be a lot cheaper! Damn church is going to cost me a mint, and both the *padre* and the preacher are trying to hit me up to donate a little extra to the churches."

Juanita slapped him lightly on the arm. "John, do not profane the church, you know the *padre* is just doing what he does."

Francisco and Toby, the ranch hand, walked in and Francisco said, "Now what did the *padre* do?"

The old man laughed again, earning glares from both Juanita and Jesse. "Oh the usual, trying to scam me out of my money!"

Exclamations of "John!" and "Papa!" sounded in chorus as the two women rounded on him. He held up his hands, "Just joking, just joking!"

Francisco, the ranch foreman, snuck up behind his wife, Juanita, and kissed her on the neck tickling her with his moustache. This prompting her to swat at him and jokingly say, "You smell like a horse. You will take a bath before you come to bed, otherwise it's the couch for you!"

He just smiled and eased around to sit down and pet Rex, as the old man jumped in, "Juanita, you know I'm only paying for one bath a week for him, so I guess…"

Juanita interrupted, "You want to be fed or not John Cronin?"

The old man bowed in defeat, and everyone laughed. Juanita bustled around the kitchen with Jesse helping get dinner ready, and quickly the meal was on the table; they enjoyed chatting as they ate, and Toby reported he'd finished the two horses Ellington wanted broken.

As Juanita was dishing up the left over cobbler and adding ice cream, the old man decided now was as good as any time to update them on what had gone on today. Some might find it strange to be discussing dead bodies over dessert, but Francisco, in addition to being the ranch foreman was a reserve deputy sheriff as was Jesse; Juanita was an RN although not working as one, and Toby was the grandson of a Montagnard family that the old man, Billy and other 5th Special Forces men had lived and fought with in Vietnam back in the sixties. None of them so much as turned a hair at the change of subject, since between ranch life and law enforcement, birth death and everything in between was seen, discussed, and dissected over the dinner table.

They discussed lighting changes, including reactivating the motion sensors at the driveway and the back gate, and putting the sodium lights down by the bunkhouse back on line. The old man decided to reactivate the motion lights at the corners of the house and just live with the occasional animal that would wander by at night and trip them. Toby suggested moving Diablo up to the first stall in the barn and leaving the door open so Diablo had access to the corral. While Toby had trained Diablo, and he was gentle as a lamb with him; anyone other than Toby or the old man got to see another side of Diablo. He tolerated the women, but neither had ever tried to ride him.

He and Francisco decided to close the back gate and open up the honey pot north of the house just in case somebody tried to sneak in that way. Opening the gate at the cattle guard, and putting down a couple of feed lot panels cut and bent into little pungi stakes just inside the cattle guard would stop any car or person stupid enough to try that entry.

On the south side, just in case anybody tried to come across the pasture, they'd stake out some tag ends of barbed wire rolls across the likely lines of approach to the pasture gate at the front of the house. The old man reminded Toby that he would have to be more careful in both those pastures in the future.

After dinner he adjourned to the office and saved a copy of the incident report from earlier onto his hard drive and copied it to one of those new 'thumb' drives as people were calling them. He figured with multiple copies, his butt was covered.

Going back to the kitchen for another cup of coffee, he casually threw out, "Oh, DEA and CBP[4] want me down at Laredo to assist with another class of new officers, so I'm going down tomorrow and will be down there Monday and Tuesday teaching."

Francisco smiled and nodded, while both Juanita and Jesse glared at him again. "Hey, they asked me, I didn't ask them. Besides, Charlie's on vacation and if I don't do it that leaves Bucky and you know how bad an instructor he is."

Jesse nodded ruefully. "Yeah, for somebody that knows as much as he does, he couldn't instruct his way out of a paper bag. You would think they'd send him to school or something!"

The old man said, "Well he is a sector supervisor, so technically he's not supposed to be teaching, just management. But if you stuck Bucky in an office, he'd go nuts. Anyway, with this new administration, they're trying to revise the instructional courses to make them politically correct; so if we're going to tell the newbies the truth, now is the time to do it."

Francisco said, "Truth is good, politics is not. But we know that don't we?"

Jesse giggled. "Oh God, I can't imagine Bucky as politically correct, nor Aaron or Matt! Speaking of Marines, Felicia called today they've been heard from! Matt heard from Aaron and they are still on track to be back in eighteen days. Felicia said Matt already has his leave approved, and she's put in for

---

[4] Customs and Border Patrol

vacation, so the three of them will drive here in Aaron's truck then Matt and Felicia will fly back."

The old man teased, "So double wedding? Is that the hold up?"

Juanita laughed, but Jesse just cocked her head. "Uh, probably not, but I think they're getting serious, although they both say they're only friends. But I know from Angelina that Felicia is pretty damn serious about Matt. She's asking Angelina what the family would think, so I'm betting if there aren't any problems we'll be doing this again in a year for her and Matt."

Juanita said, "That would be good. Felicia needs to remarry and Matt needs a good woman. I think you're right, Jesse. Do you know how many Marines are coming for the wedding yet?"

Jesse said, "I think three plus Matt to match the number of bridesmaids. When we add Trey and Beverly that gives us five of each; that's supposed to be lucky, so that's what we're going with."

The old man chuckled. "Well, Trey makes two of any normal person, so you're one behind."

Jesse reached out to slap the old man. "Hey, no making fun of Trey. He can't help that he's a big guy! He told me he's down to two-fifty from his playing weight of three-oh-five."

The old man laughed. "Still, he makes two of any of us. And it'll be interesting to see the Marines' reaction to him and Beverly."

Jesse nodded. "I really don't see a problem, Marines can and do deal with everything and everybody on any given day. As Aaron said, they're all Marine Green at the end of the day."

Juanita continued wiping down the counter and finally said, "In that case, we'll put Trey and Beverly in the guest room here, as big as he is, there isn't another bed he'll fit it. We'll give the girls the old house and we can clean up the bunkhouse and put all the Marines there."

The women went back to chatting about details and the old man made a graceful exit to go pack.

***

At breakfast the next morning Toby was wearing the Gerber Bowie that the old man had given him for Christmas, so he understood what was going on. Francisco was still working with Toby on both English and Spanish, but it was a slow process, and Francisco realized he was learning Degar almost as fast as Toby was learning Spanish. Their conversations now veered through three languages and he envied John the ability to speak Degar as fluently as he did.

Jesse wore jeans and her Colt Python on her hip. The old man looked at Juanita and she just patted her apron with a smile. Francisco and the old man discussed ranch business and they decided that either Francisco or Toby would be around the ranch at all times. Juanita and Jesse decided to split up the off ranch requirements like shopping and Jesse's work by having Juanita vary her times into town and where she shopped, and Jesse decided to alter her times to and from work and use the Suburban instead of the GTO for the time being.

The old man ruffled Rex's fur and said, "And don't forget Rex. He knows friends and he's not a bad watch dog as long as he's not getting fed by the bad guys. In this case an ounce of prevention is worth a pound of cure!"

Everybody laughed at Rex, who looked at the old man with an injured expression. The old man said, "Okay, I'll be back late Tuesday, and I'll call before I come into the driveway."

Laredo

The old man pulled into the hotel at 6 PM, and was met in the lobby by Bucky who said, "I was beginning to wonder if you'd blown me off."

The old man replied, "Nah. I made the mistake of stopping by work on the way, and the sheriff wanted a few clarifications on the report from yesterday on the body. Do you know if they confirmed it was the Guilfoile kid?"

Bucky said, "Yeah, I got a call from Brewster County. They found the kid's head in the mailbox and the hands wired to the steering wheel of the car. Thankfully the mother didn't see it, but she's pretty torn up. Huntsville is springing Eddie today, and I guess they'll tell him before they release him."

The old man shook his head. "That just sucks. Since when are kids fair game?"

"Well, it's been a way of life in *Mehico*, when you go back to the original expansion of the Medellin cartel and them going after the Federales. If they couldn't get the guy, they either kidnapped his family or took them out. Nowadays, they just kill the families first, then the Federale when he goes bat nuts and comes after them. They are coming across the border after folks, but that's mainly been over around Phoenix and Tucson and points south.

EPIC didn't have any firm data on any hit teams, so they didn't even put anything out."

The old man shook his head. "Assholes. And yet DHS is saying the border is safe. Yeah, right."

***

In Huntsville, the warden hung up the phone and looked at his deputy. "This is just the shits. That was the sheriff over in Brewster County. Guilfoile's son was murdered but they didn't get an ID until yesterday afternoon, and he wants us to make the notification prior to releasing him. I guess we better try to get the wife available to talk to him as soon as we make notification, and I want him out of here directly after that. I do not want him to go back to the cage."

The deputy warden sighed. "Yeah, that is really a shitty way to find out, and you know he's going to go after somebody for this."

The warden pulled out his wallet and reached in, pulling out what cash he had and counted it up, as he looked at the deputy. "Can you spare twenty until tomorrow? It ain't much, but I want to make sure Guilfoile's got enough to take a bus and then a taxi to get home. If I remember right, the bus stops in Alpine, and he's all the way down in the south end of the county."

The deputy warden fished around and came up with a twenty and handed it over. "Ah hell, consider it a donation... He did three years at Goree and kept his nose clean until that little dustup and he didn't kill the guy when he could have. He's been here two weeks and didn't cause any problems with anybody, he just stayed real quiet. Let him go at noon with the rest of the releases?"

"Yeah, we'll make the call to get his wife on the phone at eleven tomorrow. I'm surprised we haven't heard from her yet," the warden said.

Prisoners were normally held 24-48 hours in Walls unit in the 'cage' and then released out the front door of the forbidding brick building with a bus ticket home. Dressed in over-starched, badly-fitting clothes that came from Goodwill, prisoners didn't mind since at least they weren't prison garb. But with the clothes and shaved head, everyone who sees them, knows exactly where they're coming from.

***

Bucky was driving the old man to one of his favorite hole-in-the-wall restaurants, planning for the seminar along the way. They talked about the class schedule and how much time the old man would have to teach, and discussed using the new classroom and computer hook up to do a show and tell from the cameras. Bucky was enthusiastic about trying it, but agreed they would need to go in early and see if it was possible. He also gave the old man a rundown on the class and the students, noting that over half the class was ex-military.

The next morning the old man rolled out at his usual time, and grumbled to himself that the hotel's free breakfast didn't start until six. Finding a greasy spoon, he ate a quick breakfast and asked for a to-go on the coffee, much to the surprise of the waitress. She'd been bright and cheerful, so the old man left her a better tip and reminded himself to be nicer to folks in the mornings.

He pulled into the parking lot at the border crossing, and stood sipping his coffee as he waited for Bucky, who got there minutes later. Walking in, he greeted a few folks that he knew, and Bucky led him into the control room. The old man looked around in amazement. "Damn, somebody spent some dollars here!"

Bucky grinned. "Yeah, they're throwing dollars squared at us, and this is one of the results. Big screens, multiple cameras simultaneously, lots of new PTZ cameras and both color and IR[5] heads in the same boxes."

The old man said, "Whoa, PTZ? IR I'm assuming is infrared, what the hell is PTZ? Ah, do you still have the cameras on the other side? The ones that got placed by friends?"

Bucky said, "PTZ is pan, tilt, zoom, and yeah we've still got the extra cameras." Turning to the young kid on the console, he said, "Bring up panel… ummm, four I think it is."

The console operator said, "Is he cleared sir? You know we're not supposed to— "

Bucky interrupted, "Yeah, they were his idea, so he's definitely cleared. Now do it."

---

[5] Infrared

The old man grinned at Bucky as one of the big screens flipped to a whole new set of cameras, albeit ones with much lower definition than the ones they'd just been watching. These were showing the lines of trucks and cars awaiting clearance, and showed drivers and others milling around on the approach to the bridges and also down two of the side streets by the Cantina.

The old man said, "Have y'all seen any indication anybody has tumbled to these being over there?"

Bucky said, "Yeah, we got our friends to move one of them that the Zetas picked up on, but they don't appear to know about the others. Or they just think they are security cameras for the businesses over there, since they are visible if you look for them. The one we replaced got moved across the street and under the soffit of the *tacqueria*."

The old man nodded in satisfaction. "Now, the question is, can we remote these back to the classroom?"

The console operator looked at Bucky who nodded at him; the operator pulled up another set of screens on his console and said, "Displays nine and ten, right?"

Bucky said, "Yeah, that sounds right, push 'em over and I'll go check," as he walked out of the control room. Moments later he was back. "Yep, that worked! I killed the screens so for now just leave them on the push. I'll flip from the computer to them when we need 'em."

The operator nodded and went back to his scan, ignoring both of them. Bucky grinned and motioned the old man out of the room. "They don't like us coming in and quote bothering them unquote, and they keep lobbying for a cypher controlled door, so they can keep folks out they don't like."

The old man shook his head. "This younger generation is in their own little world, and I'm firmly convinced they would rather interact with a damn computer than another human being! Now, where's the damn coffee!"

Bucky laughed and led the old man to the break room and the coffee and donuts. "See? Only the best: day old coffee and day old donuts. You should be right at home!"

"Screw you, Bucky, and I know damn well this coffee is fresh. The night shift goes through at least two or three pots unless you fired 'em all. And I'll pass on the donuts, never particularly cared for them."

They picked up the coffee and moved to the classroom, with Bucky finally getting the computer to cooperate as he found the lesson he was required to teach this morning. He finally turned to the old man. "Lemme burn through this mandated crap and then we'll start their real education, if that's alright with you."

John nodded as the first students started trickling into the classroom, and Bucky started chivying folks into their seats, filling out the name cards on the tables, and filling out the myriad of documents to prove they'd actually attended the training. The last thing was the signup sheet circling the room so Bucky would know who was who.

The old man just shook his head, thinking back thirty years to his introduction to working with the DEA.

He'd shown up on a Monday in Jacksonville, FL was issued gear, two passports, one in his courier cover and one in his real cover and was on his way to South America on Tuesday morning as a "courier" for a diplomatic pouch carrying his equipment. When he'd arrived in Brasilia, he was promptly driven to the embassy, changed clothes, turned over his courier passport, and was back at the airport in three hours. Put on a Heli-Courier and flown out of Brazil to a camp in Guatemala, he'd been dumped on the side of an unimproved runway and sat for two hours until someone had shown up to pick him up. It wasn't until he'd been in the camp that anyone actually questioned him about his qualifications, and his training consisted of OJT in the jungles and a passing grade was that he survived.

Truly a different world today: governed by bureaucracy, paper pushers, and checks in the block along with, in many cases, CYA leadership that really didn't want the boat rocked, or at least not rocked by anyone under them. The old man was really glad he was just a deputy sheriff and didn't have to play those games anymore.

On the Podium

The old man sat in the back of the room for the first two hours and mentally cataloged the students based on their interactions with Bucky, wondering how many would last more than a year once they actually got in the field. He picked out two he figured were former Marines, and three that either had to be Army or Navy vets. One of the females had to have been military police from her comments, and looked familiar but he couldn't pick which service she'd been in. Bucky finally finished the mandated lecture material, and gave the kids a 15-minute break.

As the students filed back in, the old man was standing at the podium with Bucky off to the side. The students' curiosity was aroused even more, as the old man hadn't been introduced before and Bucky waited until they were all back and in their seats before doing so. "Okay, as you've been told, at times we bring in experts to teach classes down here, and this old fart..." Bucky waited for the expected laughter to die down, "Is one of them. Matter of fact, I'd almost say he's a dinosaur, he's so old. But seriously, this is Captain John Cronin, Pecos County Sheriff's department and literally one of the experts on catching smugglers of both drugs and people. You may look at him and think: what can an old deputy sheriff teach me? Well, lemme give you the rest of the story. Former Green Beret in Vietnam, two years with the DEA back in the bad old days, graduate of the FBI National Academy, and been catching smugglers for over twenty years worldwide. He's a DOJ[6] and FBI consultant on smuggling, loaned out to foreign countries, and a couple of months ago he helped bust a twenty-four million dollar heroin shipment and as a bonus, saved twenty-two kidnapped women and one small boy over in Thailand. In other words pay attention. John?"

The old man nodded. "Well, after that build up I have nowhere to go but down, so let's get to it. First, I don't have any of those fancy slides or pictures, or anything else till we get to the cameras."

He walked around the podium and hooked his hip on the edge of the table, "First let's talk about people and their reactions…"

An hour later, after a break, he gave them his thoughts on vehicles and other ways of smuggling both drugs and people. At noon, they called it for lunch and he and Bucky hit the roach coach outside in the parking lot. The young female the old man had finally pegged as part of the raid on the house came over. "Can I say something sir?"

He said, "Sure, sit and eat, Spears, but first I gotta know, ex-Army or Air Force? And how did you get from DHS to CBP?"

---

[6] Department of Justice

She sat and said, "Air Force, six years, one tour at Bagram. And I wanted to apologize to you for that bullshit raid we did. That was just wrong."

Cronin shrugged and, she continued. "I saw a post on USA Jobs for CBP agents, and I jumped at the chance. Used my veteran's preference and lateraled across about a month after that POS raid."

"Couldn't stand the treatment of women you saw over there or at DHS, right?"

She looked sharply at him. "How did you know?"

He said simply, "You're not the first, and you won't be the last. Any languages?"

She nodded. "Spanish, a little bit of Pashtu and Urdu."

"Okay, those will work down here. Now what was your question?"

"Well. sir, you never mentioned people that looked heavier than they should, for us that was a clue they might have a vest on. And you didn't distinguish between men and women smuggling drugs."

The old man said, "No, I didn't because you will see people wearing everything they own, and the cartels aren't much into suicide bombers over here yet. As far as not distinguishing, the cartels will use anybody, male female, dead alive or in between. They are looking at moving product any way they can, by as many means as they can. They love to use decoys to attract our attention especially with females, whom they consider disposable, just like the Middle Eastern males do."

She acknowledged his comment and the three of them chatted as they finished their sandwiches. At 1300 the class reconvened and Bucky brought up the two sets of cameras. The old man stepped to the side and said, 'Okay what you're seeing here are the bridge cameras on the right and some other cameras on the left. The ones on the left we don't talk about outside this room. Also you don't speculate on where they might be, and for damn sure when you take your walking tour across the bridge you don't try to spot them. Now the three cameras I want you to focus on the right screen are the two in the upper right leading to bridge four, which is the commercial bridge, and on the left screen the second camera from the bottom. Y'all just watch them for a few minutes and then we'll talk about what you're seeing."

After a few minutes he asked, "Anybody noticing anything unusual?"

One of the youngsters he'd pegged as a former Army SF[7] said, "Yeah, the approach camera shows some hinky-acting drivers, and others that seem totally unconcerned. I know you said it's all about profiles this morning but I really didn't understand it."

The old man said, "Okay, anybody else notice that?" A chorus of agreement sounded in response, "Okay, when I said profiling, what you're looking for is the out of the ordinary actions. Those drivers that are acting hinky, as you call it, are legal drivers

---

[7] Special Forces

who are scared shitless the cartel is going to shove something into their cabs or under their trailer somewhere and force them to be decoys while the cartel tries to sneak a shipment through. Notice the guy five trucks behind the driver in the white shirt, he's got on a red shirt? See how he appears totally unconcerned right now?"

Again a chorus of affirmatives. "He's walked off twice and left his truck completely, once walking up to the *tacqueria* and once for a coke. He's probably a cartel driver or protected driver, so they won't screw with him. The other thing to watch for is which lane the drivers go for, if one lane is slower coming through, they'll think that lane is getting more scrutiny and try to position themselves in the other lane. That is a good cue to watch them."

Looking at Bucky he said, "Bucky, you want to tell them the dirty little secret?"

Bucky said, "Sometimes we let ones we're pretty sure are carrying go through, but we throw a GPS tracker on them, and follow the trailer. We've gotten some good busts off that, and they usually don't even know the tracking bug is there. It's designed to fall off after seventy-two hours and if we haven't gotten them by then, they are probably clean."

The old man's cell phone rang, and he stepped into the hall to take the call. Bucky finished the lecture and called another break as the old man stepped back into the classroom. He turned to Bucky. "Well, don't that beat all, appears Cho needs me to come back to Thailand to testify against those Chinese smugglers and kidnapping ring we broke up last year. I guess the twenty odd kidnapped women and a few million dollars' worth of heroin aren't enough evidence; according to Cho either I come back and testify or the powers that be are going to drop the case. And it appears he did an official request through State, but I haven't seen or heard anything. Is there an office I can use? I need to call the sheriff and the FBI and see what's up."

Bucky nodded. "Sure, second office on the left is mine."

The old man went into the office, closed the door and hit speaker on the phone as he pulled out his wheel book. Dialing the sheriff's cell he waited patiently until the sheriff picked up. "Jose? John. Have you seen anything come down from the Fibbies or State about me going to Thailand to testify on that smuggling situation from a few months ago?"

Jose answered, "Not a thing, either in email or snail mail, but let me check right quick." The old man heard keystrokes in the background, then, "Nope, nothing. You want me to call or are you going to?"

The old man replied, "I'll call my contact. Something's not right here, and I don't want to stir the pot till we figure it out."

"Okay, how's the class going?"

"Good. They've got some sharp folks coming through, and I truly hope we can get some of them in our area. Lemme go make some more calls just to make sure. You've got no problem with me going, right?"

The sheriff replied, "Dammit, you know better than that. If you need to go, go!"

"Thanks. Jose. I'll let you know what falls out of this one." Hanging up, the old man next dialed the SAC[8] at the National Academy. After discussions with him, it was pretty much a done deal that State had not forwarded the request to either the FBI or to the Sheriff. Apparently they were now in the slow-roll mode on any requests that could possibly have a negative impact on any Chinese interactions, because SECSTATE wanted to control all interactions. The SAC said he would back-channel the Legate in Bangkok, but if John went it would probably be as a private citizen with no official cover.

Getting more pissed by the minute, the old man decided to go, even if it was on his dime, since he truly hated kidnappers and smugglers. Calling Cho back, he told him he would be there Sunday and he expected to be reimbursed for his time and travel, which Cho graciously agreed to do. Cho even offered to make hotel reservations and provide Som, whom the old man had first met at NA last year and had driven him during the original investigation, as the driver again.

The old man got online and made reservations for Saturday from Dallas to Hong Kong, and return in a week, thinking that in case State was really watching who went where, this would at least not be quite as obvious. He then called Cathay Pacific's 800 number and made a separate reservation from

---

[8] Senior Agent in Charge

Hong Kong to Bangkok for Sunday morning and return that allowed him to make the other flights. He requested the airline hold those tickets for pickup in Hong Kong, rather than merge the two fares.

He called the sheriff back and told him he would be back tonight and needed vacation for a week, and filled him in on what was going on. Jose told the old man to stuff it, that it was a working trip.

Walking back to the conference room, he caught up with Bucky. "Well, State is slow rolling everything, sounds like politics is being played again. I'm taking off Saturday for Thailand via Hong Kong to testify against those smugglers, but I'm going as a private citizen, can you believe that shit?"

Bucky shrugged, "With the powers that be now, yeah. You want to finish up with the cameras and intel? I can cover the rest of it so you can get out of here."

"Thanks, sounds like a plan."

Back in the classroom, the old man went back to the podium. "Okay, now we know who the player is today, so we're going to let him go through and tag him; but what I want you to watch is how he positions his truck when we jump the first driver in the white shirt. Bucky have them open the truck gates again and let's watch the fun."

Bucky stepped out and returned a few moments later, giving a thumb's up. On camera, the class could see the gates swing open and trucks begin to roll slowly into the lanes. The on-duty officers checked paperwork against cargo, weight, lights, and safety equipment for each rig. On cue, three more officers and a K-9 descended on white shirt, and the player immediately jockeyed to get over into the next lane. While the four officers worked over the truck, the adjacent lanes moved through with minimum hassles, and mostly just walk-arounds of the trucks. When the player came into the lane, he got the same treatment, with one notable exception, when the officer bent down looking at the air tanks, he palmed a small GPS transmitter to the bottom of the back tank. He stood up and gave the driver back his paperwork and he rolled out of the station.

As Bucky left to go talk to the officer, the old man asked, "Did anyone see anything different there?"

Officer Spears said, "Maybe, but I'm not sure. If there was a tag put on, how was it done? By the officer doing the inspection, or by another officer?"

The old man picked up a tag from the podium saying, "Okay, nice catch. Here is a tag, you can see this is pretty small, and you can see they are marked on the tape side with numbers. These equate to the time in hours the tape will stay attached." Passing it to the first table he continued, "Note on top there is a four digit code, this is the tracker PIN that gets entered into the monitoring system to allow it to display on the monitors here, or be pushed to units in the field."

Bucky came back and walked to the podium; after a few keystrokes the left display changed to a rolling map display with the tracker displayed in the center. "Okay, here's twenty-one sixty-four, it's on the cab of the truck, and his stated destination on the paperwork is Bellaire, Texas. We'll leave this one up in the corner and see where he really goes…"

Mixed Feelings

Eddie Guilfoile walked out of the Walls unit and down the steps in a fog. His mind was reeling between freedom and hatred for those who killed his son, and in no small measure, disbelief that the warden had given him money and they'd let him go after cutting up that enforcer. Knowing Iris was not waiting as he watched the others run across street to meet loved ones, he turned and started the long walk down to the bus station. Wrapped up in his own mind, he ignored a horn honking after he looked up and made sure he was still on the sidewalk. The car honked again, and he continued to ignore it, trying to wrap his mind around the fact that he'd never see Junior again, and that Iris was a lot stronger than he'd thought. Suddenly he heard a siren burp, and looked over in irritation, only to see Ranger Clay Boone. He walked over after the ranger motioned to him, "What do you want Mr. Clay?"

Clay replied, "Eddie, I'm truly sorry to hear about Junior, and I was over here on business and thought I'd see if you wanted a ride back home. It'd beat riding the bus all night."

Eddie straightened up and looked around, weighing his options. He wasn't really sure he wanted to spend nine hours in a car with the Ranger, but it would get him home a lot faster than riding that damn bus. And if he saved the money, maybe he could get Iris a dress to wear for the funeral and maybe pay some for a stone for Junior. He leaned over. "Sure, Mr. Clay, if you don't mind, I'd appreciate it."

Clay unlocked the door as Eddie walked around the front of the car, heading toward the back door. Clay motioned him to the front seat and Eddie shook his head then opened the front door and sat gingerly in the front, trying to not bang into the radio and computer stack in the center of the car. "Mr. Clay, do you know what happened to Junior?"

Clay glanced over trying to decide how to answer, he finally said, "Yeah, I do. Everything points to a cartel hit on Junior. They killed him but at least he wasn't tortured."

Eddie ducked his head, "But Iris said the sheriff took something out of the mailbox and out of the car." Steeling himself he turned to the ranger. "That was his head wasn't it, and maybe his hands?"

Clay just nodded, not trusting himself to speak.

Eddie slumped back in the seat and turned toward the door. Clay continued driving and they passed almost two hours without a word being said. Clay pulled through the gate at the Austin airport and into the Ranger's hangar parking area, waking Eddie up as he drove over the FOD shaker. Eddie looked around in curiosity. "What are we doing here, Mr. Clay?"

Clay opened his door. "You didn't really think I drove all the way here did you? Come on, our trusty steed awaits," he said with a smile.

Eddie grabbed his possibles bag out of the back seat and followed Ranger Boone into the hangar as Clay flipped the car keys to the sergeant sitting behind the counter. "Thanks, Mike. Did you gas up the sky pig out there?"

The sergeant reached up and caught the keys. "Yep, you're good to go Clay, topped off both the internal and the bladder so you've got enough go juice to get home. And I still want to know how in hell you got a five-hundred ND when we're stuck with the A-Stars…"

Clay chuckled. "Just gotta know which buttons to push with DEA to get that support, and being in the middle of nowhere on the border doesn't hurt." Signing the fuel chit, he filled out the a-sheet with his name as the helicopter pilot in command and filled in Eddie's name as the observer. "Okay, we're outta here, I want to get home before dark, and the Loach ain't the fastest thing in the air."

Eddie followed Clay through the hangar to the little Hughes 500ND sitting in front of the hangar, and let Clay buckle him in the back seat, taking the headset Clay offered him. Clay settled himself in the right seat, strapped in, put his hat in the retainer on the co-pilot's seat, put on his headset and started the checklist. Eddie watched in amazement, as he hadn't known the ranger knew how to fly, much less had his own helicopter. Clay turned master power on, and started the turbine as Eddie heard a pop in his headset, followed by Clay's voice. "Okay, Eddie, I've got you set up for intercom only to talk, but you'll also hear the radios as I talk to various folks.

Just set back and enjoy the ride. To answer me, click that red button on the handset in your hand."

Eddie fumbled with the handset, and then Clay heard a click followed by Eddie's response, "Yes, sir, Mr. Clay, but I didn't know you knew how to fly."

As the turbine spooled up, Clay said, "Oh, just one of those little things they teach us that we don't always tell folks, Eddie. Here we go."

Clay wiped out the controls, and came up on Ground, "Austin Ground, november niner fife[9] tango romeo at ranger's hangar, taxi for takeoff with Hotel."

Austin ground came back, "Five tango romeo, you're cleared to air-taxi to three-five right hold short. Cleared climb straight ahead to two thousand five hundred, left turn to intercept victor five-five-zero to Pinch, cleared GPS direct Alpine, squawk five-two-tree-zero. Contact tower one two one dot zero."

"Roger, readback climb straight ahead to two thousand fife hundred, left turn to intercept victor fife-fife-zero to Pinch, cleared GPS direct Alpine, squawk fife-two-tree-zero; light on the skids, switching two one dot zero." Eddie heard popping through his headset and felt the helicopter lift and teeter as Clay keyed the mic again, "Tower, november niner fife tango romeo taxiing tree fife

---

[9] Military trained pilots use tree for 3, fife for 5, and niner for 9. Civilians only use niner for 9.

right." They picked up and smoothly began air-taxiing out to the runway.

Austin tower replied, "Five tango romeo, intersection takeoff approved."

Clay air-taxied onto the runway, aligned the helo and smoothly added power. Eddie felt a sinking sensation as the helo climbed but he ignored it as he stared fascinated out the window watching the airport fall away below him. As the helo banked, he grabbed the seat, thinking they were going to fall, but they continued to climb. Eddie fumbled with his handset and keyed it, "Mr. Clay, what was all that gobbledy-gook on the radio?"

Clay glanced back. "That was how we get home, Eddie." He paused, glancing down at the controls. "I just thought of something, have you ever flown?"

"No sir, never have till just now..."

"Well, just sit back and enjoy the ride. I'm gonna be talking to folks as we fly home to let them know where we are, so try not to ask me something when I'm talking to them okay?"

"Yes, sir."

***

Compound outside San Buenaventura-

Ernesto Zapata, AKA *Cuchillo*, sat behind his expansive desk, idly fondling an old butcher knife and smiling at Roberto, his old friend and chief bodyguard, as his accountant droned through the monthly numbers. He tuned out the accountant, remembering this first time he'd killed with this very knife. He'd been eleven years old, and killed the *bastardo* who'd cut up his mother because she wouldn't do what he wanted in the way of sex.

Ernesto had heard it all from his hiding place in the back of the hovel outside Nuevo Laredo; *heard the demands, heard the pleading, then the slaps and screams, and finally the blood-curdling scream and silence from his mother. He remembered following the drunk, cutting his Achilles tendons, and listening to his begging in turn before he cut his throat. Years on the streets, and his fondness for knives had earned him the sobriquet of Cuchillo.* Suddenly, he caught a number from the accountant. "Say that again, we're down how much product?"

The accountant quailed, "Um, nine point two percent this month *Jefe*."

"So the *Norte Americanos* have gotten the two big shipments and how many small ones?" Zapata asked.

Roberto answered, "We've only lost two small *shipments*. One of those was due to the Rio being high and the stupid coyote trying to force people across. At least the bastard drowned himself and saved me the trouble of killing him; but I wonder if that includes the money we lost in the bust in Texas?"

Zapata turned to the accountant. "Does it?"

Shaking his head the accountant said, "No *Jefe*, if that money is added in we're down eleven point three percent."

Zapata turned back to his desk and rammed the butcher knife into the desktop. "*Merde*, now I have to call and explain. These are *not* calls I like making… *Vamanos!*"

As the accountant picked up his papers and hurried from the office, Roberto turned to Zapata, "How much trouble are we in?"

Zapata rocked back and sighed. "I don't know. The cartel is allowing us a ten percent loss rate, but since we're the new channel, I don't think they will let us go too long at that. But it's still better to be here than being enforcers eh, *mi amigo?*"

Roberto nodded. "*Si*, there aren't many of us left are there?"

Zapata said, "No, you and I are the only two left now since Ricardo got killed in Texas." That set Zapata off again and fuming he turned to Roberto, "Go find Jesus and bring him here."

Roberto nodded and silently left the room, returning a few minutes later with Jesus in tow. Jesus was clutching a stack of papers in his hands and looked like he hadn't slept in two or three days. Pushing his glasses back up he said, "*Jefe*, I have finally found the location of the American sheriff who has caused us so much trouble."

"Show me," Zapata demanded.

Pulling a picture from the stack of papers, Jesus passed it over. As he reached for a second picture, he dropped the whole pile of papers, and began frantically scrabbling to gather them back up.

"Who is this old man?" Zapata asked.

"*Jefe* that is sheriff captain John Cronin from Fort Stockton. We have tracked him down through the news and searching the land records. We do not have a picture of his son, Jesse, yet, but we are still working on that." Jesus answered, as he handed over a Google map showing the ranch off Highway 18.

Zapata turned to Roberto. "Put Eduardo's team on this, they did good with the boy of the *cabron* that cut up Jose. I want them dead in a week. And use the Americans that contacted us. Let's see if they really will shoot their own for money. Offer them five thousand apiece for the kills."

Roberto nodded and silently left the room as Cuchillo turned back to Jesus, saying quietly, "Why can we not find this Jesse? Is he truly such a mystery, Jesus? Or are you just lazy?"

Jesus turned pale. "*Jefe*, I have been trying! But he seems to be a non-entity. It appears the senior Cronin has purposely kept him from the media. I did find one instance of a Jack Cronin, but he seems to not exist either. I will go research more!"

Cuchillo impatiently waved Jesus away, turning back to his computer muttering. Jesus almost ran Roberto down as he left the office. Roberto slid silently back to his normal place saying, "It's done, *Jefe*. Eduardo will be in El Paso in two days and across the border in three. He's going to pick up the two *Norte Americanos* then go straight to the ranch and do the hit. He figures in and out in less than forty-eight hours. He's taking one new shooter to try him out, but it shouldn't be a problem."

Cuchillo looked up and said, "Dead, I want them dead. And their families, too. We must teach these *pendejo Nortes* not to fuck with us."

Roberto bowed his head. "It will be so, *Jefe*. I have so instructed. Eduardo will not fail you."

Shooing Roberto away, Cuchillo said, "He'd better not. I can replace him after I make an example of him. Bring me that little one, Rosa? The fresh one."

Roberto turned and grimaced, but said, "She will be here momentarily *Jefe*. Will you need me the rest of the evening?"

"No, but stay close anyway."

"*Si, Jefe.*"

***

Eddie sat back in the helicopter and watched west Texas go by as he considered what he was going to say to Iris, and how he would face the days to come. Unbidden, tears rolled down his face, and he idly clicked the handset without realizing it. Clay looked around, saw the tears, and said nothing.

Eddie clicked the handset again and said, "Mr. Clay, what should I do?"

Clay answered, "Eddie, I really don't know what to tell you, other than just do what you can to be strong because Iris is going to need to you be there for her. I know y'all don't have any family close, and I know the sheriff has had folks going by and checking on her."

"Yes sir, but dammit, I want the bastards that killed Junior!" Eddie burst out.

Gently the Ranger said, "Eddie, we don't know who did it. Pecos County was where Junior was found, and their best investigator has been working it, but honestly Junior was only dropped there. We haven't and maybe never will find where he was actually killed or who did it. All the sheriff has been able to find out is Junior didn't get on the bus after practice last Wednesday."

Eddie said, "I'll find out, I swear I'll find out!"

Clay replied, "Eddie if you do, you damn well better tell me and not do something stupid like take the law into your own hands. You've got enough stuff hanging over your head, and Iris needs you now, more than ever!"

Ducking his head Eddie answered, "Yes sir, Mr. Clay. I promise I will. I know things gotta change, and I gotta go straight. I'm hoping I can get hired to do some horse work now that I've proven I can do that."

Clay nodded as Eddie slumped back in his seat and stared out the window. Eddie slept most of the way back to Alpine, only waking up as they descended on final into the little local airport. After landing, Clay air-taxied over to his hangar and put the helo down on its mobile pad to Eddie's amazement. Clay smiled but didn't say a word as he finished the shutdown procedures for the helo, and after everything was off, he turned telling Eddie to unbuckle and climb out. Once they were on the ground, Eddie helped Clay push the helo back into the hangar. By the time they'd finished securing the hangar, it was dark and Eddie was wondering how he was going to get home.

Clay motioned Eddie toward the Ranger's Jeep as a pair of headlights pulled into the parking area. Moments later, the car pulled up next to the Jeep and Ronni, Clay's wife hopped out. "Boy am I glad I caught you, Clay Boone! You've got your damn phone turned off again and I've got a cooler of food in the trunk for you to take down to the Guilfoile's and I was not about to chase you down the damn highway!"

Holding up his hands in self-defense, Clay said, "Ronni, we just got here and I literally just walked out of the hangar, I haven't even got the Jeep unlocked or had a chance to turn the damn phone on, so cut me some slack, okay?"

Eddie leaned around the back of the Jeep. "Mr. Clay, if it's a problem, I can walk to a pay phone and get a taxi…"

Ronni looked over at Eddie. "No sir, he's going to give you a ride home. If he doesn't he's gonna be parkin' his ass on the couch for a while. We're an old married couple, and we fight like one, so just ignore us please. I've put some food up for y'all and please tell Iris I'll try to get back down there before the funeral and help her with the house."

Eddie nodded dumbly, not trusting himself to speak as Clay grabbed the cooler out of the back of the car and he and Ronni talked quietly. Clay kissed Ronni and she got back in the car and left. Clay loaded the cooler in the back hatch and Eddie threw his bag in beside it, motioning Eddie to jump in up front. Clay started the Jeep, turned on the radios and hit the road for Eddie's house in the south part of the county.

Eddie was quiet for most of the ride, but finally turned and asked, "Mr. Clay, why are y'all giving us food? I mean, I'm a criminal and all, it sounds like your wife…"

Clay held up his hand. "Eddie, you and I may not go to church every Sunday, but our wives do. And it is the Christian thing to help out in times like this, and yes Ronni's been down a couple of times to help Iris out. They don't really give a damn that we're on different sides of the law, all they see is a family in need. And that's also the way I look at it, which is one of the reasons I gave you a ride home. I didn't have to, and I probably violated quite a few procedures by flying you in a government helicopter, but I've seen enough death and destruction that if I can do a simple thing like this get you home quicker, I'm going to do it. You may not realize it, but your family is well liked down here, because of Iris and how Junior behaved. It didn't hurt that he was a good athlete; it was the fact that Junior was an all-around good kid. And folks knew that, Eddie, and they know that deep down you're not a bad man. You've always been polite to folks, never drunk and a troublemaker. You just made the mistake of trying to smuggle drugs through this county, and that ain't gonna fly."

Eddie nodded. "Thank you for that. I'm scared, 'cause I don't know… I just don't know if I can hold up… I mean…"

Compassionately, Clay said softly, "Eddie, there's no shame in crying. That's bullshit that grown men can't cry. And remember Iris is gonna be as scared as you are, and she's going to be afraid you're gonna blame her for Junior getting killed."

"NO! It's not her fault. Oh God, how could she even think that… If I'd let that Mex kill me, Junior would probably still be alive… So I guess it's really my fault." Eddie put his head in his hands and sobbed.

A few minutes later, Clay pulled into the ramshackle old house that Eddie and Iris owned, thanks to Eddie's parents having paid it off years ago. It needed work, but Clay could see where somebody had been doing a little bit here and there and he wondered if that had been Junior or Iris. He knew Iris worked in town, but he'd never had occasion to cross paths with her. The porch light came on as Eddie got out and Clay saw the front door crack open. He heard a wail of anguish, but didn't know which one it came from as they met at the top of the steps. Clay eased out and got the cooler and Eddie's bag out of the hatch and set them on the steps. Neither Eddie nor Iris even noticed, and rather than interrupt Clay walked back to the Jeep, closed the hatch and left them standing on the porch in an embrace.

Bangkok (Again)

After two days at home, the old man got caught up on all the little bits and pieces. He and Jesse had gone over the ranch accounts, filing the quarterly taxes and once again listening to Jesse bitch about the oil royalties that they had to figure out the taxes on. He just hoped she understood why he was turning all the ranch stuff over to her, and that reminded him he needed to call Billy Moore, his old Green Beret team-mate and now big time lawyer, who took care of all the Cronin's legal needs, and update his power of attorney data too.

After an early drive up to Dallas, four hours to LAX and twelve hours from LA to Hong Kong, the old man stretched and groaned. He made a mental note that once again that even with the upgrade he was stiff as a board, tired as hell and getting too old for this crap. He knew he had a few hours to kill and decided to go ahead with his plan of actually getting off the airport and getting a few hours of sleep *and a little misdirection for State in case they were looking for him*. He did the cattle lines at customs and immigration, and finally made it to the taxi line. Once in the taxi it was a quick trip to the Conrad Hong Kong, where he checked in for his "three" day stay. After a few hours of sleep, he woke up even grumpier than when he'd gone to bed, cussing his body clock and lack of decent rest. He went back down, checked out and bless them for being on time, caught the hotel shuttle back to the airport.

Checking in at the Cathay Pacific counter, he picked up his ticket to Bangkok, did the customs and immigration drill, and was once more ensconced in business class for the two-hour flight up to Suvarnabhumi Airport on the outskirts of Bangkok. His bag was one of the last bags to show up, as usual, and he got the proverbial wrong line at customs and immigration, as usual.

Finally outside, he looked at the chauffeurs waiting to pick up incoming passengers, looking for a sign for him. He finally saw one that just said 083. Walking over, he noticed two familiar faces. One being Som, his driver from before, and the other being Phan, the FBI agent from the Embassy. As he walked over, Phan walked off, completely ignoring the old man. He greeted Som, "Penance again Sam? At least this time it's not the middle of the night."

Bowing, Som said, "*Sawasdee krup*, I actually volunteered this time." Then he grinned.

As Som grabbed the bag and began walking out, the old man said, "Thank you. It's nice to see a familiar face, but I'll warn you I'm tired and grumpy!"

They walked to the chauffeured car park and Som placed the bag in the trunk of the black Mercedes along with the old man's briefcase. As Som bowed the door open for the old man, he slipped a note into the old man's hand, then closed the door. Running around to the driver's side, he jumped in and put a finger to his lips as he looked back at the old man, who nodded.

He unfolded the note to read the following:
You're not here, you didn't call us, you didn't visit. Your phone doesn't work here. You didn't stay at any hotel we could find. You didn't go in the front door. YOU are in a world of shit with State. Low profile, snake's belly if you can.
/s/ JS Bach

The old man looked up, to see Som repeating the gesture, and he slumped back wondering what the hell he'd just walked into. An hour later, Som pulled through the gates on a compound on the outskirts of Bangkok, and Som led him into the house. Inside, Colonel Cho Wattanapanit, director of the Central Investigation Bureau and the old man's classmate from the FBI National Academy, dressed in a suit and tie, awaited the old man in the foyer. "John, thank you for coming. Apparently your presence is not being liked by your government. They have been calling asking if you are here, and whether you are going to testify at the trial. We have told them nothing, but they are snooping around all the hotels and have an observer from the Embassy sitting in the back row of the courtroom each day, who seems to be more interested in who comes in the back door than the hearing itself. For this, I am sorry."

The old man shook hands. "Joe, I don't give a shit about those Foggy Bottom types. We did the right thing, and I want to see justice done. And I have no problem getting on that stand. I got a note from a secret admirer that says pretty much what you

60

said, so the next question is where can I bed down, and how's the hearing going?"

Cho wobbled his hand. "So-so, they have good lawyers trying to tear down our case. I must get back to the court as the hearing will be starting again in an hour. I've arranged for you to stay here and we will figure out a way to get you into the hearing tomorrow, as that's when I believe your testimony will be required."

"That quick?" the old man asked.

Cho nodded. "It is moving quickly. This judge does not like delays and is determined to do the right thing. He's one of the few. I must go. Som will take care of you."

The old man said, "Okay, I'd like to study my statement from the original takedown to make sure I have all the facts in order."

Som pointed to the living room. "Sir, your statement and all pictures and evidence documents are in there, waiting for your review. Would you like some lunch?"

"Sure, why not, Sam? And some coffee if you have it," the old man said as he walked into the living room and realized the murmuring he'd heard wasn't a fountain, but another operations center set up. He saw a coffee table set up to the side and chair behind it, guessing that was for him, he sat and flipped open the first folder, which was his statement.

A couple of hours and four or five cups of coffee later, the old man came up for air, and decided he really needed the little boy's room. He noted that his bag had disappeared, and he had no clue where it was. Wandering down the hall, he found a bathroom and made use of the facilities. As he came out, he realized something smelled pretty good and he wandered further finding the kitchen and three older Thai ladies busily cooking something in a big pot. They ran him out of the kitchen, reminding him of Juanita and how women ruled the kitchen.

Back in the living room, he found Som with another Thai in a business suit, and the old man's mind said *Lawyer!* Som introduced him as Pip and confirmed he was a lawyer and would be the lawyer questioning the old man in the morning. They put in another hour or so with Pip running through the expected testimony, including how he'd found the secret access to the bilges and the discovery of the kidnapped women. The old man's ass started to hurt in sympathy as the questioning continued. Then it was Pip's turn to explain what to expect from the defendant's lawyer. Finally, the old man turned to Som. "I need to get some rest, and I think I'm about questioned out. Any idea where my bags went, and what the chances are of some chow?"

Som turned to Pip and they chatted for a moment in Thai, then turned back to the old man. "Pip believes you are ready and concurs on resting. I will show you to your room, and have some food sent. I'm afraid it will be curry chicken, as that seems to be all the evening crew wants to eat."

The old man said, "*Da nada*, that's fine and I just need something in my stomach to offset some of the coffee."

Som led the old man to a bedroom at the rear of the house with a fountain splashing cheerfully outside the sliding doors. His bag was sitting on the bed, along with his briefcase. Som showed him how to close the shutters but recommended he leave the doors open and said he would send food immediately. The old man unpacked his bag, hung up his suit, took off his boots, and sat down with a sigh.

There was a soft knock on the door, and a younger Thai woman came into the room with a covered tray that she set on the table by the doors. She bowed out and the old man awkwardly bowed in return. Getting up, he walked over to the table and took the cover off the tray, inhaling the smooth scent of curry and spices. He realized he was hungry and sat down and dug into the food. After about two bites, he decided the Thais were almost as sneaky as the Mexicans with the spices. He grabbed the glass of iced tea and drained about half of it trying to put out the fire in his mouth, knowing it wouldn't work, but trying.

The old man decided to try again to send a text to Jesse to let her know he was okay and would be testifying, but he couldn't get any bars and dropped the phone back on the bed in disgust. Deciding he would fight that battle tomorrow, he took a shower and called it a night.

The next morning after a quick shave and a shower, the old man followed his nose and wandered into the kitchen, only to be chased out again. He walked into the living room/ops center and sat at the same little side table, picked up his statement and idly flipped through it. Som came in, followed by an older lady with a tray, which she placed on the table and Som asked if he wanted coffee.

"Oh hell, yes, Sam, I need coffee to get functioning in the morning! And I need to send a quick message to Jesse to let her know I got here. Can you get me on a computer for a couple of minutes?" the old man asked.

Som said, "Of course, Mr. Cronin, finish breakfast and we will do that. I will get your coffee from the kitchen, much fresher than in here."

The old man nodded and dug in, noticing the eggs seemed to be more orange than the eggs at home. After eating and now working on a second cup of coffee, Som logged into a computer and turned it over to the old man. Opening his email link, he quickly typed a generic message, saying he'd arrived and was doing well, and hoping to be done by tomorrow but expecting Wednesday at the latest. Signing off, he thanked Som and went back to reviewing his statement.

***

At the Ranch-

Jesse walked into the kitchen closely followed by Rex, she shivered saying, "One of these days I'm going to check the damn weather before I volunteer to pick up a shift. That roast smells *good*! And I

64

can't believe Papa hasn't sent the first email or text. It's like he is just *gone*."

Juanita laughed. "John will be back when he gets back. He's been doing this for a long time, and he just forgets. As far as the weather, you did it to yourself, so there is nobody else to blame. I found your rain jacket right after you left; but your phone was off, so I guess you never got the message. And the motion sensor didn't go off when you came in— Rex, no!" Juanita said, swatting at Rex's nose. "This is the last of that old brindle steer, and with this weather, I figured it would be a good filling meal."

Rex sniffed and pulled his nose back from the edge of the table where the roast was cooling, and padded back to curl up next to Jesse's chair.

Ruefully plucking at the large blue and orange jacket Jesse said, "Well, it did keep me dry at least, and thankfully the only time I was out of the car it wasn't raining! I think the rain might have shorted the sensor out, remember that was the one we had trouble with last year, and as nasty as the weather is, *I* am not going back out and screw with it now. Did Francisco get back from Ellington's yet? I saw him heading up that way with the trailer a couple of hours ago."

Jesse's phone dinged with a message tone, and she dug it out, "Huh, Papa *finally* decided to communicate with us, and is guessing he may get back in a couple of days, maybe by Tuesday or Wednesday or is he a day ahead? I never can keep track of that."

Juanita laughed. "Oh that's good, Francisco and Toby had a problem getting the mare into the trailer, so it took a little longer than usual. I think she just didn't like the weather, much less that old trailer. Toby's out in the bunkhouse sulking since Francisco wouldn't let him go, but you know how much of himself he invests in every one of those…"

Outside, Eduardo opened the door of the van quietly, motioning for the driver to stay there. He slid the side door open, motioning the four in the back out, he lined them up behind him with the blond kid directly behind him as they stepped quietly up the edges of the steps onto the porch. He pulled the screen door slowly open, and had the third man hold it as he reached down and gently turned the doorknob and pushed the door open.

Rex suddenly bolted for the front door growling and barking in an attack mode as the front door slammed open. Jesse started to get up, but her boot slipped in the puddle of water on the floor and she was momentarily caught between the table and chair as she fought to get at her pistol. Juanita reached in her apron as a burst of automatic rifle fire sounded stunningly loud in the living room and Rex suddenly went silent.

Eduardo led the shooters into the house, pointing the kid and one of his new shooters down the hall.

Jesse managed to get untangled, but it felt to her like it took forever. She drew her Python and slid around the table to the center island, dialing 911, when dispatch answered she whispered, "Lisa, we're under attack at the house, at least a full auto AK[10] and we need help." Jesse set the phone on the floor behind the island and hit the speaker, hoping what happened would be recorded, regardless of how this ended.

In dispatch, Lisa immediately punched the emergency tone and said, "Any units, officer needs assistance; shots fired. Respond to Captain Cronin's ranch, they are under attack by unknowns with full auto rifles. I say again any units respond to Captain Cronin's ranch shots fired, shots fired."

The radio broke into a confused cacophony of sound as multiple units tried to respond. Lisa said, "This is dispatch, get off the damn radios and drive! First unit there call on arrival." She reached over and flipped the switch to the law enforcement common, going out to everyone on the channel, "Any units, respond to Captain Cronin's ranch on highway eighteen, they are under attack by unknowns with full auto rifles. I say again any units respond to Captain Cronin's ranch, shots fired, shots fired. Be aware county units are en route."

Crouching at the corner of the island, Jesse looked at Juanita as she took the other side. Not the best defensive position, but at least there were pots and pans in the island and it was good hard wood construction. Juanita shook her head, as another round of automatic fire laced the wall causing a powdering of dust to spray into the air. They both turned to the door as a voice in Spanish said to search the house and kill everyone.

---

[10] AK-47 Russian Kalashnikov rifle

She didn't hear any acknowledgement before a Hispanic male swaggered through the kitchen door with an AK held casually in his hands as he started spraying rounds across the kitchen counter and rising. Jesse and Juanita both shot him. Time seemed to slow down and Jesse focused the large moustache and realized she'd put a round right through it.

One down and how many to go she thought as she crouched lower; suddenly an AK appeared around the doorframe and full automatic fire sprayed the kitchen again. Thankfully, neither of them was hurt, but Jesse never even registered the gunfire. Jesse tried to return fire and hit the rifle, and it was quickly retracted. Juanita fired and they both heard cussing as if from a great distance coming from the living room, and muffled conversation but they couldn't make it out.

Suddenly, there was a scream and more automatic fire from the living room, but it wasn't directed into the kitchen. Juanita looked over and mouthed, "Toby?" Jesse nodded and thought Toby was now probably dead and braced the Python on the side of the island, waiting.

Unbeknownst to them, Lisa was frantically trying to get them to answer, as she could hear the automatic rifles fire through the speaker, but Jesse nor Juanita ever heard her calling out to them.

Another AK fired but they had no shot since the shooter was firing blind from the living room. They ducked again, and as they did, another shooter rushed the kitchen door firing his AK on full auto.

Jesse got off one round, hitting the shooter in the chest and took a round in the vest from the other side of the door that sat her back on her butt as the second round hit her in the left shoulder. She looked up to see a blonde haired kid with an AR pattern rifle staring at her over the sights from the left side of the kitchen door. She had time to realize he was a lefty too, and her last thought was *Papa, I'm sorry...* as his shot grazed her head, spraying blood from the side of her head. Her spasmodic reaction flipped her pistol out of her hand and onto the island top as she arched up and fell back to the floor.

Juanita looked over, seeing nothing but a limp body and blood pooling under Jesse's head, she screamed, stood up and emptied her revolver into the other shooter bent over in the kitchen door. The blonde-haired kid killed Juanita with two rounds to the chest that dropped her right behind the island and next to Jesse.

In the sudden silence, Lisa's disembodied voice was heard coming from the phone, "Jesse? Jesse? Oh God, Jesse? Somebody talk to me, please!"

***

Cho came in a half hour later saying, "John, we will probably want your testimony to be the last, so we will pick you up at three. We are going to smuggle you into the courtroom via the CIB access. Pip will be your questioner, and I am assured you are ready to testify."

"Okay, if that's what it takes, I'm in your hands. Now, I've got another six hours to kill, maybe I'll try to get some more sleep, my body clock still has no idea where it is!"

Cho and Som chuckled politely and nodded as the old man walked back down the hall.

At two-thirty, the old man came back into the living room in his suit and with briefcase in hand. Som nodded to him as the young lady brought a cup of coffee, "Are you ready, sir?"

The old man said, "As ready as I'll ever be. Being an expert witness is never fun, regardless of which side of the argument you're on. And throwing in multiple languages just makes it more problematic when you have to depend on translators to actually get the gist of what one says translated correctly for court documents. That's why I always like to have my report entered directly into the trial record anywhere I testify."

Som replied, "Yes, we have the same problems with some of the cases where Cambodians, Laotians and Burmese are involved. If you're ready, I will take you to the court and we will go in via our entrance."

The old man quickly finished his coffee and picked up his briefcase and followed Som to the car. An hour later, they pulled into an underground garage adjacent to the court, parked, and Som lead the old man through a myriad of corridors into a small office manned by two CIB officers in uniform. Another cup of coffee, and Cho walked through the door, "John, they are on a fifteen minute recess. You are the only witness left, and the State Department person is watching the doors like a hawk. The lawyer for the Chinese believes he has the case near being thrown out, and will *not* like your testimony. He will do everything to discredit you and make you look the fool."

The old man waved his hand. "That's been tried by the best, and I just let it roll off like water off a duck's back. I've done this drill before. Let's get it done." He opened his briefcase, took out his folder of notes and said, "My briefcase will be okay here, right?"

Cho bowed to the old man and led him through more passageways, ending up at the judge's chambers. The judge came out with a curt nod and made a shooing motion to Cho, indicating they should precede him now.

Cho led the old man into the courtroom and they made it to the first row of seats without the embassy watchdog noticing, because he was concentrating on the rear doors. When the judge had been seated, Pip called for the old man to take the stand, the embassy watchdog started, and almost stood up, then slumped back in his seat.

As Pip started leading the old man through his credentials, the watchdog got up and left the courtroom, reaching for his cell phone. After almost an hour of testimony on the initial search for drugs on the ship, and finding the hidden bilge access, and another hour on the discovery of the kidnapped women and the shooting that followed, all with multiple objections from the lawyer representing the

Chinese, his testimony was completed. The lawyer for the Chinese defendant tried to cross-examine him, but couldn't shake the old man's testimony as he refused to answer without referring to his notes, and never rose to any of the bait or accusations the lawyer threw out. Disgusted and throwing his hands up, he finally sat down and the judge gaveled the court closed. The watchdog came to the railing and peremptorily motioned to the old man.

The old man ambled over, and the watchdog all but hissed, "Cronin, you were told *not* to come testify and you disobeyed State! Your ass is going to hang for this, because you have royally screwed up *our* work at an international level."

The old man continued until he was inches away from the watchdog and leaned into him, saying very quietly, "Listen, dickhead, you're a fucking flunkey so let me spell it out for you. I was *never* told not to come or testify. I have *never* been contacted by anyone at state or FBI concerning this incident since the debrief I did when I left months ago with the Legate here. Pan Wattanapanit requested my testimony as an expert witness and as a participant in the takedown on the ship. *That* is what I'm testifying to, and if that is fucking up your almighty *dealings* with the Chinese, then you're really stupid! Now get out of my face and do not bother me again, *do you understand?*"

The watchdog physically recoiled from the old man. "You can't talk to me like…"

Dispassionately the old man said, "Fuck you." Turning to Cho, he said, "Let's get out of here before I teach this flunky a lesson."

Aftermath

Eduardo walked into the kitchen, heard the phone and stomped down on it, shattering it. He casually picked up Jesse's pistol off the top of the island where it had landed, and fired two rounds into Jesse's chest. When the gun clicked on an already fired case, he threw the gun down, muttered under his breath and stomped on her left leg, breaking it, but seeing no reaction.

"*Putas* are dead now, we should cut them up, but they probably called the cops. Let's get the hell out of here. I guess the old man and the boy are going to have to wait. But this should make them good and crazy," he said as he turned and stalked out of the kitchen.

The kid said, "What about the other men that were supposed to be here?"

Shrugging the leader laughed. "We'll get 'em both, maybe at the funeral. Yeah, we'll do them at the funeral. That way all they have to do is flop them in the same hole!"

The kid laughed mimicking his boss. As they strode by the bodies of the three hit team that had been killed, one by Jesse and Juanita; one by Toby, who had almost decapitated the second one, and the third Juanita had killed, the kid asked, "What about them?"

The boss said, "Leave 'em, just grab the guns. I don't want to have to smuggle anymore full autos across the border."

The kid slung his AR, and picked up the AKs lying on the living room floor, one had the pistol grip broken and he held it up. "Busted, looks like one of the bitches got lucky."

Eduardo looked over. "Bring it anyway, we can get parts. Now move, I hear sirens."

Running out the door, he jumped in the passenger's seat of the van as the kid opened the side door and dumped the guns on the padding in the back and jumped in behind them. The driver punched the gas and headed for the gate, "Which way?"

Eduardo replied, "South, and take it easy, we've got every right in the world to be here, remember? Kid, make sure you've got a gun ready to run if we need to shoot."

The kid nodded, pulling his AR off his shoulder and checking that a round was chambered. He flipped the safety on, and pulled another magazine from his back pocket and replaced the one current in the rifle as he leaned back against the back of the passenger's seat as the van pulled onto Highway 18 and headed south just under the speed limit.

Moments later, Francisco slid into the driveway behind the house, jumping out gun drawn; he raced frantically to the back door. Hesitating, he yanked the screen open and put his ear to the door. Hearing nothing, he eased the back door open and slid in as low as he could. To his horror, he saw both Juanita and Jesse lying on the floor and neither moving. He dimly heard sirens, but all he could do was stare at Juanita. Mechanically he rose, checked the house and came back to the kitchen. He laid his pistol on the center island and slumped to the floor, cradling Juanita in his lap while holding Jesse's hand, never realizing Jesse was still alive.

As they met the first sheriff's unit, the shooters pulled to the side like any good driver would, and then continued south escaping into the night. Eduardo looked over and said, "Find us a cheap hotel on I-10, and get a single room. We will stay and wait for three maybe four days. If anybody asks, we work for the oil field company. Understood?" The two nodded.

***

Once in the room, Eduardo went into the bathroom. The kid turned on the TV and leaned over whispering, "Al, I don't like this worth a shit. We done what they wanted, he should pay us and we should…"

Al replied, "Hey, cool it. We said we were in for the duration, and it ain't over yet, 'sides there may be more money. Ain't like you got any place to be right Leo?"

The kid said, "Ain't like downrange, but I don't like sitting around here."

***

Deputy Hart and the sheriff found Francisco in the same position when they entered, guns drawn. Francisco was sobbing, tears rolling down his face as he slowly rocked Juanita's body; he never acknowledged them, just continuing to rock Juanita and hold Jesse's hand as he prayed in a low voice. Jose reached down to check for a pulse on Jesse, and was startled to feel a weak pulse in the neck. He keyed his radio, "Dispatch, code three the ambulance, one alive with gunshot wounds; alert the hospital to expect a code on arrival. Five signal sevens. Advise Doc Truesdale and get the Rangers coming."

Dispatch responded, "10-4."

The sheriff pulled his phone out and called dispatch. "Lisa, Jesse's alive for now, Juanita and Toby are dead along with three shooters. Pass that via phone to Clay and activate the unknown shooters protocol, notify DPS[11] and the other counties, tell them this was a hit, unknown perps armed and dangerous. You know what to do, get on it."

Hanging up, he immediately dialed John's phone, but it went immediately to voice mail. "John, call me immediately, there is an emergency at the ranch. Jesse is alive. *Call me!*"

Doc Truesdale beat the ambulance to the ranch, and he took one look at the situation and started making phone calls even as he started working on Jesse. He very gently took Jesse's hand from

---

[11] Department of Public Service (Texas Highway Patrol equivalent)

Francisco, and turned her head so he could get a look at the entry wound. Cussing, he chose not to do anything, as the blood seemed to be clotting fairly well, he just placed a 4x4 Quik Clot patch over the entry. He started peeling the jacket off, noting the holes and powder burns through the center of it. He sat back with a sigh when he realized Jesse had her vest on, then cussed again as he tried to get to the shoulder wound. Pulling his shears out, he started cutting away the jacket and vest, until he'd at least exposed the wound and he could get his stethoscope underneath the vest. He knew in the back of his mind he was screwing with a crime scene, but he really didn't care and wasn't going to stop. Gently probing under the vest, he was glad there was no blood on the mid-line- apparently the chicken plate had done its job. Rolling Jesse gently he determined the bullet to the shoulder had gone all the way through, and manipulation didn't reveal any broken bones, but he'd need x-ray to actually determine that and look for bone fragments. He bandaged the shoulder with what he had in his go kit, as the ambulance crew came through the door with a stretcher and full crash kit. "Head wound left frontal, left shoulder through and through anterior to posterior, haven't gotten to the left leg yet, but it's also broken, no blood evident. Possible broken ribs, BP eighty-five over sixty, falling; she's O-Pos there's a pint of plasma in my bag that I grabbed on the way out the door. Get two big bores started, one in each arm and push some normal saline while I set up the plasma. Jose, need some help over here, I want to get Jesse loaded and gone."

The sheriff and Hart came around the island and with the medics and Doc stabilizing her head, got Jesse on a backboard and on the stretcher. He looked at Francisco, and pulled the sheriff to the side, "Jose, I'm going to sedate Francisco, he's catatonic, and I'm afraid of how he will react if you try to take Juanita from him right now. When the other unit gets here, have them load him and transport and I'll meet them at the hospital."

He followed the medics out and piled into the back of the ambulance, back on his phone and coordinating with the hospital for an operating room and a team to support him on arrival.

Clay Boone passed the ambulance heading back into town and said a quick prayer, hoping that Jesse was still alive, glancing in the rearview mirror he saw another ambulance chasing him down the road. He pulled past the cattle guard, parking on the highway, as the ambulance turned into the driveway. Belatedly, he wondered if there were any tire tracks, as he collected his evidence kit and walked carefully down the side of the driveway and around the sheriff and Deputy Hart's cars.

He saw a deputy stop the ambulance short of the house and make them turn around, so he guessed somebody had thought of it. He saw the medics grab a stretcher and hurry around the house toward the back door, and Clay picked up his pace. Setting his case on the porch, he walked carefully out to the driveway, looking for any tracks and was rewarded with set of evidence flags and a clean set of tracks that were only marginally washed out. Taking pictures, he gently laid his ruler across the tracks, then parallel to them, noting that all four tires matched and looked fairly new. Looking at the weather, he decided not to try to take a cast, as the odds were it wouldn't set up in time to actually be any good.

Once back on the porch, Deputy Hart had him sign into the scene book with his time of arrival and handed him a set of booties along with a set of nitrile gloves. Clay asked, "Is it that bad?" And Hart nodded. Shoulders slumped, Clay stepped carefully up to the door and started taking photographs, starting with the burst lock on the front door and bullet holes through it from the inside. With his tac-light, he looked at the floor and saw where others had stepped, did the same, dropped a number 1 step plate and took a panoramic series of the living room, now littered with bodies; including that of Rex facing the door with a snarl still on his face. He also noted a set of bloody footprints coming back through to the front door and took close ups of them, after dropping an evidence marker #1.

The sheriff stuck his head around the kitchen door, "Hey, Clay, Hart and I are in here. Doc stomped through the middle of the scene, and we tried to stop him."

Clay looked up. "Okay, I'm pretty sure I'm following y'all's footsteps here, and I'm dropping markers for each step. I'll worry about Doc's footprints later. Looks like a damn war zone in here.

Spent cases everywhere, I'll get there in a few, let me get some more pics in here first."

The sheriff nodded and disappeared back into the kitchen. Clay looked down, then took a close-up of Toby partially under what he mentally thought of as Hispanic perp #1. Noting their position relative to the front door and the bullet holes, he mentally lined up a probable shooting position and again shined his light to look for footsteps. Finding two options, he stepped left and dropped a number 2 plate, took close ups of Hispanic perp #2, noting at least one round through the face and three through the body. He turned back and took photos toward the door, then did another step to the right, dropped plate #3 and took pictures of Hispanic perp #3, who had at least two to the upper chest and a bloody hand. Scanning with his light, he found another wet set of tracks, stepped to there, dropped another plate, and took more pictures looking back toward the door. Satisfied this was *probably* the position from which Toby was shot, he looked at the floor and realized there was no way in hell to pick out which rounds had been fired from where, but as he looked he saw two cases lying almost side by side and they were different sizes. Picking the smaller up with a pencil after taking the picture, he saw 5.56 on the headstamp and called the sheriff, "Jose, got an interesting one here, somebody was using a five-five-six, is there one in the kitchen?"

The sheriff replied, "Nope, both Juanita and Jesse were armed with pistols, Juanita with a Smith and Wesson model ten in thirty-eight, and Jesse with her Python in three fifty-seven. Jesse's gun is empty, so is Juanita's, but no evidence of any reloads. Okay the ambulance crews got Francisco out the back door, you need to see this and let me walk you through what we found while it's still fresh. Granted, we've contaminated the crime scene all to hell and gone, but needs must."

Clay continued methodically taking pictures and documenting as he moved into the kitchen, and winced as he saw Juanita sprawled in death. It was bad enough when you didn't know the person, but *much* worse when you'd sat at the table, broken bread with them, and considered them friends. He knew he was going to have to tell Ronni, and truly hated that thought, as the women had been close for years. The sheriff walked Clay through what they'd done, with Clay putting down more evidence markers, especially where Jesse's body had lain, and what they believed was Juanita's actual position before Francisco had pulled her into his lap. Finally Clay had to step out, as he knew he was going to need help to document everything. Violating procedure all to hell, his first call was to Ronni, breaking the news as gently as he could. Ronni's scream echoed as she hung up and Clay damn near lost it then. Steadying himself, he quickly called Major Wilson, briefed him and requested Major Wilson call Austin for assistance from HQ Company for evidence documentation and guarding Jesse who was the sole witness.

Clay tried John a couple of times, but it kept going to voicemail, and he finally stopped, figuring the sheriff had gotten the message through and John was on his way back. Knowing Doc Truesdale was the coroner, and knowing he was in surgery with Jesse, Clay called the Alpine County coroner, Doc Grayson to come up and assist.

By the time the doctor had arrived, Clay had the basics of the scene mapped and documented, and Doc Grayson pitched in with the bodies. Hispanic perp #1 was fairly easy, as Toby had sliced his throat from ear to ear, and perp #4 or #5, or maybe perp #3 had shot both Hispanic perp #1 and Toby. He was including one shot that went through Toby's forearm, through the perp and hit Toby in the mouth. Grayson called that the death shot. Hispanic perp #2 was found to have four hits, two to the face, and two to the upper chest. Hispanic perp #3 was found to have three hits to the upper chest, and one graze to the back of the right hand, possibly while holding a rifle, as pieces of what they believed was a hand guard and pistol grip were scattered near the right side of the doorway. A ninth round was found embedded in the hallway wall toward the left side of the kitchen door frame, and a tenth round was embedded in the wall above the center of the kitchen door. Once the bodies were transported, the sheriff along with Clay made the determination to seal the scene and continue on Monday, as the other Rangers wouldn't arrive until sometime in the morning.

The fifth and sixth rounds from Jesse's Python would not be found until three days later when Jesse's vest was checked by the Rangers from HQ, and they determined that two of the three rounds embedded in the chicken plate were in fact from her .357.

***

At the hospital, Doc Truesdale and the surgical team were deep into trying to keep Jesse alive, Doc's almost constant stream of cussing as he gently probed Jesse's temple under magnification went almost unnoticed; a second team was finishing setting the left femur and starting to look at x-rays on the light table in the corner to see what if anything needed to be done to Jesse's chest and shoulder. It appeared there were only some cracked ribs and massive bruising from the three shots that impacted directly on the chicken plate, and the shoulder wound was a clean through and through.

Finally, Doc stood up and groaned. "I think I've got all the fragments I can see, and other than localized bleeds, I've cleaned and debrided the site up as well as I can, but I don't want to close it yet. Y'all want to jump on this shoulder while I look at these x-rays again?"

Doc Vaughn said, "Okay, leg is in traction and splinted. We can look at rods or nails later if needed. Christine, lets jump to the shoulder with a fresh set of instruments," as she and her nurse stepped up and draped the shoulder.

Looking at the CT scans on the light table Doc Truesdale asked the anesthesiologist, "What've we got?"

The anesthesiologist replied, "BP one fourteen over seventy, stable; respirations twenty, pulse eight-two. She's equal but not reactive on the pupils, and comatose. No response to stimulus, and I'm not pushing anything to her, other than just enough to keep her under and the normal antibiotics and pain meds."

"Shit. I can't tell if there is any actual contusion here, just the epidural bleed that we've drained already. Entry was on the anterior supraorbital margin laterally; looks like the bullet deflected some, but impacted and cracked the lateral temporal. I've cleaned up what I can see through the scope, but I need to get a neuro guy here. After Vaughn cleans up the shoulder, we need to get an EEG to see if we've got alphas at eight plus, theta, and gammas. And I guess we better put in a bolt," Doc said.

The anesthesiologist said, "Since we've already shaved half, I'll shave the other half and get them run as soon as I bring her out of the anesthesia, but we're gonna have trouble with the theta due to lack of symmetry, and probably all of them because I can't put a full set of sensors on with the wound location."

Doc sighed. "Do the best you can, I've gotta go make some phone calls and get some help."

What now

The sheriff sat at his desk and tried to collect his thoughts. Punching the speaker he hit redial again on the old man's cell, and got the voicemail again. Rather than leave yet another message, he picked up his phone list and scanned down it till he found Billy Moore's cell. Sighing he hit the speaker and dialed the numbers. After three rings he heard Billy answer and said, "Mister Moore, this is Sheriff Rodriquez over in Fort Stockton, I've got a major problem. There's been a raid on the Cronin ranch, Juanita and Toby are dead, and Jesse is in ICU here in Fort Stockton with some pretty bad injuries. She's been shot at least twice, but is alive as far as I know."

Billy broke in, "Where's John?"

The sheriff replied, "I think he's in Bangkok, and I can't get through to him, it just goes to voicemail. I need to have somebody authorized to take control of the ranch and give the hospital their pound of flesh for insurance."

Billy replied, "I can do that, but what about Francisco? Is he?"

The sheriff said, "No, Francisco is alive, but he's sedated, comatose was what Doc said."

"Comatose or catatonic?" Billy asked.

"Ah, Catatonic, that was the word. He was just sitting on the floor rocking Juanita and holding

Jesse's hand when we got there. He apparently got there just after the shooters left. He never fired a round. Jesse was comatose, I think Doc said."

"Shit... I'll, hang on, I'm getting another call. Lemme see who this is," Billy said. A minute later he was back, "Sheriff, you there? Doc, you there?"

When both answered Billy said, "Okay, Doc's found a neurosurgeon up in Dallas that's willing to fly in, I'm going to go get him, and I should be in Fort Stockton in three hours. I'm assuming the investigation is ongoing at the ranch, but with nobody in a caretaker status, I'm going to need to find somebody to at least look after things till we can get in touch with John and get him back here or Francisco comes around. Jose, is there anybody you can recommend? And has anybody called Aaron to let him know? What about guards for Jesse?"

The sheriff scrubbed his face. "I can call Felix Ortega; he is a good man. He and his son know the Cronin's and they've been friends for years. I haven't tried to call Aaron yet; I need to get in touch with John first and foremost. As for Jesse, I've got no spare officers. I don't know..."

Billy interrupted, "Private security, I'll authorize payment for it, I'll also call China Post One to see if anybody is in the area. Did you try calling the CIB office in Bangkok? It's probably the middle of the day there; somebody should know how to get hold of John. Break, break- Doc you need anything or anybody else? If not I'm going to get off here and head to the airport. I'll dig around and see if I have any numbers that might reach him."

Doc answered, "No, nothing else right now. Just prayers. Thanks Mr. Moore." And dropped off the call.

The sheriff said, "Thanks, Mr. Moore, I'll keep trying John, and I'll call Aaron too."

Billy said, "Jose, don't be surprised if, when you get ahold of John, he doesn't react the way you'd think he would."

"What do you mean?"

"You know I've known John thirty-plus years, right?"

"Yes," the sheriff replied.

The sheriff heard a sigh, then Billy continued, "In Nam, we did things people shouldn't have to do. Killing another human is one of those things. We had to keep our emotions under control all the time in the field, if we didn't we would have died. For lack of a better term we called it the 'Black Hole'— that was where we shoved emotions to get the job done. John was one of the best I ever saw at keeping his emotions in check, regardless of the situation. I doubt that you will see or hear any emotion out of John. Doesn't mean he doesn't have them, it's just that he'll have buried them deep until this is all done."

The sheriff said, "Okay, I always wondered about John, and how he never seemed to react. Lots of folks think he's just *cold.* I can't think of a better word than that."

"And the other thing is, don't get in John's way. When he gets like that, there isn't much differentiation between friend and foe. He's going to do what he thinks is right. I'll try to be there, and I'll do what I can to mitigate anything that comes up. Okay, I'm outta here for the airport."

"Thank…" The sheriff realized he was talking to a dial tone.

Pushing the speaker off, the sheriff sat for a minute. Then keyed the speaker again, he tried the old man one more time with no luck, then tried Aaron. Aaron's voicemail picked up and the sheriff left a message for him. Frustrated, he dug through his phone list, and found Matt's phone number, dialed and left him a voicemail also.

Leaning back in his chair with a sigh, he thought of all the things that needed to be done, and realized he didn't have either the manpower or the expertise to do it. He called Ranger Boone and heard the ring tone as Clay walked into his office.

Clay glanced at his phone and smiled grimly. "I'm guessing we're on the same page here Jose. Any luck with John?"

The sheriff shook his head. "No luck with John, Aaron or Matt. Apparently, Billy Moore is on the way to Dallas to pick up a doc to assist Doc Truesdale and Trey, you remember him? The big black nurse that went to school with Jesse and played ball at Texas? Billy and I are arranging for Felix and his son to watch over the ranch till we can get in touch with John. Clay, I've got a problem. With John gone, and this involving his family and place, I don't have a qualified investigator to put on it. I know you've called in the folks from Austin, but do we need to get DPS involved too? I've been racking my brain and I can't for the life of me remember whether they have an investigator in this region or not."

Clay said, "Yeah, I remember Trey. One helluva defensive lineman till he blew the knee. Still hard to believe he's a nurse. As far as DPS, they'll have to bring somebody in from Austin too. I've sealed the scene until our guys get here in the morning and I asked Hart to run the scene for us, hope you don't mind. As far as bringing in DPS, it wouldn't hurt from the PR side of things. Has anybody got anything on the BOLO?"

The sheriff slammed his hand down. "Not a damn thing. I'm wondering if we drove right by the sonsabitches on the way in. Apparently nobody saw the vehicle they used, and I don't know if they're still *in* that vehicle or changed to another one. Hell, I don't even know how many people we're looking for!"

Clay replied, "I got what I *think* are a good set of tracks, and I sent that off to the FBI, hopefully we'll get an answer on that soon, but I'm betting either a pickup truck or a van was used. I've also sent the photos of the perps to everybody I can think of, hoping to get some ID, since not a damn one had any pocket litter at all. Doc Grayson thinks they are all from Mexico though. He'll be doing the autopsy's tonight and said he'd give me a call if anything interesting turned up."

The sheriff asked, "Where are the bodies now? Over at the hospital?"

"Yeah, he's using Doc's equipment and one of the ORs to turn them pretty quick. One of your deputies, Mason I think, went over there to take notes. Hope he's got a strong stomach."

Smiling, the sheriff said, "Yeah, Mason is a good kid; but he's probably puking in a trash can about now. I'm going to stay here, there's a bunk available down the hall if you want to crash for a few hours Clay. It's not much, but at least you wouldn't have to try to drive home."

Clay looked at the ceiling. "Sure, why not? Lemme call the old lady and tell her."

Rallying the troops

Gunnery Sergeant Matt Carter walked back into the range office and dropped his ear muffs on the desk. Going to the coffee pot he poured a cup as Sergeant "Toad" Moretti came out of the back room. "Gunny, your phone has been goin' batshit for the last fifteen minutes, but I didn't see it, so I didn't answer it."

Matt eased himself into his chair with a sigh. "Thanks, Toad. I'll get to it in a minute. I'm glad we finally got that last relay done and more or less on time even."

Toad said, "Yeah, these kids are ready to go and…"

Matt's phone started ringing again, and Matt pulled his drawer open picked up the phone, "Carter." Matt visibly paled, and set his coffee cup down very carefully. "Felicia, slow down I can't understand what you're saying." He paused for a couple of seconds. "Honey, please, I don't understand Spanish when you speak that fast. What about Jesse and Juanita?"

Toad started to walk off, and Matt snapped his fingers, calling Toad back, mouthing that Jesse had been shot. Toad slumped into the chair across from Matt and stared at the floor, shaking his head.

After a couple of minutes, Matt said, "Okay, let me get things wrapped up here and I'll be at the apartment in a half hour. I'll meet you there."

Punching the phone off, he looked up at Toad. "Jesse and Juanita have been shot and apparently Juanita is dead, Jesse is in ICU in critical condition and they don't know if she is going to live. Apparently there was a shootout of some kind at the ranch."

"Oh shit. What do they want you to do?"

Matt replied, "I don't know. Lemme see what these messages are." Pulling up his voicemail, he played the first and second messages from Felicia, both of which were almost unintelligible due to the crying and Spanish. The third message was from Sheriff Rodriguez in Ft. Stockton saying that Jesse had been shot and was in ICU; he also said both Juanita and Toby were dead at the hands of the killers. The sheriff wanted Matt to make the notification to Aaron, since the sheriff knew Aaron was overseas right now. He also indicated it appeared to be a planned murder, but that Jesse, Juanita and Toby had accounted for three of the killers. He also said he was worried about being able to guard Jesse with the small group of deputies he had and asked Matt to call him as soon as possible.

Toad looked up. "Can I go, Gunny?"

Matt sat forward. "What do you mean, Toad?"

Toad stood up and came to attention. "Gunny, if she needs guards, I'll volunteer. I've got plenty of leave, and I just need to know where to go and how to get there. 'Sides, I know you're gonna go."

"Shit, Toad, sit down. Right now I don't know what any of us can do. I need to call sar'major on this one. He can make the wheels turn to get Aaron notified." Reaching over, Matt picked up the desk phone and dialed the sergeant major's direct number. "Sar'major, Gunny Carter I need to see you ASAP. Can I come over now?" He listened and then replied, "I'd rather tell you when I get there. Okay be there in ten."

Hanging up and grabbing his cover he turned to Toad. "Lock it up, will ya, and I'll call you later if we figure out how to do this Toad, and thanks for volunteering."

Toad nodded. "Well, she might as well be one of us, isn't the wedding scheduled for three weeks from today?"

Matt nodded as he hit the door on the way out. Five minutes later, he pulled up in front of headquarters and hurried into the building. Turning into the sergeant major's office, he knocked on the inner door. Sergeant Major Eberhart looked up and said, "Enter! What's got your tits in a wringer Carter?"

Matt laid out what he knew, including the upcoming marriage of Aaron and Jesse, and played the sheriff's voicemail for the sergeant major. Eberhart immediately got an administration sergeant in and dictated an email and Navy message for the sergeant to get out immediately to Aaron's parent command, the 1st Special Operations Battalion. He also told the sergeant to take the message down to the adjutant for release, and email the first sergeant at 1st SOB immediately. Turning back to Matt he asked, "What now, Carter?"

Matt replied, "Sar'major I'd like to request leave to go down there. If the sheriff needs help, I can do that. And Sergeant Moretti is also willing to…"

Eberhart held up his hand. "Carter, do you actually believe this shit? I agree she's been shot, and she's almost a Marine wife, but the rest of this seems a little farfetched at best. And what do you and Moretti think you're going to do down there? Go port and starboard until you fall over?"

Matt leaned forward. "Sar'major, I know this is fact, and I think it's all because of that shootout Staff Sergeant Miller and Miss Cronin were in. I know Captain Cronin was worried about the fact that their names had been put out there, and the sheriff is no shrinking violet. He'll do what he can, but they are a fairly small department in a big county. They use a lot of reserves like Miss Cronin to gap-fill for the regular officers. I'm trying to think of any retired guys that I know within reasonable distance to call. If I could, I'd get them to help guard her."

The sergeant major leaned back in his chair. "Okay, if you're serious, get me chits for both you and Moretti here tomorrow morning. But you're going to have to ID reliefs for you and Moretti and they are going to have to pick up the training load. Let me make a few calls tonight and see about some help, if you really think that's necessary. Now get out of here."

Matt thanked the sergeant major and hurried out of the office. Driving back to his apartment, he gave the sheriff a quick call and told him he'd started the notification chain and was looking at taking leave to come help guard Jesse.

Two hours later, Matt's phone rang as he sat at the kitchen table with Felicia trying to console her. He didn't recognize the number but the area code was Texas, so rather than cut Felicia out, he punched speaker and sat the phone on the table. "Matt Carter."

A gravelly voice came from the speaker, "Gunny, Gunner McMurtrie and Colonel Muir here, we're with the Marine Corps League down here in Texas and understand there is a little situation down in Fort Stockton that we might be able to assist on. Can you give us a sitrep please? Understand we're on an open line, so if something needs to be left out, we can get that later."

Felicia looked at Matt with a question in her eyes, but Matt held up a hand for silence. "Gunner, Colonel, what we've got is a situation where a young lady engaged to a Marine out here has been shot in a cartel-related shooting. Apparently, the shooters thought they killed her and are not aware of her actual identity. She is a reserve deputy sheriff, and was involved in two takedowns of drugs and drug runners including shooting and killing two of them. The sheriff down there, Jose Rodriquez, is afraid they will find out her identity and come after her in the hospital. He freely admits he doesn't have the manpower to guard her twenty-four seven like she needs, and he's looking for help. Me and my armorer are planning on taking leave and flying out tomorrow to help out with the guarding…"

A second voice interrupted. "Gunny, Colonel Muir, what good do you think that will do? There are only two of you and how long do you expect to stay?"

Felicia bristled at the question and started to say something, but Matt cut her off with a calming motion. "Colonel, she's engaged to my best friend, and I'll be damned if I'm going to sit on my ass here and do nothing. As far as leave, I've got sixty days on the books and I'm prepared to use every damn one of them. I don't know how many days Toad has, but I'm reaching out to some other guys…"

A raspy laugh came from the speaker, "Spoken like a typical fucking Marine there, Gunny. That's why you need folks like us. You young bucks never think anything through. I need two things: first, gimme the sheriff's private number, and second, you and your armorer don't do shit unless we tell you to."

Now, it was Matt's turn to bristle, but a cold spear of logic stopped him. Matt scrabbled through the papers on the table. "Gunner, the sheriff's number is 555 900 1515, and why don't you want us to come?"

The gunner replied, "Because we can have at least eight people there tomorrow, and we've got the ability to set up our own command post, and we can roll people in and out. You on the other hand would have to find cover for you and the armorer, right? Got any spare folks handy that can do your job on a day's notice? We've got over two hundred retirees down here bored to tears. My biggest problem is going to be fighting off the volunteers. Capiche?"

Colonel Muir said, "I've got the sheriff on the land line, he'll take all the help he can get. Charlie I'm going to start with the locals and work out from there. Concur, you two sit tight. We'll call you if we need you. Is the range house still 760 555 2121?"

Matt sat back surprised, "Yes sir, it is. How…"

The colonel chuckled, "Charlie and I spent a little time there. Tell Eberhart the situation will be handled, and not to let you two go unless we tell him. And tell Juan Ortega he still owes me a forty-five."

Matt said, "Yes sir." And realized he was talking to a dial tone. He leaned back and looked at Felicia. "Well, that was not what I expected."

Felicia reached across and took Matt's hand. "What was that all about, and they can have people? Tomorrow?"

The phone rang again, and Matt hit speaker, "Matt Carter."

"Gunny, this is Sheriff Rodriquez, I just got off the phone with a couple of retired Marines, and they are bringing in folks tomorrow to help guard Jesse. They were pretty insistent you not come."

Matt sighed. "Yeah, sheriff, I got the same orders, so I won't be coming. I'll warn you they will probably all be armed. I hope that isn't a problem."

The sheriff said, "I hope to hell they're armed! That's the whole damn reason I wanted extra folks to guard her. I was going to deputize you and whomever you brought, so I'm just going to do the same thing with them. And there was no change tonight in Jesse's condition, still in a coma. But Doc's got some specialist coming in to look at her."

Matt looked at Felicia. "Okay, sheriff, thanks for the call. And deputizing them is a good idea. I guess I'll go back to work as usual tomorrow, but please let myself or Felicia know if anything changes."

"Will do, Gunny. And thanks for the help!" With that, the sheriff hung up.

Matt leaned back in his chair and looked at the ceiling, just shaking his head. Felicia said, "Matt, what is it? What's wrong?"

Matt looked at her. "Hon, I want to go help in the worst way, but there really isn't a damn thing I can do right now...

They were both startled when the phone rang yet again, this time showing an unknown number. Matt hit the speaker again and said, "Hello?"

Aaron's voice, scratchy and broken came back, "Matt, Aaron. What the fuck is going on? I got called in by the first. Jesse's been shot?"

Matt relayed what he knew to Aaron, and Aaron cussed a blue streak, finally saying, "I'll get out of here today, one way or the other. I'll call you when I hit LA, can you meet me with civvies, and take the deployment crap back to the apartment?"

Matt looked at Felicia who was biting her hand to keep from crying, "Aaron, let's think this through.

You've got what a week, ten days left on the det[12]?
Right now Jesse is still in a coma…"

Aaron over-rode him. "I don't give a shit! I'm
outta here as soon as I get a leave chit signed. I'll
send you the flight info as soon as I get it. Just meet
me at customs at LAX when I get in, okay?"

Matt sighed, "Okay, we'll meet you at customs at
LAX. I'll pack your bag tonight."

"Thanks, man." And they heard only dial tone.

Felicia gave a tentative little smile. "He really
does love her doesn't he?"

Matt replied, "I've known Aaron for now six
years, and yes, he loves Jesse. She is the woman he
wants to spend his life with. And he's probably
going to screw himself up with the command by
leaving early, if they'll even grant him emergency
leave in this case. They may not, I just don't know."

Felicia banged her hands down on the table,
"What do you mean *may not* grant him leave? That
is his fiancé, they damn well better!"

Matt held up his hands. "Whoa, calm down!
Legally, this situation doesn't qualify for emergency
leave. They aren't married, yet, so she's not
immediate family, which is the actual requirement in
the DoD[13] regs. I don't know how hard Aaron is
going to push it, and the command does know about
the impending marriage, so they may grant him some

---

[12] Slang for Detachment- A temporary assignment
away from the main base.
[13] Department of Defense

leeway . I'm just hoping he doesn't do something stupid if they don't."

Felicia cocked her head. "Stupid? Like what?"

Matt sighed. "If they don't I wouldn't be surprised if Aaron didn't just go UA[14] and come anyway, and that would totally fuck up his career. I'm hoping the call from the sheriff will work in lieu of the Red Cross notification."

***

Back in Texas-

Later that night, Clay's cell rang, fumbling around he finally found it and answered. It was the FBI Lab in Quantico, telling him the tires were the same brand that had been sold on Ford one ton vans for the last two years. They estimated about fifteen thousand miles had been driven, and there were no distinguishing marks on any of the photographs that would tie the tires directly to the ranch location. Clay thanked them and hung up.

Clay stumbled down the hall to the bathroom, took a quick shower and dressed, thankful that he always kept a change of clothes in his bag in the car. Wandering down the hall, he found the coffee pot and poured himself a cup. He told the sheriff the results on the tire tracks and asked if he'd gotten in contact with John.

---

[14] Unauthorized Absence

The sheriff said, "Not yet. I just got an email that woke me up from Billy Moore, he thinks its Colonel Wattanapanit's direct cell number. I'm going to try that in a minute."

Clay answered, "Okay, I'm heading back out to the ranch, the Rangers from Austin should be here now, and I want to get a jump on it early. What are we going to do when John gets back? Are we going to allow him access to the scene? And where is he going to stay? I know the old house isn't an active part of the crime scene, but I don't know the DA up here."

The sheriff scratched his head. "Ah… Shit, lemme call him as soon as he gets in and see what he wants. I'll call your cell if I have an answer, and also if I can get in touch with John. I did finally get hold of Matt last night, and he's coming in along with some Marines, well *retired* Marines, to help guard Jesse. Apparently Aaron is overseas, but Matt is working through channels to get a message to him. Felix Ortega is going to be managing the place until John is back. I think you know him, don't ya?"

Rinsing his cup in the sink, Clay said, "Okay, I know the Ortegas. They won't be a problem. Just keep me in the loop if you will."

"Will do."

Coming back to Texas

Cho came into the old man's room holding his cell phone out, "John, you need to take this. It is your sheriff."

The old man took the phone with a questioning look, said hello, and sat down hard as he heard the news that Jesse had been shot. The sheriff wasn't pulling any punches, telling him they'd tried for twelve hours to get in touch with him, and left multiple messages on his cell phone. The old man finally broke in telling the sheriff that his cell didn't work this far out of town. The old man listened and finally said, "I'll get back to you as soon as I have something."

He handed the phone back to Cho saying, "My granddaughter has been shot and is in intensive care, status unknown. My foreman's wife has been shot and killed and my ranch hand has been shot and killed. They've been trying to get hold of me for twelve damn hours. Joe, I need to get out of here as quickly as I can, to somewhere in the states. Can you help?"

Cho said, "John, we'll get you out of here as soon as we can. Let me work this for you. Is there anything else?"

The old man just shook his head, "No, I just need to know when I can leave…"

Cho started to put it back in his pocket, but changed his mind, holding it back out, "John, here make any calls you need to make. From here it's zero one one then one and the ten digit phone number. I'll be back as soon as I know something."

The old man said, "I don't even know who to call at this point. Jose is doing all they can, and apparently Francisco had to be sedated, I guess he lost it when Juanita was killed." Taking the phone, the old man nodded his thanks and turned away so Cho wouldn't see the tears he couldn't hold back.

Cho started to reach out, but turned quietly and left the old man to his thoughts, amazed that he hadn't appeared to even be angry or upset.

The old man paced and bounced the phone thinking, *my God, why? Why couldn't it be me rather than Jesse? Has anybody told Aaron? How the fuck did they get surprised?* Thoughts spiraled through his head and he finally clamped down on the thoughts and focused on what he had to do next. First was get a way back to the states, next was get back to Texas, third was find the sumbitches that did this and kill them.

Plain and simple, he was going to kill them. No more tears now, he felt himself slipping back into a calm, cold, deliberate place that he hadn't been in for years… It wasn't a pretty place, but he knew the place well, no emotions just doing what needed to be done. He'd done it before and was going there again.

He pulled out his wheel book, sat down and wrote out a list of questions. When he'd finished, he used Cho's phone to call Jose, then Billy, and finally Clay. By the time he'd finished those calls, he had at least an outline of a plan in his head. Jose confirmed Felix was to look after the ranch house and secure the place, and he'd had Billy authorize expenditures as required out of the operating accounts. He thought about calling Bucky, but decided to hold off until he was back home.

A half hour later, Cho came back in with a printout, handing it to the old man, "I'm sorry, I cannot get you out of here until tomorrow morning John, it's already too late this evening and nothing going west gets you home any quicker. Did you want us to make reservations for you from Los Angeles to Dallas?"

Taking the printout, the old man responded, "Thanks, I'll take care of getting home from LAX. How much do I owe you for the tickets Joe?"

"Nothing, John, nothing. CIB has paid for them from our funds and you will be in first class to Los Angeles. I am sorry we cannot do more. Please know that we will pray for Jesse, and those you have lost. And I truly apologize for this, had I not asked you to be here..."

Waving the printout the old man said, "Stop it, I was here because I *wanted* to be here. We had discussed something like this occurring, and had measures in place; apparently, they didn't work as well as we'd hoped. Putting bad guys away is what we do."

Cho bowed and left as the old man started dialing. When the sheriff answered he said, "Joe pulled some strings and I'm leaving at 0730 on Thai Air flight TG six nine two Bangkok, Seoul, LA arriving at noon; get ahold of Billy and tell him to get something to LA to pick me up and bring me straight to Fort Stockton, I'm guessing probably a Lear would probably be the quickest. Tell him to take the charges out of the operating account."

The sheriff replied, "Got it John, and I don't have any updates on either Jesse or Francisco. I'll pick you up…" and realized he was talking to a dead phone, the old man had hung up.

Calling Billy Moore, the sheriff passed the request and directions, and got confirmation that the old man would be met at LAX and escorted directly to the Lear, which would fly him directly to Ft. Stockton, and they should be on deck at 1500 local.

***

Arriving at LAX almost twenty hours later, still in a deeply morose frame of mind, the old man started off the airplane, to be met by an older gent in a coat and tie, and a young Customs agent. They older gent said, "Captain Cronin?" The old man just nodded.

He continued, "I'm Barry Melton, I'm the head of C&I[15] here. Come with us please, we'll expedite your arrival and get you over to the GA[16] ramp where your airplane is waiting." Without waiting for

---

[15] Customs and Immigration
[16] General Aviation

an answer, the younger agent punched a code into the jet bridge door, and they went down to the ramp in into an SUV sitting there. The younger agent got in the back, opened a briefcase and said, "Captain, can I have your passport and customs declaration please?"

The old man reached in his pocket and pulled the passport and form out, handing them back, "Here, the form's folded inside."

Meanwhile, Melton was steering the SUV across the ramp in and onto a perimeter road away from the main terminal. The younger agent finished stamping the passport and kept the customs form, handing the passport back. "Thank you sir, and I wish it was a better welcome home."

The old man just nodded, not trusting himself to speak. Melton pulled up in front of a Lear 35 sitting on the ramp with one engine already turning. "Here you are, captain, and I just want to say we're all praying for your grand-daughter. Have a safe trip home sir."

The old man reached for the door handle, but then turned. "Thank you, I don't know what to say but thank you. I…"

Melton said, "Don't worry about it; we take care of our own. DOL[17]." The old man shook his head and got out of the SUV.

Walking over to the Lear, he was met by the co-pilot, ushered to a seat and strapped in. The door

---

[17] De oppresso liber- Motto of the Army Special Forces

was closed and the aircraft immediately started taxiing. The co-pilot came back, "Mr. Cronin, we'll get you home in about two and a half hours. We don't have a flight attendant on board, so if you need anything just key the intercom."

The old man just nodded and turned to look out the window as the Lear taxied to 25 Left. After liftoff, he fumbled around and figured out how to recline the seat and slumped back, running all his options through his mind. He had to work to keep the deep feral anger from coming to the fore and taking him over. He been there before and he knew it wasn't pretty, and he really didn't want to let *that* particular part of his psyche out of the mental box he'd locked it in and buried many years before. He realized he hadn't called and checked on Jesse during the stop at LAX, but it really didn't matter at this point. *Whatever condition she was in, there wasn't much he could do until he got there.* Two and a half hours later, the PA woke him up as the pilot said, "We're descending into Fort Stockton now, please make sure you're strapped in and your seat is fully up please."

***

The sheriff met the airplane when it taxied in, shaking the old man's hand and handing him his gun belt and badge. The old man slipped the badge onto the belt and slung the gun belt on as he asked, "What's the status Jose? I didn't bother calling in

LA because I got a rush by Customs from one airplane directly to the other."

The sheriff replied, "No change. Jesse's still in ICU, and Doc is still hopeful. But I don't think anybody knows what's going to happen."

Grimacing, the old man said, "Okay, let's go, I gotta do this before I chicken out."

The sheriff dropped the old man at the front entrance to the hospital and told him he would park and be right up, but the old man was already through the doors and gone. Checking with reception, he was told Jesse was in ICU on the third floor. Savagely punching the buttons until an elevator arrived, he rode up in silence. Getting off the elevator, he saw two older gents in blazers and gray pants sitting in chairs by the entry to ICU and a young couple turning toward him as he came off the elevator.

Stalking down the hall, he realized the two were not a couple but were apparently law enforcement. The man held up his hand with an ID in it. "Mr. Cronin, you need to come with us. We need to talk with you right now."

The old man started by him with a growl, and the man reached out to grab him. The old man locked up his wrist, forced the man to his knees, and had his .45 out and pressed to the man's head without saying a word. The woman recoiled, and looked like she was going to reach under her jacket. The old man stopped her with a word, "Don't."

About that time the sheriff walked off the elevator, saw what was happening and grabbed his phone and called the SAC. "Bill, your two agents just fucked up big time over here, and you need to call them off right now!"

The SAC asked what he meant, and the sheriff replied, "Well, John has the male on his knees with a .45 planted between his eyes right now, and I'm not sure he won't pull the trigger."

Cussing the SAC hung up, and the sheriff continued walking toward the situation. Suddenly, the man's phone started ringing, and Jose said, "John, you might want to let him loose, I think that calls for him." At the same time the woman's phone started to ring.

The old man shoved the man down and turned toward the entrance to ICU, realizing the two men there were standing and smiling but had made no move to help the two agents. Looking at the sheriff, he nodded toward the two men.

"Marines, retired Marines actually; I couldn't think of what else to do, so I called Matt. He got in touch with somebody in the Marine Corps League, and they put the word out. Right now we've got nine of them stashed out at the hotel three on a shift, twelve on twenty four off and two more living in a camper in the parking lot and running a command center out of it. I've deputized them all. Hell, I didn't know what else to do…"

The old man nodded and walked to the ICU entry saying, "Thanks for being here, guys, I'll make it up to you."

Inside the door, he saw Angelina, the head nurse motioning him toward the right rear module.

Suddenly tentative, he slowed and resigning himself to the worst, stepped into the module. Trey looked up from the chart he was working on and stood, looming over the old man. "Mr. Cronin, I'm sorry you've got to see her like this, but this is all we've got right now."

The old man almost stumbled as he looked down at Jesse, pale, all of her hair gone and a huge bandage covering the left side of her head with tubes coming out of it, tubes running in her nose and mouth, her left leg in suspension and what looked like a cast from thigh to ankle. Monitors beeped softly and he had to look twice to make sure Jesse was breathing. Leaning over he kissed the uninjured side of her head and murmured, "Oh honey, what did those bastards do to you?" He picked up her hand to hold it and noted that it was totally flaccid, no return grip at all. How long he stood there unconsciously rubbing the back of her hand, he didn't know...

Saying a quick prayer, he wiped his eyes and looked around, to see that he and Jesse were alone. He walked out of the module to the nurse's station to see Angelina, Trey, Doc, and another individual all standing there. He looked at Doc Truesdale. "Thank you for saving Jesse's life, Doc. I owe you big time."

Doc waved him off saying, "John, let me introduce you to Dr. Hoffman from Parkland. He's really the one that saved Jesse. He's a neurosurgeon in Dallas and also a professor at Memorial Hermann, Baylor's school of medicine in Houston."

The old man shook Doc Hoffman's hand. "John Cronin, and thank you for saving Jesse. Is there anything you can tell me? Please, be honest."

Hoffman pointed to his eyebrow. "The shot entered just to the outside of the eyebrow, and *skipped,* for lack of a better word, along the side of her head to here," he said, indicating his temple just above the ear. "At that point, it appears to have tumbled and impacted the skull, fracturing it in a small area, prior to fragmenting and spraying out to the left side." Hoffman shook his head slowly. "Honestly, I don't know when she will come out of the coma, if ever. Neurosurgery is still an inexact science, even with all the technology today, we still know very little of the inner workings of the brain. Jesse's injuries include possible damage to the portions of the brain with motor function, speech and associations; that is short-term memory, equilibrium and emotions. Dr. Truesdale and his team were very busy for quite a while repairing the initial trauma, and he was quick to get a bolt in to monitor the pressure in her brain, and run the correct EEG tests, however they remain inconclusive, as a full set of sensors could not then, nor can they now be placed on her. Trey called me and asked me if I would assist, since Dr. Truesdale was not confident he'd gotten all the splinters and foreign media out of the cavity, so a Mister Moore picked myself and Trey up in the dark of night and flew us down here. After further x-rays and another CT scan, it was determined that the cavity was in fact clear. We monitored her for twenty-four hours and I had to

112

relieve some pressure on the brain, so we removed a section of skull where the original injury was, and that has stabilized her to this point."

Turning, he picked up a cup of coffee and sipped then continued, "We are monitoring her condition closely, and thus far have seen no change. Her other injuries, the shot to the left shoulder was a through and through, and it's doing fine. Three ribs were broken and contusions were caused by two maybe three rounds that impacted her chest protector, and those are doing fine. Her left leg was traumatically fractured, probably by an individual stomping or jumping on her femur based on the footprint left on her pants' leg. That has also been repaired and placed in both a cast and traction. Right now she is on minimal medications mostly antibiotics and some steroids to help her heal. She is also on a low dose of pain medication, mainly to allow the body to relax."

The old man nodded to Angelina as she handed him a cup of coffee. "Thanks, doc. So basically there isn't a hell of a lot that can be done at this point by me, you or anyone else. Is that what I'm hearing?"

Hoffman looked at the old man. "Mr. Cronin, I don't know that I'd put it that..."

"Bluntly? Doc, I need straight answers not bullshit. Sounds like you've given me straight answers and I appreciate it." Turning to Trey the old man said, "Trey, I need some down time. What's the status of a watch on Jesse? I know you're doing the electronic watch, but what about a human being?"

Hoffman bristled but Trey answered, "Mr. C, we're looking in on her on a regular basis. Don't have anybody to sit with her full time, but I do my best. Miss Ortega and some other ladies have been coming by during visiting hours, and Doc Truesdale and I are on opposite shifts along with Doc Hoffman and Angelina."

Chewing his lip for a couple of seconds, the old man said, "Thanks, Trey." Turning the old man walked out of the ICU without another word.

Dr. Hoffman exploded, "What a fucking asshole! I can't believe that cold son of a…"

Angelina interrupted, "Doctor, you do not know Captain Cronin, *do not* make the mistake of believing that you know him. *We* know him. *We* know what he has done here. *Do not go there.*" She ran out of the ICU after the old man.

Hoffman physically recoiled from Angelina's intensity, and looked at Trey, who said, "She's right doc. *Don't* go there."

Angelina caught up with the old man in the hall, staring blankly and sipping his coffee, "Angelina, where is Francisco?"

She answered, "He's down in room twenty-four. He's sedated because Doc T is scared he might go further off the deep end. Doc will be in, probably around eight tomorrow to relieve Hoffman. He wants to see you and discuss what to do with Francisco then. Come on, I'll take you down so you can look-in on him."

As they walked down to room twenty-four, the old man thought back to the shootout with the drug smugglers and remembered that Jesse had been in that same room then. Angelina opened the door quietly, and she and the old man walked in to see an older Hispanic lady sitting in the visitor's chair. Angelina turned and whispered, "My grandmother. The women have someone here every day in case Francisco needs something. They are all mad as hell about Juanita being killed."

The old man said, "Good evening, Miss Lopez, thank you for providing comfort to Francisco and for being here."

The old lady said, "*De nada Senor*. We are here for him." Fiercely she added, "We want Juanita's killers taken care of. Do *not* let her die in vain John Cronin."

"I won't," he said in a voice that sent shivers down Angelina's spine. Going to the bed, he leaned over and took Francisco's hand, feeling a bit of resistance, unlike what he'd felt with Jesse. He looked down and said, "Francisco, I need you. I'll be back, my friend. We *will* take care of this." Nodding politely to the women, he walked quickly from the hospital after taking a few moments to talk to the retired Marine on the outside watch.

In the car he asked, "Jose, what was that shit with the two fibbies?"

The sheriff said, "Apparently you've mightily pissed off State, and Bill's new ASAC[18] sent a couple of the newbies down to get you without talking to Bill. I've talked to Bill and explained the

---

[18] Assistant Senior Agent in Charge

situation and it's not something that has to be handled now. He said he'll bury the paperwork for a while, but you need to talk to him."

"Fuck them. I told that little shit from State to go pound sand in Bangkok, and I'm not in the mood to listen to a pile of shit from them."

"I told you Bill will bury it for now, but sooner or later…"

The old man waved off the comment saying, "Later is right."

Picking up his Suburban from the sheriff's department the old man headed to the hotel to meet Master Gunner McMurtrie. Pulling into the parking lot, he saw a large motor home sitting in the back corner of the parking lot and pulled over to park near it.

Getting out, he walked slowly toward it, trying to think of what to say when the door was suddenly opened when a gravelly voice said, "Cronin?"

The old man noted that the voice had come from the darkened opening, and smiled, "Yeah, John Cronin, Jesse's grandfather. Permission to enter?"

The lights were flipped on and he saw a figure move from the doorway, and he could have sworn he heard something to the effect of "Don't start that shit." But maybe not. Stepping into the motor home, he saw one man sitting back down at the dinette in front of a bank of radios, and another older, hell *all* of these guys were old, man in shorts and a T-shirt sitting in the corner with a cup of coffee, and three other men dressed in blazers and slacks also with cups of coffee in hand. The one at the dinette with the gravel voice said, "Coffee is on the counter, cups in the first cabinet on the right, grab a cup and let's chat. I'm McMurtire."

The old man did as he was told, and moved into the dinette/living room area, noting a cocked and locked 1911 lying next to McMurtrie. After shaking hands with McMurtrie, he turned to the others, "I'm John Cronin, and I can't thank you guys enough for what you're doing. I'll cover all the bills while you're…"

The one in shorts and a T-shirt stood up. "Chris Muir, I'm one of the watch coordinators with Gunner."

To which McMurtrie said not quite sotto voice, "And he's a colonel too," provoking laughter from the other three gents.

Muir said, "These gents are Sergeant Major Lopez, Master Gunnery Sergeant Lopez and First Sergeant Rodriques." The old man shook hands with each of them in turn with a thank you at each handshake.

McMurtrie said, "They're our Mex crew," prompting more laughter.

The sergeant major said, "We figured we'd be the best crew for night shift, since many of the service employees are Hispanic, so we are making friends and finding out what is really going on in the hospital. Most of the employees are really angry about the woman…"

The old man supplied, "Juanita."

"Yes, Juanita's death, and are sad about Francisco's condition. They all move very quietly around his room, and very quietly around the ICU, I think because they are scared of the big black nurse Trey."

John laughed. "Hell, *I'm* scared of Trey. I wouldn't want to get him on my bad side!" Everyone laughed again, then the three trooped out to go relieve the watch, leaving McMurtrie and Muir with the old man.

The two of them detailed how the watches were structured, and their emplaced comms links and plans to roll people in and out as they were available. They also said they'd had more volunteers than they could possibly use.

After a half hour of discussions and multiple yawns on the old man's part, McMurtrie finally told him to leave; with another round of thanks, the old man headed out to the ranch thinking over what he'd just seen and been briefed on.

At the Ranch

The old man pulled into the ranch yard in front of the old house and was met by Deputy Hart who apologetically told him as they walked around to the front porch of the new house that he would have to escort the old man and he'd have to sign in and put on booties and gloves before he could go in, and he was limited to going directly to the bedroom and getting his clothes and that he'd have to be escorted.

The old man said, "Fine, let's do this. And I understand, Hart. Not blaming you." After gearing up and signing the crime scene book, he opened the door and heard a murmur of conversation coming from the kitchen. He also was hit immediately with the smell of old blood, and an underlying smell of spent gunpowder. Automatically taking in the scene markers, he carefully stepped through the living room, and stopped at the door to the kitchen. Looking at the damage and the spent shell casings, he was amazed Jesse survived at all. The Ranger and DPS trooper looked up from their work and both greeted him and asked after Jesse. He told them no change, and went on to his bedroom, followed by Hart. Picking out enough clothes for a week, he stuffed them in a bag from the closet, unplugged his alarm clock, phone charger, and radio charger with the MT1200 still sitting in it and threw them in the bag too. Zipping it up, he looked around the room and its normalcy, compared to the devastation in the front of the house and thought *How in the hell can I deal with this. What if Jesse… No! Don't go there. Positive… Positive… Gotta stay positive. Yeah, I'm positive I'm going to kill that sumbitch.* With a grimace, he picked up the bag and retraced his steps. Stopping again at the kitchen door, he asked the Ranger, "Hey Roy, not trying to rush, but any idea when you're going to release the scene? I'd like to get the house cleaned up. Also did y'all remove Rex's body in addition to all the others? And if so, where is it?"

The Ranger said, "I think we should be done by probably tomorrow." Looking over at the trooper, he added, "Sarge, you think that's about right?" The trooper nodded in agreement and the Ranger continued, "As far as the dog, you'd need to ask the gent that's keeping an eye on the place. He's staying in the bunkhouse."

The old man said, "Thanks, guys. I know you've got a job to do, and it's not like I don't have any place to go, but…"

The other two nodded in unison and the old man continued to the door. Stepping out, he deposited the booties and gloves in a dump bag there and signed out of the scene book. Turning to Hart he said, "Thanks, I appreciate what you're doing, and I know I can't be nosing around. Tell the sheriff I'll see him sometime in the morning after I see Jesse and talk to Billy Moore."

"Will do, captain. And I'm truly sorry we don't have the shooters yet."

The old man shrugged and stepped off the porch and headed around the house. As he walked toward the old house, Felix Ortega and his son stepped through the corral gate, "*Senor* John, welcome home. I hope you are satisfied with us keeping a watch on the property and taking care of the stock."

The old man said, "Felix, Ricky, I truly appreciate your stepping up. Please let me know how much I owe you for the time…"

Felix waved him off. "*Senor*, please do not insult me. Ricky will be paid, I will not."

The old man said, "Understood, and my apologies. I'm tired, it's been a stressful day, and I'm not thinking clearly. One thing before I go to bed: where is Rex's body? I want to put him in the cemetery. He deserves that for trying to protect the family."

"It is taken care of, *Senor*, we buried him up there as soon as they released his body to us. I put together a small casket for him and we buried him with the other pets. I also made a cross for him and put it at the head of the grave. Do not worry about the stock or anything else. We will take care of it. Rest and take care of Jesse, and please let us know when we can start cleaning and repairing the house."

The old man looked at Felix for a moment. "I'm not sure what I want to do, and there are other considerations…"

Felix said, "*Si, Senor*, we are patient. My wife has cleaned the old house, sheets and towels have been washed in all bedrooms as we were not sure which room you would use."

"Thanks, I'll use the back one. Good night," he said as he walked away.

Sitting on the side of the bed, the old man said a short prayer for Jesse and Francisco, then turned off the light and laid down.

Rolling over, he felt like he'd been asleep for ten minutes, only to hear his alarm going off. Slapping at it, he sat up and stumbled into the bathroom. After finishing his business, he went into the kitchen and fired up the coffee pot. Out of habit, he walked over and pulled the window shade back and looked to the east. It looked clear and a light wind blew, rustling the pear tree next to the barn. The coffee pot beeped, interrupting his musings and he poured a cup savoring the taste and smell of the freshly brewed coffee. He wandered back into the bathroom, intending to grab a quick shower, but heard the cell phone ringing. Cussing, he set the coffee cup down and scrambled back to the bedroom. Tapping the speaker he said, "Cronin."

Clay Boone said, "Bout time you're up. Meet me at the truck stop in thirty."

"Okay." Hanging up he finished cleaning up, pulled out a pair of washed out grey Dickies and dressed quickly. Flipping his gun belt and badge on, he headed out the door, then stopped and came back into the kitchen. Taking a to-go cup he poured a cup of coffee, cleaned the pot and set it on the drain to dry.

He drove down to the truck stop and found Clay sitting at a booth in the back. "Morning. You got anything for me?"

Clay waved the waitress over and gave her his order, followed by the old man. Once she'd left he leaned forward. "Well, this was definitely a drug hit. Bucky's folks ID'd two of the three as low level enforcers, originally working down around Nuevo Laredo, but they disappeared about six months ago. Figure they went over to the new channel that we've been hearing about. Looking at everything, there were at least two more, maybe three involved. Didn't see any indication of the driver ever getting out of what we think was a Ford van. Weapons used included AKs and at least one AR, but that is an estimate based on cases found. The AR only fired five rounds. Bad part is four of those were hits, two on Jesse, two on Juanita. Ninety some AK rounds fired, including some that went through one of the perps to get Toby. For what it's worth, I don't think Toby or Juanita suffered at all. One odd fact, both Jesse and Juanita's guns were empty, but we can only find ten hits with them. Both Jesse and Juanita got rounds into one perp, putting him down, Juanita got another, and Toby got the third one. "

The old man bowed his head for a moment, and then wiped his eyes. "*Who* sent them, that's what I want to know! I'm gonna…"

Clay broke in, "Whoa, John, don't say another damn word. Bucky thinks this 'Cuchillo' Zapata might be the sumbitch that ordered this, but he hasn't gotten any firm word back from any of his CIs yet."

The conversation was interrupted by the waitress bringing their breakfasts and refilling their coffee cups. The old man asked for a glass of orange juice, and they sat quietly until she brought it. Desultory conversation with fits and starts continued as they ate slowly. Finally, Clay asked, "What are your plans now?"

"Well, go to work now, go see Jesse at nine, back to work after that. Any idea when they are going to release the house?"

Clay leaned back. "It should be this afternoon. We let the ladies in and they got most of the blood up, as soon as they could. I think the kitchen is going to need a good bit of work, but other than patching a few holes in the hall and by the front door, the rest of the place is okay. Are you going to repair it?"

"Right now, I'm trying to decide whether to fix it, or burn it down. If Jesse dies, I'll never set foot in it after that. Just wouldn't be able to..."

Picking up the check, the old man went to the counter and paid for both of them, over his shoulder, he said, "You get the tip, I've got this."

As they walked out, Clay said, "If anything comes up, call me okay? And as soon as we can release the house, I'll call you."

"Thanks. If you turn up anything else, let me know. We've got some funerals to plan and I've got to go back to North Carolina to bury Toby. They'll want to do that pretty quickly. Oh yeah, can I get Toby's knife back? Uncleansed? The 'Yards will want it for his memorial."

Clay nodded. "I'll make it happen."

They parted company, Clay back to the ranch, and the old man to the sheriff's office and the whirlwind of work, visiting Jesse, planning Toby's funeral with Billy Moore, and multiple conversations with the sheriff on evidence, the APB that had now gone statewide, and the apparent tie-in with the murder of the Guilfoile boy and Juanita and Jesse.

Late in the afternoon, Clay finally called to say the house was released, and told the old man that Felix wanted to talk with him. The old man called Felix, who said people were standing by to clean the house, if that was alright with the old man. Not knowing what else to say, he told them to go ahead. Late in the afternoon, he went and sat with Jesse for a couple of hours, then hit a burger joint on the way back to the ranch. Standing at the kitchen sink, he ate without tasting much, while talking with Billy Moore. Billy had already called the Cronin's insurance agent and gotten the okay for repairs as required, and finally convinced the old man to let Felix and his folks do the repairs. Billy also confirmed that Toby's body had been received at the funeral home in North Carolina, and the funeral would be in two days. He'd also been in touch with the local Hispanic community and the *padre*, and the intent was to bury Juanita in the family plot on Friday, if John agreed.

The old man did, and hanging up, he walked slowly back to the bedroom. Climbing into bed, he said a quick prayer for Jesse, Francisco, and another for Toby and Juanita.

Toby's Funeral

The old man stood waiting with two suitcases as Billy's jet taxied in to the FBOs ramp. As one engine spun down, and the door came open, Billy hopped off and walked over to the old man. Leaning close he yelled, "Let's go, I want to get wheels up as soon as we can. Francisco not coming?" He grabbed one of the suitcases as the old man took his hat off and picked up the other bag.

With the bags stowed, the old man sat across the table from Billy and buckled in as the airplane started taxiing out to the runway. "Thanks, Billy. I appreciate the ride, and your help in getting some cows to support the funeral. Francisco just can't handle it, he's still damn near catatonic over Juanita, and I just don't know what he'd do…"

Billy just nodded as the jets spooled up and took off. After it had climbed out and the air was smoother, Billy pulled up his briefcase and opened it; taking out a stack of papers. "How's Jesse?"

"Jesse's still in a coma, and nobody is sure if she's going to come out of it, there's still swelling in the brain. They brought a cutter in from Dallas to relieve the pressure. Doc's been living at the hospital and Angelina and Trey finally threw him out. Right now it's hurry up and wait," the old man replied.

"Shit." Billy shook his head and whistled. "You want a status update?

Leaning forward the old man said in a tired voice, "Yeah, but lemme tell you what we've found first, and then you can fill me in." Billy nodded and the old man continued, "So far we've managed to ID two of the DOAs. They were low-level gunnies from an offshoot of the Zetas. They were apparently well known to the Federales, but still managed to get across the border without any problem. Neither had a gun on them, but they were both carrying switchblades and both were wearing the same tennis shoes. There were over sixty rifle rounds fired in the house, from at least five different locations. Four of the five were AKs, and at least two of the shooters changed magazines. One weapon was probably an AR, as the sheriff and Clay found five-five-six cases mixed with the seven six two by thirty-nine. Looks like the AR shooter fired five times, and he's the one that took Jesse down. Rex was killed right at the front door, looks like by an AK on full auto. From the entry wounds on Juanita, she was hit by fire from three different locations, one to the right side of the kitchen door, one from the center of the living room straight through the door and the killing shots were also five-five-six and tightly grouped fired from the left side of the door. That tells me they had at least one pro there."

The old man twisted in the seat for a minute, grimacing. "Jesse was hit from the left side of the door, and the shooter braced on the door frame for at least a couple of shots. We got prints they are running now, but nothing has come back yet. The other two are unknown, but they were wearing the same shoes, 'cause one of them tracked blood into the living room, and he was the one that picked up Jesse's pistol and shot her with it."

Billy winced at hearing that. "Thank God she had the vest on."

The old man nodded once. "Yeah, and a miracle the shooters didn't notice it. Apparently, the round through the shoulder and the blood from the head wound convinced the shooters she was dead. I'm just thankful the five-five-six ammo wasn't the eight fifty-five steel core stuff, just the normal fifty-five grain, otherwise it'd have penetrated the chicken plate in the vest from that range. The one that shot Jesse also got into the front seat of the van while the other guy got in the side door with the extra guns he'd taken from the DOAs. It appears they were in a Ford van if the tires weren't stolen, and there apparently was a driver who stayed in the van the whole time, but the way it was stopped, he apparently missed seeing Toby come up on the front porch and in the front door. Toby came in the door, and took the one guy to the left of the door with the Bowie knife. Damn near took his head off, but shooter number one apparently saw him and hosed him down, again on full auto. He even popped three rounds into his own guy."

Billy wrote a note and said, "Any indication his guy might have been alive?"

The old man shook his head. "Nope, Toby took him ear to ear. That was absolutely insane to charge guys with full auto guns with a knife! He was covered in this guy's blood in addition to his own. I think Toby might have still had an arm around his throat when he was shot, because one round went through his forearm.

Billy said, "The Montagnards can do some crazy things when they decide they need to. And Toby was trying to protect the women. Francisco?"

The old man leaned back. "Yeah, we've seen that before haven't we? Well, I've asked Doc to bring Francisco out of the sedation, we need to bury Juanita in two days, and I need to find out what Francisco saw. Apparently they had to sedate him to even get Juanita's body away from him. Doc said he'd be conscious and alert by zero eight hundred on Friday."

Billy got up and went forward, coming back with a thermos and two cups. Pouring coffee for them both, he sat back down and started flipping through his notes. "Okay, I got hold of Harrington, he's meeting us at the airport. He's also coordinated the beeves, and he's been the interface between the church, funeral home and the 'Yards. I went ahead and had Bartlett fly the body back east yesterday, and they are going to have the service this afternoon. And, no, you don't owe me anything for the beeves or the flight, dammit."

Taking a sip of coffee he went on, "I took what I could get from Jose and Clay, and plugged into my network. I also talked to Bucky and he's been digging through the DEA side and Bill has been honchoing the Fibbie side. Right now everything points to one Ernesto Zapata, who calls himself Cuchillo." Billy pulled out a picture and slid it across the table. "He was the one who put the hit on you and Jesse, based on that damn US attorney's bullshit leak and the fact y'all have stopped two big shipments of his. Zapata was originally an enforcer and his brutality got him moved up to a mid-level guy in the Zetas. They apparently let him go on his own and set up a separate distribution channel because the Zetas were getting nailed way too often at Laredo. Based on what Bucky says, and the folks over at EPIC, he's running a subset of the Zetas based out of San Buenaventura and running mules up through the Sierra Madres to the Bend."

The old man leaned back. "I'd really like to get a shot at that damn US Attorney, Deal wasn't it? He's the sumbitch that caused this!"

Billy replied, "Oh, he got taken down, apparently thanks to the US Attorney in San Diego. He took it directly to the general counsel, who apparently had Deal pulled back to DC. As soon as he got back, the GC and professional conduct types got his ass in an interview room and the bastard cracked like a cheap piece of shit he was. Apparently, his *rabbi* was one of the civil rights types that decided since they won the election, they could do what they wanted. And since Deal had been going after cops in New York, intimidating a lot of them into leaving the department, and getting nice settlements from NYPD against these so called illegal searches, seizures and arrests of Bravo Mikes and illegals, they put him in Dallas. Turns out that bunch was in the middle of replacing all the US Attorneys from Texas to California with their butt buddies in a concerted effort to stop the prosecution of drug runners, smugglers, and illegals in the Border States. Once Deal caved, they fell all over each other trying to claim it was by *direction...*"

"I'll direction his ass. If Jesse dies... I'll just add his ass to the list."

"John, stop that shit! Jesse is a long way from dead, and she's got the best care we can get for her. You and I both have seen people come back from a lot worse! As far as Deal is concerned, I'm also filing with the ABA[19] on his ass, and I'll guarantee you he'll never be able to get a job with a reputable law firm if *I* have anything to do with it."

Satisfied, the old man leaned back and Billy ran through the rest of the plan for the funeral. Two hours later, Billy and the old man stepped off the airplane at the small private airport near Raleigh and for once Billy was quiet. Retired Sergeant Major Harrington, looking like he could still do a twenty-mile ruck march stood waiting at the corner of the FBO's building. While Billy dealt with the pilots, the old man walked slowly over and said, "Mike, I'm truly sorry about Toby. If there was anything I could have done..."

Mike Harrington held up his hand, "I know there was nothing you could do, and I don't blame you, John. I truly appreciate what you did for Toby, and you probably did more to give him some satisfaction

---

[19] American Bar Association

with life than he'd have ever seen here." Turning to Billy, he said, "'Preciate your coming too, Billy. The three of us and Mattson will be the only ones allowed to attend the funeral, since we all knew them since they were kids."

Billy said, "Did you get the beeves for the funeral ceremony?"

"Yep, I bought four and Deng came up with the money for two. That will feed everybody and be enough to satisfy the 'Yards that will be here and expecting a traditional funeral ceremony. Did you bring anything of Toby's for the tomb offering?" Harrington asked.

The old man held up a suitcase. "Got his hat, boots and the knife he took out the shooter with."

Harrington nodded. "Thanks, John, that will bring Deng some peace, and she's got a burial blanket that she'd made for herself that she's going to use for Toby, and she'd hoped you'd bring something of his back. Gonna be a church service, then a traditional burial on their land. Deng's husband has been brewing beer, and I understand they got some dancers together to do the traditional funeral dance too."

Billy asked, "Do you need us to do anything? Everything set with the funeral home, church and..."

Harrington turned away for a second, wiping his eyes he replied, "It's all taken care of, and I owe you both. The thing I want to know is *why*?"

Billy said, "Mike we've always known there were bad people out there, hell we spent a good portion of our lives fighting them. This… Well this was just plain evil."

***

While the church service was sparsely attended, it seemed as if the entire extended Montagnard population showed up for the traditional burial. Deng, as the mother, wrapped Toby in the traditional burial blanket, and he was put in the ground. His hat, boots and still bloody knife were placed on top of the grave, much to the appreciation of the 'Yards. The traditional clay pots of beer were tapped, and the dancers did the traditional funeral dance, and the beer and food flowed freely. A number of 'Yards came up to Deng and complimented her on Toby and the food, causing her to alternately beam in happiness that she'd met expectations and sob in grief knowing Toby would never come home again. Billy, the old man, Mattson and Harrington participated in the rituals as they could, and seeing the crowd starting to get restless, decided it was time to bow out gracefully. Deng broke down when the old man hugged her, and she thanked him in Degar for Toby's life and giving him the chance to succeed. Tears flowed freely on both sides, and Harrington finally persuaded Deng's husband to take her back inside while they left.

After the funeral, Mattson bowed out, saying he needed to get back home, so Harrington took them to a local bar to get a little time with just the three of them. Desultory talk about the funeral and how much the kids had grown seemed to be the extent of the conversation until Harrington banged the beer mug down. "Dammit, I know you're going to do something, and I want in."

The old man looked over at Billy then said savagely, "Are you sure? I'm going to kill that sumbitch Zapata and anybody else I can find down there. I'm going to teach those fuckers a lesson about fucking with me or mine. I'll get all I can get, and honestly, the odds are we're going to end up dead."

Harrington looked beseechingly at both of them. "John that was my grandson they killed. I'll never see Toby again. How can you not let me go? We've always taken care of our own, you know that..."

Billy looked at both of them and said quietly, "Can you be ready to go in a week? Affairs in order?"

Harrington nodded, not trusting himself to speak.

The old man said, "It's going to be five days of hard riding just to get there, and if we survive five more days coming out probably under fire."

Harrington grinned, "Just like the old days in other words. At least this time it won't be through the damn jungle!"

Billy cautioned, "Yeah, but those old days are damn near forty years ago."

Harrington replied, "Shit, Billy, I never thought I'd survive them, so I figure the last forty years are gravy. If I gotta go out, I'd rather it be this way than in a damn bed somewhere."

Billy looked at his watch. "Okay, we need to get going. Be ready in four days from today, and I'll send the airplane back for you. Low profile, don't tell anybody, understood?"

Harrington nodded silently. Finishing their drinks, they piled back in the car and Harrington dropped them at the airport with a quick handshake for Bill and the old man.

Back on board, the old man turned to Billy. "I don't like this, Billy. I know Mike wants to be in on taking down Zapata, but I just don't know…"

Billy leaned back. "Yeah, I hear you, but I can also see his point. He's got a vested interest. Also if he goes then the community feels like they're involved. You know how they think…"

The old man sighed. "Yeah, revenge and tribal honor drive a bunch of stupid shit."

Billy replied, "I know, but if they hadn't done that stupid shit, you wouldn't be here today John. Remember that."

The old man threw up his hands. "Oh, *I get it*, I just don't have to like it. I know how well I work with Francisco, and I haven't seen or worked with Mike in thirty plus years. Ah shit, I'll make it work somehow."

They spent the remainder of the flight going over details and planning a way to get down into Mexico with the least chance of being detected, and methods of communication that might work. In the final plan, it was decided to go in on horseback, and only communicate in emergency or on pre-planned times.

Plans and More Plans

While the old man and Billy were in North Carolina, the women in the community had completed the funeral preparations for Juanita. Since Francisco and Juanita had no family locally, nor any to support the wake, the women had once again taken charge and the wake was in full swing. The *padre* had set aside the time at the church for the Mass in the morning, and the funeral home had prepared a gravesite out at the ranch in the family graveyard. Since Francisco was still in the hospital, Felix and his son were honchoing two crews: one doing repairs to the kitchen and one cleaning and laying out tables for the meal and reception after the burial.

In the sheriff's office, a meeting was in progress with Jose, Clay, Bucky, Doc Truesdale, and Deputy Hart over how to handle the situation surrounding the funeral and transport. They had managed to keep who lived and who died out of the papers and without titillating details, the story had died.

It was pretty much agreed that the shooters were still in the area, they would probably make a try tomorrow at Francisco and the old man. How to defend it was the question at hand. Jose pounded on his desk. "Dammit, I have no idea how many people are going to show up tomorrow, and I'm pretty sure from Belinda that half or more of the Hispanic community is going to turn out, along with every rancher in two or three counties, and who knows how many LEOs are coming in either. This is going to be a royal clusterfuck... The church is nowhere big enough!"

Bucky made a calming motion with his hands. "I can get you at least ten shooters, put five on each location at dawn, and with the number of police cars in the caravan. I think the hit is either going to be tried in town, or once we get to the ranch."

Clay said, "And sure as hell if we try to put bodyguards on either John or Francisco, they will go bat nuts, so that's off the table. At least we're not trying to move an invalid to the service. Speaking of which, Doc, any change with Jesse?"

Doc shook his head. "Nope, the specialist looked at her again this morning. Swelling in the cranial vault is stable to reducing slightly, but she's still in a coma. The leg is coming along, and I got good color and autonomous response cues to pain this morning. Actually, I'm more worried about atrophy than anything else right now on the leg. She's fighting, and Angelina says she's seen rapid eye movement, so that indicates there is brain function across all levels. Problem is, till we can bring her back, there isn't shit we can really do to help her right now."

The sheriff said, "Yeah that reminds me, the retired gunner told me they'll have two new guys coming in today. So I need to get them in here, deputize them and then turn them over to him. He said he'll run the integration into their watch bill on the door and grounds."

Deputy Hart asked, "Can we maybe get them to help for the funeral?"

Doc shook his head. "No, they stay on Jesse."

Jose got up and brought back an aerial of the town. "Okay, Bucky, if you're giving us five, we need to decide where they make the most sense. One covering the back of the church, here." He stabbed the map with his finger, "And the rest covering the intersections at Main and Hornbeck, and Hornbeck and Front. Anybody got a problem with that?"

Hart asked, "What about the underpasses on I-Ten? Or do we put a couple of reserves out there?"

Bucky said, "Leapfrog the ones from Main and Hornbeck. That makes the most sense, one car on each side."

The sheriff pulled down another aerial. "Okay, for the ranch, we'll need to cover primarily highway eighteen, and the ranch itself. Clay, can your folks handle the highway?"

Clay replied, "What we'll do is get the troopers to block the road at Gomez for an hour, and also up at fourteen-fifty. That should keep traffic off eighteen, and we'll put a car or two just north and south of the ranch. I'd put the shooters out with horses rather than tie 'em down, that's a lot of property, and they'd be hard pressed to cover it with only five folks. I think any tries that get made are gonna be in town, myself."

The sheriff shrugged. "Well, all we can do is the best we can do."

Everybody nodded and with that the meeting broke up.

***

Late that evening, Billy's jet landed at the Ft. Stockton airport, and the old man quickly deplaned. Walking into the hangar, he fished his keys out, threw his bag in the back of the truck and drove slowly to the hospital.

Sitting in the truck in the hospital parking lot, he called the ICU. Trey answered in his deep bass voice. "Trey, John Cronin. I'm back. Any change?"

Trey said, "No sir, nothing new. She's stable and other than some meds for pain, all we can do is wait right now. Both docs were here about twenty minutes ago and they didn't change anything. Shoulder is doing good, leg is doing good and they think the pressure is down a bit in her head."

Hanging his head, the old man replied, "Thanks, Trey. How is Francisco doing?"

"Well, doc brought him out of the sedation this afternoon, and he seems to be coherent and functional, but we're going to keep a close eye on him. He was asking about the arrangements. So's not to upset him anymore, I told him everything was handled. But I don't know where his clothes are."

The old man replied, "I know where he keeps his suit and good boots, I'll go get them and bring them…"

Trey interrupted, "Mr. Cronin, you go get some rest. Ain't a damn thing you can do here but worry, and we've got a bunch of overqualified worriers already here. Jesse don't know who's here anyway, so you get some rest and nothing is going to happen until ten in the morning. You can bring his suit when you come in tomorrow. Or do I have to come sit on you?"

The old man chuckled. "Alright, Trey, I'll do that. But I damn sure better be called if *anything* and I do mean anything changes!"

Smiling, Trey said, "Yessir, boss, I'll be doin' that," and hung up.

The old man shook his head, realizing how good Trey was at dealing with people. You wouldn't expect it out of an ex-second team All-American guard who stood six feet six and weighed almost three hundred pounds. The more the old man thought about it, he came to understand that Trey really *was* a gentle giant. And it somebody really did piss him off, he could just pick them up and throw them halfway down a football field.

Driving back out to the ranch, he pulled in the back gate and then closed it behind him before pulling up next to the old house. Looking over at the new house, he wondered what to do. It had taken the Rangers and DPS three days to process the house and he'd only been back in once to get his clothes. He jumped when Felix asked from behind him, "Are you alright, Mr. Cronin?"

Gathering himself back up, he turned. "Felix, I honestly don't know what to do. The kitchens pretty well tore up, and so are some of the walls. If Jesse dies, I may just burn the sumbitch to the ground and be done with it. We buried Toby today, and that was hard. Tomorrow is going to be worse. But Francisco is awake and seems to be dealing with things, so I need to get his suit and boots to take in tomorrow morning."

"Mr. Cronin, if you want, we can fix the house. You know I do woodworking, and we've got some others in the community that would be more than willing to pitch in."

Bowing his head, the old man said, "Felix I can't tell you how much that means to me. But I'd have to pay you for everything, and I wouldn't want to impose."

"Mr. Cronin, you and yours have been friends with us for damn well over a hundred years. We know what you'd done, along with your father to help folks out around here. This would be our chance to give a little back."

Felix stopped for a second, then continued, "You've never asked for much from us, and you've always treated the men and the kids you stopped fairly, maybe too fairly. Jesse's never turned up her nose at associating with us, either. Hell, Lupe is one of her best friends and they've been that way since kindergarten. Y'all have walked the walk as far as we're concerned. That means a lot to the community; actions speak a lot louder than words."

"Thank you, Felix, thank you." The old man turned away so Felix wouldn't see his tears. Walking slowly to the old house, he went directly to bed and fell into a deep dreamless sleep.

Juanita's Funeral

Waking automatically at 5 AM, the old man detoured into the kitchen area and turned on the coffee pot before heading to the bathroom for his morning ablutions. Coming out, he was pouring his first cup of coffee when there was a knock on the door. Picking up his .45, he walked cautiously to the front door, and peered out. Seeing Felix, he opened the door, keeping the .45 behind his leg. "Morning, Felix, what can I do for you?"

Felix held up a garment bag and a Styrofoam to-go plate. "I have the clothes for Francisco, including socks and underwear. And I also brought you breakfast from the truck stop. It's not home cooked, but it's the best I can do under the circumstances."

The old man stepped back in. "Come on in. Put the clothes on that chair and I'll take the food back to the kitchen. What time did you get up to get all this done?"

"It's no problem. Ricky and I are staying in the bunkhouse, so I got him up and sent him for breakfast while I got a shower and picked out the clothes for Francisco. He's eating now, and as soon as he gets a shower he'll take care of the horses and head up to make sure the cattle are up in the North Forty and out of the way before he opens the fence by the cemetery. We will manage the parking and

save places for the hearse and cars in the funeral
party right below the cemetery. The other folks may
have to walk a bit, but that's the best we can do.
Elena will attend the services for Ricky and I
because we don't want to leave the ranch
unprotected. Jose will bring some officers up to
block the gates starting at nine-thirty, and we'll
move up to the cemetery then. Afterward, the
women will come back here and set out the foods
that have been prepared and the Rios brothers are
bringing over some brisket and some pulled pork."

The old man said, "Thank you, Felix. I
appreciate it. I'm going to eat this right quick and
head in to the hospital and see Jesse and Felix. I'll
be bringing Felix to the church and I guess I'd ride in
the car with him out here."

***

Eduardo and the other two sat in a booth at the
truck stop eating breakfast after checking out of their
single room in the hotel. As they were getting ready
to leave, three troopers and two of the DEA snipers
came in and picked up their to-go orders. Since the
booth they were sitting in was close to the cashier,
they were able to overhear the officers discussing the
plans for the morning. Eduardo's frown deepened
with each new comment, until he heard one of the
troopers ask, "Anybody heard how Cronin's
granddaughter is doing?"

Another trooper said, "She's still in ICU at the
hospital here, and apparently still in a coma. I hear

143

they may transfer her over to Houston if she doesn't come out of it soon." The rest of the conversation was lost as the troopers and snipers moved out of the restaurant.

As they cleared the restaurant, the kid asked, "Okay, now what Eduardo? It's apparent they're going to be waiting on us at the church and up at the ranch."

Eduardo held up a hand. "Wait." Once they were back in the truck Eduardo turned to the kid, "You are going to *visit* the granddaughter in the hospital and kill her. I don't know how she survived, but she will not survive this day. And that should bring the sheriff Cronin to us."

"How do you want me to kill her?" the kid asked.

"Preferably a bullet between the eyes, but silently would be better. It's not like anyone else there will have guns, and we will be waiting in the parking lot when the sheriff comes in," Eduardo answered.

Laughing, the kid asked, "Can I take flowers? That way I could put them on her chest after I do her!"

The driver turned. "Lilies, that's what you need to take. I saw a florist last night. We can go by there on the way."

Eduardo laughed. "A fitting touch. Let's go."

***

The old man pulled into the parking lot and reached in for the garment bag in the back seat.

Steeling himself, he walked toward the main doors and noticed an older gent in a blazer and grey slacks. The man nodded to him, then spoke into his cuff mic, as the old man saw the earpiece cord running out of his collar. His glance automatically went to the gent's waist and he noted the bulge there. Nodding to himself, he needed to remember to go out to the hotel and pay for the Marines' rooms and thank them in person.

Inside the front door, he waved to Cindy behind the reception desk, and continued back to the elevators. Getting off at the second floor, he noted two older gents in blazers and slacks, and these two also had earpieces, high and tight haircuts and bulges at the waist.

He noted they remained tactically separated, effectively boxing him in as he continued down the hall to the ICU door.

As he entered the ICU, Angelina came out from the cubicle where Jesse was, her eyes red. Fearing the worst the old man stopped dead. Angelina saw him and rushed over. "No Jesse is not gone, but there isn't any change either. It's just that Francisco is holding her hand and praying for her, and apologizing to her for not saving her. It's tearing him up, and it's tearing me up too. I'm afraid for his mental state when Juanita is actually buried."

Doc Truesdale and Trey came in behind the old man, and quietly shook hands with him. Doc went in and brought Francisco out of the cubicle, and the old man first shook his hand, then enveloped him in an embrace after seeing the tears in Francisco's eyes.

He said softly, "Francisco, there was nothing you could have done, it's not your fault. I need you here and now my friend, I need you to be strong for Juanita and Jesse. I need you to help protect me, my friend. Can you do this for me?"

Francisco gave a quick hug back then stepped back, new determination came into his eyes, and he looked straight at the old man, "It is time. I have said my prayers and made my peace with Juanita and Jesse. Thank you for bringing in my suit and good boots. Juanita would not want to see me in those old boots." Turning to Angelina he asked, "My dear, do I need an escort back to my room?"

Angelina looked up and said, "No, no you don't Francisco, and welcome back."

The old man went into the cube that Jesse was occupying, and tried to understand the back and forth between Doc and Trey as they discussed Jesse. His anger started rising as they talked about her as if she nor he was there, but just a piece of meat. Then he understood they were only doing the same thing he and other officers did at scenes to de-personalize the environment and allow them to keep feelings out of the job. Finally, Doc turned to him, "John, the only good news today is pressure still seems to be decreasing in Jesse's skull; I think we might be able to get her closed up in the next couple of days. I think Francisco will be okay, but I'm going to be passing off coverage today so I can be there if something happens."

Trey leaned over in his deep bass rumble and said, "Mr. Cronin, I'm going to stay here and keep an eye on Jesse, I hope you and Francisco understand."

The old man said, "Understood, Trey. Thank you. Doc, as soon as Francisco gets changed, I'm going to take him over to the church, so he can talk to the *padre*."

***

At the church, the *padre* took Francisco into the rectory and discussed the arrangements while the old man, sheriff and other pallbearers moved Juanita's casket from the hearse to the nave of the church. The women had decided that it would be a closed casket during the services and at the cemetery, but the *padre* brought Francisco in for one last look. Francisco caressed Juanita's face one last time, leaned over and kissed her cheek gently, then turned away. The old man knew in that moment that Francisco was really back.

The sheriff stepped outside and keyed his radio, confirming all the plans and officers were in place over the route and that DPS and the Rangers were standing by for escort and traffic duties to support the funeral. He looked around and saw people everywhere, and was glad they'd decided to run the external speakers out both the front door and side doors. Otherwise there would have been a lot of folks that wouldn't be able to hear the eulogy and Mass. Walking back into the church, he was surprised to see a number of husbands getting up and leaving, until he noted all the women coming in and sitting with friends.

After a short but touching service, the pallbearers carried the coffin, followed by Francisco who kept his hand on the coffin lid until it was placed in the hearse. As Francisco and the old man walked to the limousine, the sheriff radioed the teams to shift to the next set of route locations and call when they were in place. All the DEA snipers called in immediately along the route, and both DPS and the Rangers radioed in ready within a few minutes. The sheriff led the procession slowly out of town, and up Highway eighteen.

Pulling into the pasture by the family cemetery, they parked and waited for everyone to arrive before the pallbearers took Juanita's casket up to her gravesite. Francisco again followed behind, resting his hand on the casket and praying. Setting the casket in place, the pallbearers lined up behind the *padre* as he intoned the first prayer. The old man looked over at Francisco seeing tears rolling freely down his face as he twisted his hands in his lap.

Lupe Ortega stood and took the *padre's* place at the podium, giving the eulogy for Juanita in both Spanish and English, finally turning directly to Francisco and saying, "Francisco, many times Juanita told me how happy you made her for all the years you've shared together, and that her marriage to you was truly blessed by God. Know that she's gone across the river to Heaven and will be waiting for you on the other side. God Bless." With that, she stepped over to Francisco and hugged him before returning to her seat.

***

Eduardo had the driver pull into the hospital parking lot and stop before he got in range of the cameras at the main entrance. Backing up, the van pulled into visitor parking and the kid exited the van, walking slowly toward the main entrance, carrying the vase of lilies. The kid kept looking around and tugging his jacket down, catching the attention of the retired Marine on outside patrol. As the kid entered the hospital, he keyed his radio. "Base, Gilbert post one here. Got a strange one, young blond kid; twenties, skinny, 'bout six feet. High and tight haircut, khaki pants, brown jacket, flowers in a vase in the left hand. But something just ain't right."

"Post one, base. Copied all. Post two/three you copy?"

Two mic clicks sounded then post three said, "Morton, post three, copy."

Base came back, "Post one base, vehicle?"

"Base, white Ford van, it's parked out in short term parking. Has writing on the side, but I can't see it from here. Looked almost like they were avoiding the cameras at the door. Might be two others in the vehicle, I *think* the kid got out the side or rear door."

Inside the hospital, the kid walked up to Cindy, very politely he asked, "Ma'am, can you tell me where Miss Cronin is? I know she's in the hospital, and I wanted to take her some flowers, since I just found out about her being in here."

Cindy looked up, saying, "Well, Jesse is up in ICU. Where do you know Jesse from?"

The kid drew a blank, then said, "Oh I was in school with her."

Cindy's radar went off suddenly, and she casually asked, "Oh you went to A&M too?"

Relieved, the kid nodded, "Yes, ma'am. ICU you said? Thank you very much."

As he turned away, his jacket thumped into the edge of the reception desk. As Cindy watched him walk away, she noticed he kept looking back at her. She ducked her head, seemingly ignoring him, until the elevator doors closed. Hitting the PA she keyed the security beep then said, "Doctor Weaver, Doctor Weaver, Code Red, ICU, Stat."

Dialing 911, she looked up to see the Marine from outside standing in front of her asking, "Blond kid? Strange action?"

Cindy nodded, "Didn't know what school Jesse went to. And like a fool I told him where she is. And his jacket thumped against the desk."

Keying his radio, he said, "Gilbert, Post one. Blond is on the way to ICU, possible weapon in jacket or on belt. Have reception calling 911."

Lisa answered the incoming 911 call. "Dispatch, 911 what is the nature…"

Cindy overrode here. "Lisa, Cindy at the hospital. I think I just told a guy that doesn't know Jesse where she is. And he might have a gun! The Marines told me to call."

As the kid got off the elevator, and started walking down the hallway toward the ICU, the hair on the back of his neck started standing up, and he knew from his time in Iraq that his subconscious was trying to tell him something. He started to reach into his jacket pocket when a gravelly voice behind and to his right said, "Don't try it, kid. Just stop where you are."

***

As the *padre* completed the service for Juanita with a final prayer, the old man heard alerts going off on the sheriffs and other deputy's radios. He stepped back beside the sheriff as he pulled his radio from under his jacket and heard, "Dispatch to all units, possible attempt to access hospital by person or persons unknown. One whiskey mike, blond hair, estimate mid-twenties, slim build, estimate six feet. Wearing khaki pants, brown jacket, possibly armed. Initial response Code Two."

The sheriff and the old man looked at each other and both said, "Jesse!" The old man glanced over at Francisco to see him making a shooing motion, and the old man turned and ran after the sheriff.

***

Looking back over his shoulder, the kid saw another old guy in a blazer and slacks, but this one had what looked like a pearl-handled 1911 held at the low ready. As he was trying to decide how to

151

react, a second old guy came out of an alcove ahead of him, with what looked like another much more utilitarian 1911 in *his* hand. As he looked back and forth, he thought frantically of a way to get out of the predicament he was in.

The old guy behind him said, "Set the flowers down kid, and get down on your knees. Morton, tell base we've got him contained, and make sure the cops are on the way."

Morton said, "Got it, Tom, nice setup." As he used his cuff mic to call in but the kid didn't hear the crackle of a radio, so he figured they were using earpieces. Not knowing what the response was, he decided to comply and set the flowers on the tile in the hallway. Backing off half a step, he raised his hands and sunk to his knees.

As Tom stepped up behind the kid, he watched Morton step closer, then press his hand to his earpiece. Feeling Tom grabbing the pocket of his jacket, and starting to slip his hand in, the kid brought his elbow down and back, catching Tom on the top of the head and stunning him.

He saw Morton's eyes widen as he put a hand down and pushed off like a sprinter out of the blocks. He hit Morton's arm just as he swiped the safety off, and the 1911 went flying down the hall. Continuing to sprint down the hall, he hit the alcove with the stairwell, yanked the door open and pelted down the stairs, as he heard Morton yell, "Base, he got away from us, heading down the middle stairwell. Get him Gilbert!"

The third retired Marine, Gilbert, was still standing at reception with Cindy when that call came over the radio and he told Cindy to get down behind the desk as he moved to where he could cover the door to the stairwell. Looking around the lobby, he confirmed it was clear and drew his 1911 saying, "I'm in the lobby, have the stairwell covered."

Upstairs, Morton had retrieved his pistol as Tom groaned and climbed to his feet, "Why didn't you shoot his ass Tom? What if he'd gone for the ICU instead of the stairs?"

Tom replied, "I had a bead on him, Morton, but I never shot anyone in the back in the Corps, and I was debating whether I wanted to now; when he zigged to the stairwell. I didn't know what I had for a backstop there, so I didn't shoot. Let's go see if we can back up Gilbert."

Morton hit the stairwell as they heard a door bang open one floor down. Tom said, "He went down, be ready Gilbert. Base, where are the cops?"

Base replied, "They are on the way, lights only so maybe we can get this guy before he realizes the cops are there."

Gilbert knew he'd heard a door bang open in the stairwell, but the kid hadn't come out. Going back toward the front door, he saw the kid running past a window heading for the parking lot. Gilbert yelled into his mic, "Kid's outside running toward the parking lot. I'm going for the front door to try to cut him off."

Morton came down the stairwell and went out the exterior door, but didn't see the kid. He turned toward the parking lot and followed at a jog, pistol at the low ready. Gilbert made it out the front door before the kid rounded the corner. Stepping behind one of the supports for the overhang, he checked his line of fire, and waited.

The Chase

The sheriff and the old man jumped in the car and the sheriff grabbed the radio as he spun out of the pasture, "Dispatch this is the sheriff, go out on common and let DPS and the Rangers know what's happened. We're southbound on eighteen now."

Deputy Martin called in, "Dispatch, two-oh-two, two minutes from the hospital. Do we have anything on a vehicle?"

***

The kid rounded the front of the hospital and fired twice in the direction of Gilbert. Gilbert ducked and got off one round before he lost a good backstop. In the parking lot, Eduardo heard the gunfire and looked up, "Start the van, head toward the exit so we can pick him up and keep going!"

The driver nodded, started the truck and backed out of the space, moving slowly toward the exit. Gilbert ran out toward the parking lot but knowing he had no cover, stopped behind the last car in the ER area, "Base, late model white Ford van, Harris Services El Paso on the side. Kid is running to it now. I don't have a clean shot."

The sheriff and Martin heard a new voice over the radio. "All units, Marine base. Vehicle is identified as late model while Ford van. Field Services, El Paso on the passenger's side. Still in hospital parking lot."

Martin responded, "One minute out."

The kid bailed into the side door of the van, which then accelerated out of the parking lot and turned right. Gilbert reported that and base passed it along as the sheriff said, "We're a mile north of Ten, let's see if we can get road blocks up…"

Martin came over common, "Two-oh-two, suspect vehicle just turned north on eighteen, lighting him up now."

***

In the van, Eduardo turned to the kid, "Did you kill her?"

Panting the kid answered, "Nah, I never got there, they've got guards with guns. I was lucky to get out of there alive."

Eduardo banged the dash, cursing in Spanish then told the driver, "Head to the ranch, maybe we can get the old man yet."

They all heard the siren start behind them, and the kid looked out the back door, "Ah shit, it's a cop car."

Eduardo reached down and picked up one of the AKs, shoving it at the kid, "Shoot it. Shoot the car. Kill the damn cop."

***

Moments later the deputy yelled, "Shots fired, shots fired! I'm backing off! Van is still north on eighteen, passing twenty-first!"

The sheriff stomped the brakes and slewed the car sideways across Highway 18 just north of the frontage road, keying his mic on common, "I'm going to block right here, try to force him to go west. All units converge on ten."

As units behind him slammed on brakes and tried to keep from crashing, the driver saw all the police cars coming south at him, and panicked. Yanking the steering wheel, he tried to turn west to the access ramp for I-10, as Eduardo grabbed another AK and was trying to force it out the window to shoot at the police cars. The van teetered on two wheels, then started rolling over, followed by a second or two of fully automatic rifle fire as the van rolled, two then three times. Finally coming to a stop on its side in a cloud of dust, the engine died as everyone watched in amazement.

Coming out of their trance, the sheriff, the old man, Clay Boone and two DSP troopers all ran toward the van, stopping about fifteen feet away as they tried to figure out how to approach it. With the top facing them, they could see a string of bullet holes in the top, but had no visibility into the van itself. Finally, the old man said, "Ah fuck it. Somebody take the rear, I'll go to the front. Just don't shoot my ass."

Easing forward, the old man drew his 1911 and snicked the safety off. Rather than walk directly up to the van, he moved out about ten feet and cut the pie as he stepped around to view the windshield. His first thought was to wonder why the windshield was red, then realized it was blood on the inside of the windshield. Stepping closer he observed one body hanging in the driver's seat, secured by a seat belt. Looking through the blood, he could see what appeared to be a second body crumpled on the passenger's side door. He heard Clay yell, "Clear back here, and one down in the back. Got weapons all over the place."

The old man said, "Two up front, no movement seen. Can't see shit but there's a lot of blood on the inside of the windshield."

A trooper and the sheriff came around the bottom of the van and looked at the windshield, guns drawn, so the old man said, "Sheriff, if y'all will watch here, we'll see if we can get in the back and check the bodies."

Jose nodded, and the old man walked to the rear of the van. Clay was crouched looking in through the broken window so the old man took out his handkerchief, reached over and tested the upper door. It opened with a groan, and Clay released the lower door. Sliding in, Clay stooped and felt the neck of the blond kid lying in the back, "Hey, got a pulse on this one!" Moving forward he reached up and felt the neck of the driver, as he looked down at the body on the passenger's side door. He said, "Both these are dead. Looks like half the one on the passenger's side is under the van."

A deputy brought over a board and they propped the upper door open as Clay collected weapons and passed them out to the old man, who safed them and lay them in the dirt. After all the weapons had been removed, they allowed the paramedic and EMT to get in and work on the kid lying in the back. A backboard was brought up and the paramedic and EMT removed the kid from the back of the van. The sheriff asked, "He gonna live?"

The paramedic shrugged. "Dunno, he's beat to shit and been shot at least once. It'll be up to the docs if they can save him."

The sheriff, Clay and the troopers looked at the weapons. "I'm betting these were used to hit your ranch, John. Six AKs all full auto," Clay said, pointing to one with a busted hand guard. "I'm betting we'll get blood off that one that matches one of the shooters at the house. And I'm betting that AR is the one that was used to shoot Jesse and Juanita."

The sheriff turned to the trooper sergeant. "You want to have the wrecker get this thing back on the wheels so we can get to the other body, and make this scene easier to work?"

The sergeant said, "Sure, lemme get a few more pictures in situ, then we can go from there. I need a round count and where y'all fired from on this too. We've already disturbed the scene to the point that I'd be worried if there was going to be a lawsuit involved, but I don't think that'll happen in this case. Oh yeah, we ran the plate and this van was reported stolen Monday morning from the Field Services yard over in El Paso."

The old man snapped around. "Monday?"

Holding up his hand the sergeant said, "*Reported* Monday, we don't actually know when it was taken yet. Got a trooper on the way to meet with those folks right now."

The sheriff had canvassed the officers that were in on the original attempted stop, the blocking of Highway 18 and the subsequent roll over, not a single officer had fired a round. When he told the trooper the trooper replied in amazement, "That dumb ass did all that himself? Shit, he probably shot the driver which caused the wreck to start with then. And the kid in back took a round or two sometime during the roll over. Guess we won't get blamed for too much force on this one."

After he finished taking pictures, the trooper told the wrecker driver how he wanted the vehicle to be righted and stepped around to the front to get pictures as the vehicle was lifted. As the vehicle came up, it was apparent the third body in the passenger's seat had been crushed by the van at some point as it rolled. As the van banged down on four wheels, a shot rang out, causing everyone to duck and go for their weapons. The old man looked at Clay saying, "Looks like you missed one there."

Clay dropped his head. "Well, I wasn't climbing into that mess in front. I didn't see one though. Guess we need to go through the vehicle again."

The sheriff called, "Hey you guys come around here. Y'all need to see this!"

When the van had landed back on all four wheels, the windshield had popped out and the sheriff pointed to the body in the driver's seat.

"Guess we know where that full auto fire went. I just wonder if that was accidental or if the guy in the passenger's seat was trying to kill him. Lot of rounds went through him and out the driver's side door, the roof and the back looks like."

As the morgue crew started taking the bodies out, the old man told them, "Watch your selves on that one in the passenger's seat, there's a loaded gun there somewhere that's already gone off once."

The older crewman leaned over and picked up an M-9 covered in blood from the stretcher, "Found this one stuck in the driver's back pocket. Safety is on."

The trooper took it, cussing as he tried to get the slide back and magazine out. "Damn blood glues all kinds of shit together... Ah..."

As he cleared the pistol, the crewman called, "Found another pistol, you want to come get it?"

The trooper laid the M-9 on the hood and stepped around to the passenger's side, "Damn, didn't these sumbitches believe in holsters?" Chuckling he added, "If this one had still been alive, that woulda left a mark, since it shot him in the ass when it went off."

The old man looked around and finally saw the sheriff standing off to the side talking on his cell phone, walking over as the sheriff hung up he asked, "Can you give me a ride back to the church, I want to get the truck and get back out to the ranch."

"Sure, DPS and the Rangers have got this. I was just checking on the status of things. Looks like these may have been the shooters that hit your place. Let's go."

After the sheriff dropped the old man off, he waited to see which way the sheriff went, then drove over to the hospital. Getting out of his truck he saw eight of the retired Marines standing in a group at the side of the parking lot. He went over and said, "Don't know if y'all are aware, but we got the three that were in the van. Well, actually they got themselves, but two are dead, and one was brought here about an hour ago. Don't know if he made it or not. I owe y'all a debt of thanks for keeping Jesse alive."

Tom stepped forward saying, "Actually, you oughta be kicking our asses, we had the little sumbitch and he got away from us. Matter of fact, I'm the one he got away from. I'm truly sorry, captain."

The others chimed in, in a babble of voices, only to be waved to silence. "No, y'all did your best, none of y'all are trained LEOs so maybe you didn't do the right things, but you were alert enough to recognize a problem and act on it. *My* bottom line is Jesse is still alive because y'all were here. *That* is what counts. I'm not sure the situation is resolved, so I'd like y'all to stick around if you're willing until we get some resolution."

Colonel Muir said, "Can you give us a few minutes, captain?"

The old man answered, "Yep, I need to go check on Jesse then I'll be right back out."

With that, he continued on into the hospital and up to the ICU. Doctor Hoffman and Trey were deep in an argument when the old man walked in, with

Trey obviously dissatisfied with the answers he was getting from the doc. The old man finally cleared his throat just to get them to pay attention. The doc nodded curtly and left the ICU without a word. The old man turned to Trey. "What in the hell was all that about?"

Trey related that when the shots were fired, Angelina and Doctor Hoffman had looked up at the sound of gunfire, then at each other. Trey was watching Jesse and saw her left hand seeming to clench on its own when the gunfire started. When there were no further shots, the hand relaxed. He'd been trying to explain to the doc that response was real. When the old man asked what kind of clenching response, Trey had mimicked a grip but with some other movement. The old man cocked his head, thought for a minute, and said, "Something like this Trey?" as he made a partial fist and moved his index finger.

"Yes, *exactly*, that was exactly what she was doing with her left hand! How did you know? And what is that movement?"

The old man smiled grimly. "She was pulling a trigger, that's what she was doing."

Trey reached over and picked the old man up in a hug, "Thank you! I goddamn well *knew* she was reacting!" Realizing what he'd done, he gently set the old man back on his feet, a look of fear on his face, "Oh my God, I'm sorry Mister Cronin, I'm so… I didn't mean to…"

The old man shook his head. "No harm, Trey. Just don't do it again, okay?"

Trey relaxed. "Thank you, now I gotta go find that damn doc." He bolted from the ICU.

At the sound of snickering, then outright laughter he turned to see Angelina, hand over her mouth standing at the entrance to Jesse's cube, "Oh my God, what I wouldn't have given for a picture of that. The look on your face was priceless John!"

The old man just looked at her as she walked back to the nurse's station still chuckling. He went into Jesse's cubicle, looked at her and picked up her hand, thinking it was not as limp as it had been before. Or was he just imaging things? Leaning over, he kissed her head and whispered, "Hon, I think we got them for ya. But I know you're in there and still fighting. Come on back to us Jesse, please."

He went out, waved to Angelina and met Doc Truesdale coming down the hallway. The old man stopped him. "Doc, what's the status on the kid from the van they brought in?"

Doc looked up. "He didn't make it. Two rounds in him, plus multiple broken bones and internal injuries. He kept mumbling something about Cuchillo should have paid him. And he kept asking Al to get him out. Out of what, I don't know."

The old man looked sharply. "Cuchillo? You sure that's what you heard?"

"Yeah, he said Cuchillo a couple of times, and guess you'll find this interesting: he had a military ID card. US Army," the doc said, as he held up the baggie with pocket litter in it. The old man pulled out his wheel book and wrote the info from the ID card, finally getting it to separate from the other crap and flip over inside the baggie.

Reading from the wheel book, he said, "Leonard Hightower, age twenty-two, E-four, and this ID is still current. What the fuck is going on here? Does the sheriff know yet?"

Pulling out his phone, the old man dialed the sheriff and hit speaker. "Sheriff, John and Doc Truesdale here. The patient didn't survive. Got an ID though, you ready to copy?"

The sheriff replied, "Go. Has the morgue wagon got there yet, Doc?"

Doc answered, "Yeah, I was just on my way down to meet them."

The old man continued, "Info as follows, ID matches victim Leonard Hightower, age twenty-two, E-four, current military ID."

The sheriff said, "Shit. Standby." They could hear him shuffling through something on his end; then heard, "Gahdammit, I don't need this shit. The driver was military, too, Alonzo Marquez, twenty-six, E-six. I need to go call Fort Bliss and see what the MPs have. The third guy had no pocket litter at all."

Prep and Departure

After turning off Highway 118, Felix and Jose bumped down the rutted dirt road with the horse trailer bouncing heavily on its springs. Felix muttered, "Don't need a damn horse with a busted leg, not now."

Jose said, "I think it's less than a quarter mile to the old Harris place, and last time I was down here, the barn was okay. If the horses make it, they'll have one day to rest before *Senor* Cronin and the others arrive, and I've got hay and oats in the trailer for them."

Another fence and cattle guard loomed out of the darkness, and Felix eased over it, then spotted a broken down house in the headlights. Pointing to the left Jose said, "Go that way, there's enough room to turn around over there."

Felix jockeyed the truck and trailer around and with relief got it lined up with the barn door. Using hooded flashlights, Felix and Jose checked the sturdiness of the stall doors and stalls themselves. Reassured, they moved the horses one by one into their respective stalls, and unloaded the hay, oats and boxes from the back of the truck.

Felix and Jose buttoned up the trailer, and Felix got ready to drive out. Jose reached in and grabbed his sleeping bag and 30-30 Winchester from behind the seat, the last thing was a paper bag of food off the front seat. "Okay, get out of here. I'm good to go until *Senor* Cronin arrives, and then I will bring his truck back to the ranch. I'll get your boy to give me a ride home from there."

Felix nodded and Jose shut the door, disappearing into the darkness.

Jose spent a quiet night and day with the restive horses, but he didn't want to chance them being seen, so he kept them in the stalls and bribed them with carrots and apples. Finally about nine that evening, he heard a truck rumbling down the track to the place; he picked up the Winchester 94 and eased over to the corner of the house away from where the truck would pull in, crouching and ready if this wasn't the old man.

The truck eased into the ranch yard and turned around facing out toward the road. The old man climbed out of the driver's side as Francisco eased from the passenger's side with his rifle calling in Spanish, "Jose? Don't want to shine a light, you know who we are?"

Jose recognized the voice, lowered his rifle and stepped away from the house. "Si Francisco, all is ready here, except saddling the horses and pack horse."

The old man said, "Thanks, Jose. We'll take it from here, just let us get the gear out of the truck and you can head out. Just drop the truck back at the ranch, and Felix or his boy will give you a ride home."

"*Si Senor*, I will help."

In just a few minutes the truck was empty, and Jose left with a quick wave out the window. The old man and Francisco started saddling the horses and were fighting with the pack frame and loading when another truck was heard and headlights came bouncing down the track.

Francisco stayed in the barn, and the old man moved over to where Jose had crouched, as the carryall pulled into the ranch yard. Leaving the engine running, Billy got out and walked in front of the headlights. "Okay, I know y'all are here, so put down the damn guns and come on out."

Shaking his head, the old man came around the corner. "Dammit, Billy, there's nothing like announcing your presence with this big white wagon, what is up with this?"

Harrington stepped out of the passenger's side as the back doors came open and four more bodies stepped out. Stunned the old man said, "What the fuck, Billy? You were only supposed to bring Harrington and an intel update, who ..."

Realizing the four were all Montagnard, he glared sharply to Harrington. "Is this something you did?"

Harrington held out his hands. "No, John, they found out I was coming and when Billy showed up to pick me up they were there. It's a matter of honor to them, and they want to be in on the vengeance for their tribesman. You know that, you saw it before."

Helplessly, the old man turned to the 'Yards, and told them in Degar that he didn't have horses for them, nor did he have food for them. And they were probably not going to survive this mission. The elder, probably in his mid-50s answered in Degar that they were responsible to see the vengeance done, and not to worry about them. They didn't know how to ride, and would walk, just like before.

"Okay, this cluster is just getting worse," the old man said to Billy. "What intel have you got?"

Billy motioned them to the hood of the truck as Francisco came up with the horses. "Bucky has you a gap south of here for forty-eight hours, until tomorrow morning, and another forty-eight hour gap in ten days. Now Zapata appears from all the intel to be holed up in his compound down in San Buenaventura, but he's only got people out patrolling the local roads that we know of. Nobody is going into the hills on a regular basis, which either means cameras, which I doubt, or he figures any approaches will be by road. He likes to come out on his balcony at sunset and smoke a cigar, usually accompanied by the guest in residence, if there is one or one of his prostitutes. He's always got at least three security people with him, and this guy Roberto who seems to have been with him for a long time. He's been stung by the drugs you've stopped, since they were contract deliveries for the Zetas, and apparently vowed to kill anybody that stops a shipment. And the failed raid on your place can't be sitting well either. We tracked the two Army IDs turns out both of them were AWOL from Bliss, and the one, Marquez, was an ex-gangbanger from LA. Looks like the ex- part didn't take. DEA ID'ed the other Hispanic as Eduardo Cortez, last seen in Nuevo

Laredo about a year ago. Known associate of Zapata and one of his enforcer crew when he was with the Zetas, so it's assumed he went with Zapata when he moved up."

Francisco asked, "Any sign of the Federales?"

Billy answered, "Only the occasional truck that runs across twenty, and apparently one small office in Múzquiz. No action against Zapata or any other cartel members in this area, so they are probably in Zapata's pocket. Here are the pictures we've come up with."

Laying pictures out on the hood he continued, pointing to each picture in turn. "Here's the compound, here are the approaches and roads, this is '*Cuchillo*' Zapata, and he's a short little shit. Roberto his right hand man, thought to be ex-Federale, but has known Zapata since they were kids. Jesus, the Brain--he's apparently a US educated mathematician who used to teach at Mexico City University until his coke habit got the best of him. The best estimate is about thirty guards in the compound, and I don't have a clue on how many more in town, but I'm guessing they monitor the approaches to the compound from town. After a few questions, the pictures were gathered up, along with the topo maps and the old man put them in his saddlebag. Billy asked, "John, what guns are you taking? Just in case I need the info."

"I've got my old sniper rifle, the Model seventy in thirty-ought-six, and my 1911; Francisco and Harrington have two of the ARs out of the safe. Francisco you carrying your Colt?"

Francisco answered, "Yep, my .357 Trooper."

Harrington chimed in, "My old 1911 over here."

Billy scribbled the list down, collected serial numbers and started packing his briefcase back up.

The old man, with Francisco's help, finished loading the pack horse and made one more check of the barn. Figuring they had everything, he looked at the small group standing there, "Okay, last chance. Anybody that wants out now is the time. What I am going to do is go take my best shot at killing Zapata. This is all on me, nobody else." He looked at the Montagnards and repeated his statement in Degar.

No one said anything, and with a sharp nod, he said, "Alright, dump any cell phones with Billy, and let's get moving. I want to get across the river and as deep as we can tonight into the Sierras. We'll hole up sometime around daylight and see what is moving before we make any further decisions. Billy, I'll carry the satphone, but I don't plan on turning it on other than five minutes each morning at zero seven hundred as agreed."

The old man handed his cell to Billy, as did Francisco and Holloway. The 'Yards didn't carry phones, and all of them were checking their dhas[20] to make sure they were secure in the sheaths. Francisco looked with interest at one 'Mikey' was carrying, and Mikey obligingly handed it and the sheath to him. Francisco pulled the sword out and said, "Interesting that the tang is longer than the blade. Is this a one-handed or two-handed sword?"

---

[20] Montagnard Sword equivalent

He re-sheathed the sword and handed it back to Mikey.

Mikey took it and grinned at Francisco as he flipped the sheath away and took a fighting stance, gripping the sword in a two handed grip that looked like a cross between the Japanese style, and a baseball batter. Chattering happily in Degar, he proceeded to demonstrate various moves as the old man translated, "Basically, he's saying he can cut, stab and hack, all from the same grip. And with the grip he uses, it not only cuts, but slices deep depending on the angle he takes. He's also looking forward to personally blooding this blade, since it came down from his grandfather and father, but he hasn't killed anybody with it yet."

Francisco just shook his head in amazement. "Toby wasn't this blood thirsty was he?"

"Nope. Toby was a tad different… Okay, let's mount up and get this show on the road." Shaking hands with Billy, and a few quiet words later, the old man swung up on Diablo and quietly led Francisco, Harrington and the four 'Yards into the darkness.

The Rio Grande was low enough they were able to ford it with no problems, and the Yards never got beyond hip deep, even as they hung onto the stirrups and straps of the various horses. Quickly moving to higher ground, the old man pushed as hard as he dared in the darkness, with Francisco occasionally offering a quiet suggestion. At first light, they cleared the crest of the ridge and found a slight depression with a trickle of water and some sparse grass. The old man called a halt and told everybody to rack out after they'd stripped the horses and hobbled them.

He climbed back to the military crest with his binoculars and started scanning the surrounding countryside to see if there was any movement. Eight or nine miles to the southeast a thin stream of smoke rose in the early morning light, and he was glad they'd decided to get over the ridge during the night. Looking at his map, he calculated they'd made almost fifteen miles and marked the location. He figured the smoke was either Coyotes running illegals up to the border, or a group of drug mules. In either case, they wouldn't be an issue now.

Everything to the south and west was as dry and barren as expected, and he was relieved to be able to ease back down to the depression and grab a couple of hours of rest. Waking about 9AM, he roused the others and they munched on protein bars while waiting for the purification tablets to act on the water in the canteens. Francisco went back to the crest and glassed the area again, coming back and saying there was no movement to the south and west.

The old man pulled out the map as everyone gathered around. He pointed out the route he expected to take for the day, and in Degar instructed Mikey and Deng, the two older 'Yards to pair off with Fred and Elmer so there was some *adult* supervision for the two younger ones. He reminded everybody to drink as much water as they could stand, and told everybody to mount up.

The 'Yards led off, scrambling up the ridge and separating to each side of the trail as if they were back in the jungle, and he worried they would forget they were as visible to others, as others were to them.

At a quick lunch break, they split MRE's amongst the group and everyone got a few minutes of rest. Francisco and Harrington chatted quietly with the 'Yards and Francisco came back saying, "According to Mike, the 'Yards are some tough little fuckers and they're adapting to the push fine. He was a little worried about Elmer, where *do* they come up with these names by the way? Anyway, Elmer seems to be holding up fine, and he's apparently sweating out all the beer he usually drinks."

The old man chuckled. "Montagnard's names are unpronounceable at best, and incomprehensible at worst. They take American names that have some phonetic resemblance to what their real name is. They may be little by comparison to us, but I'll guarantee when we're falling over from exhaustion, they'll still be going strong. I don't think I've ever seen anyone other than maybe the Tarahumera down here that are their equals for sheer endurance and determination."

Francisco added, "I was a little worried about their ability to keep up, but it's looking like we're the ones that can't keep up. I thought Toby… I thought Toby was a bit strange with his work ethic, but now…"

The old man replied, "Yeah." Raising his voice he said, "Okay, mount up and let's get this show back on the road."

The day passed slowly, as they eased down through various canyons and small ridges crossed Highway 20 and climbed back up to the higher elevations. The horses were beginning to show the constant riding, and as they got closer the tension ramped up as they looked for lookout points, and outriders from the gang.

Trailing South

Pushing hard, they'd made almost fifty miles in two days, and were in a dry camp just after dark when a voice called out, "Hello the camp, can I come in?"

The 'Yards not on guard had already disappeared into the darkness, and the old man, Francisco and Harrington eased into defensive positions, weapons in hand. The old man said, "Come friendly, and come in with your hands where we can see them."

The slow clopping of a horse was heard and a small man came into the light on a grey gelding. Stopping in the light of the camp he said, "I'm friendly, and y'all are pushing damn hard…"

Francisco rattled off a challenge in Spanish, but the only reply was, "Sorry, I don't speak Mex that good, and I'm not a Mex anyway."

The old man asked, "Well, who the hell are you, and what are you doing trailing us?"

The man said, "I'm Eddie Guilfoile, and you're gonna go kill Zapata, and I want in on it."

The old man shook his head. "Okay, Guilfoile, get down and tell us why you want in."

Eddie asked, "Can I put my hands down first, so's I can get off this horse in one piece? And tell your Indian friends not to shoot me in the back, okay?"

Harrington told the yards to come back in, and they slowly filtered back into the camp, but with hands on their dhas, not sure about Guilfoile. Eddie stepped down from the gelding; ground reined him and looked around the camp. He nodded and stood quietly as the old man got up from his position and walked over. "What do you mean we're going to kill somebody?"

Putting his hands up defensively, Guilfoile answered, "You don't drive by my place, sneak into a deserted homestead at night and drop off horses. Then sneak in two trucks full of people and leave the same night unless you're going to do something to somebody. When you leave a trail a blind man can follow and the border patrol disappears for two days that means somebody has connections. Mr. Sheriff, I know who you are, and I know you were the one that figured out who my boy was and saved my Iris from finding his head in the mailbox. But what you couldn't and didn't do was find the killers. Maybe your granddaughter got a few of them, but I think you're going after the head man. I want in."

He sobbed, "They kilt my boy for no damn reason, other than they were pissed off at me. That ain't right!"

The old man threw up his hands, "Ah screw it, welcome to the traveling circus. You don't do *anything* without letting either me or Francisco know first. Understood?" Guilfoile nodded mutely.

Time passed slowly, as the now larger group eased down through various canyons. In a small hanging valley the old man called an early halt, and directed everyone to picket the horses and let them graze and water for twelve hours. He hoped this would renew their stamina and he knew all of them needed a break. He watched Harrington dismount slowly and asked, "Mike, you going to make it? Looks like you're having a rough time."

Harrington replied, "Come hell or high water, I'll be there at the end. Don't you worry about me. I got my Tylenol, and it ain't the first time I've been stove up on an op. Makes it easy to stay alert don't ya know."

The old man smiled. "Okay, you know what we're up against, but I just wanted to ask. How are the 'Yards doing? Mikey is the only one that ever says anything to me."

Harrington said, "Oh, they're doin' okay. Just want to get it stuck in and kill themselves some drug dealers. They don't see much beyond black and white, so far's they are concerned, they need to do this to regain the family's honor. And the more they pile up, the better for Toby's trip to the next plane."

At midnight the old man rolled out, stretched and took the watch from Francisco with the desultory small talk that only occurs in the middle of the night watch turnovers. Rather than wake Harrington at zero four hundred, the old man continued to prowl around the camp, never looking directly at the small pocket fire, now burned down to embers. His thoughts vacillated between Jesse, wondering how she was doing; what he was planning, and how to approach the compound with this crowd. He just wanted one shot, but he wasn't sure Francisco,

Holloway, Guilfoile or the 'Yards were going to
agree to that. Guilfoile was a mystery of sorts, he
didn't say much just trudged along on a stolen horse
like he didn't have a care in the world. *I wonder if
Clay is missing Dusty yet. And what about
Guilfoile's wife, Iris? Yeah, Iris... What's she
thinking? But I guess he's got as much reason to be
here as I do, maybe more...*

The old man made one more check of the horses
as the first light of dawn showed in the eastern sky,
and the ridgeline above the camp became visible.
The two youngest 'Yards, Fred and Elmer, came
back into camp at the same time, chattering happily
and carrying AK-47s. When asked, they told him
they'd found a camp just over the ridgeline early in
the morning with three 'bad guys' in it; 'bad guys'
being defined as people with guns, so they killed
them and took the guns. They'd disposed of the
bodies in a crevasse saying they would never be
found. They'd also wiped out all traces of the camp,
and brought a bag containing tamales and other food
back to camp. The old man questioned them in more
detail as Mikey and Deng returned to camp, and
discovered they'd found the camp because the bad
guys were smoking pot and telling jokes. Parceling
out the food, the old man also discovered a VHF
radio stuck in the bottom of the bag, turning it on, he
saw that it was on a preset frequency, and had almost
seventy percent of its battery left. He turned on the
satphone at seven am, heard nothing and turned it
back off with a sigh.

As everyone rolled out, he made the decision to push hard, knowing that somebody would come looking for these three sooner or later. He just hoped it was later. "Okay, we've got it stuck in now, so we're going to pick up the pace a bit. Grab a tamale and let's get to it. We've got miles to go, and the terrain is fairly easy today. Tomorrow, we'll be moving into close proximity to the compound, and I want to have plenty of time to recon the approaches."

Quickly repacking the pack horse, Francisco took the lead rope and started up out of the hanging valley, settling the AR over his shoulder as he moved. Harrington mounted slowly, settled his rifle and followed with Guilfoile next and the old man bringing up the rear. The old man noted that Guilfoile rode with what looked like a suppressed .22 on his saddle bow, and had a weird looking little axe on his belt. Guilfoile saw the look, "Winchester sixty-nine A match, old K four on top, and I built the flower pot can myself. I scrounged a couple of ten round mags to go with it. I can punch a half inch all day long at a hunnert yards with it. And no serial numbers," he said with a smile.

The old man smiled. "I know nothing, I see nothing, but don't shoot unless you have to."

The 'Yards had moved off fanning out on each side of the trail, and changing the order so that there was an AK on each side of the group now. The old man was a bit worried about them using the AKs rather than knives, but decided to just let it ride, as there wouldn't be much he could do about it.

Late in the afternoon, they crested a low ridge and were met by eleven folks walking up the trail from the south. Francisco was back in the lead, and talked to their leader. As it turned out, they were Guatemalans, trying to get to the border where they were supposed to meet a coyote who was going to take them across into Texas and a new life. For only five thousand dollars apiece.

Francisco convinced them he was escorting a hunting party who were out for the big mule deer, and asked if they had seen any. After getting the location where the Guatemalans had seen some earlier than day, the parties separated and continued on their respective ways. The old man rode up next to Francisco. "You think they believed you?"

Francisco shrugged. "Don't know, but walking where they are, they've got at least four or five days to get anywhere close to the border, and we'll be in and out in the next forty-eight hours, so I really don't think it makes much difference."

The old man said, "Yeah, you've got a point." Pulling the map out of his saddlebags, he passed it over to Francisco and pointed to a point a couple of miles ahead. "I think this is probably a good spot to lay up, good visibility on three sides and the cliff to the top of the ridge behind us. Maybe find some water there too. I know the 'Yards need a break, they didn't get much sleep last night."

Francisco glassed the area after looking at the map. "Okay, if we get up above that scree slope ahead of us, it looks like there is enough of a ridge that we can follow it all the way in."

Francisco led off, and they scrambled up the
ridge then down into the bowl, finding a spring and
good grazing for the horses. A dry camp was made,
and MREs handed out with the portable heaters.
Splitting the MREs between two people gave them
enough calories to keep going, but didn't fill them
up; as the old man mentally calculated how many
were left, he realized they were going to run out long
before they made it back, if they made it back, to
Texas. Harrington and Guilfoile volunteered to take
the watches, and Harrington also told the 'Yards to
flake out and get a good night's rest. The old man
pulled the saddle off Diablo, gave him a rough rub
down, and leaned back against the saddle; his idea to
do some mental planning didn't work out, as he was
asleep in minutes.

Rolling over eight hours later, the old man stifled
a groan and sat up slowly. The first light of dawn
was touching the top of the peaks to the east.
Looking around, he saw Guilfoile moving slowly
through the horses, mumbling to them and touching
them to keep them calm; Diablo didn't even react
when Guilfoile reached up and stroked his nose. The
old man noted that Guilfoile really did have a way
with the horses, almost as well as Toby did or had.
And that brought the old man fully awake with anger
boiling up; *WHY? Why in the hell did Juanita and
Toby have to die? Why couldn't they have picked on
him instead?* Tamping down his anger, he retreated
into himself, to that cold dead place where no
emotions were allowed. *He had a job to do, and he
was damn well going to do it or die trying.* He

levered himself up and walked over to the supply packs; reaching in he laid out enough MREs for everyone to share again, and grabbed the binoculars off the top of the pack. Climbing up to the top of the ridge, he eased up and glassed the areas to the south, east and west, noting some road traffic on Highway 22, and lights in the distance that had to be San Buenaventura. Directly south, he noticed two small streams of smoke that were rising and determined they were further down the hills from the route he intended to take. Turning back to the northwest, he saw clouds moving in their direction, and figured they would be getting at least some rain before the day was over.

Satisfied, he eased back down the ridge to their camp, and Francisco handed him half an MRE and a cup of lukewarm coffee. When everyone had finished eating and all the trash had been buried, he dug out the satphone and turned it on, then pulled out the map and gathered everyone around it. Pointing to the path he planned to follow, he said, "Okay, we've got about ten maybe twelve miles to go to be in position. I want to be there by sunset and get some idea of the lay of the land and angles to the compound. Francisco, you'll be spotting for me. Harrington, I want you and the 'Yards to pull security; Guilfoile, you'll have the horses. If we run into anybody, take them if you can do it quietly; I don't want to advertise our presence until we have to."

Guilfoile asked, "How close are you going to get, Sheriff?"

The old man answered, "As far away as I can and still get a reasonable shot, and I think five to six hundred yards and the height of the ridge will give me that. I don't want to get down on the flat with the compound, we wouldn't stand a chance. If we stay up on the ridge, at least we've got a chance of getting out of this alive."

"But are you sure you can hit him from that far away?"

The old man just looked at Guilfoile, who shrugged as if to say, *I had to ask.* The old man looked at Francisco, who shook his head, Guilfoile who said nothing and Harrington who merely nodded. "Let's do it," he said.

The old man turned to Mikey and the other 'Yards, asked them if they understood and received no questions in return. He folded the map and said, "Okay, let's pack up and get on the trail. Francisco's lead, then Harrington, Guilfoile with the pack horse, and I'm bringing up the rear. Locked and loaded, but don't fire unless you're fired on."

He turned off the satphone with regret, wondering again as he saddled Diablo, how Jesse was doing, and then buried those thoughts. He helped Francisco load the packhorse, and handed the lead rope to Guilfoile who was already up on his horse. Harrington had sent the 'Yards on ahead, again splitting them to each side of the track, and they had disappeared into the scrub and early morning light. Looking off to the west, he took in the desert, looking pink and fresh in the morning light and somberly beautiful. He swung up on

Diablo and nodded to Francisco, who took the lead and climbed out of the bowl. After one more look at the desert, the old man turned away and concentrated on riding trail and watching for movement of any kind further up the ridges.

Aaron's Return

Aaron stepped off the C-17 into the bright sunlight at NAS North Island a week after he'd received notification about Jesse's shooting. To put it mildly he wasn't in a good mood, but at least he was back on US soil, and once he'd cleared the cargo onto the trucks back to Camp Pendleton, he was officially on leave. Looking across the ramp toward base ops, he saw Matt waving at him. He waved back and addressed his sergeant. "Okay, I'm gonna go find the trucks and see what the plan is, you guys hang loose, get the personal bags off the airplane and stack 'em under the wing."

Walking toward base ops, he spotted a group of flatbed trucks parked next to a small building, veering that way, he saw a group of Marines and picked up to a trot. Arriving at the group, he picked out the sergeant. "You guys here to pick up the gear from 1st SOB?"

"Yep, we're your guys. How many pallets?"

"We've got nine pallets of cargo on this one. I've got four guys that will need to ride back with you to bed the stuff down at the warehouse once you get back to Pendleton. Is that doable?

"Yeah, no problem. We all came down as singles, so there's room for us to take your guys back. All we're waiting on now is the chief to tell us we can go on the ramp, and where he wants us to line up to receive the cargo. We can load two, two, two, two and one on the pallets and that will give every truck a similar load. I want to put the heaviest load on as a single."

Aaron thought for a second. "Okay, talk to the loadmaster, he'll have the weights. I *think* the heavy pallet is either number six or seven."

About that time, a Navy chief walked around the corner of the building making a wind it up signal. The sergeant said, "Okay, troops, let's do it."

Aaron turned away and trotted over to where Matt was standing, the handshake devolved into a bear hug and back slapping with Aaron asking, "Any word?"

Matt shook his head. "No change. Jesse's still not conscious, but apparently they think she's getting better. Felicia and Angelina are talking pretty much on a daily basis if not more. Trey is still there, along with that doc that Trey talked into coming down."

Aaron scuffed a boot. "Fuck! Why can't they… Ah shit, I'm not trying to beat you up, Matt. It's just that this week has been hell. Lemme go grab my shit off the airplane, and check out with the major and we can get out of here."

As Aaron trotted back to the airplane, Matt made a quick call to Felicia telling her Aaron was on deck, and they'd be there in an hour. Ten minutes later, Aaron came back with his pack and seabag, dumped them in the back of the truck and silently climbed in. Matt turned to Aaron. "Well, at least you're here. I was worried you'd go UA if they didn't let you go

187

immediately…"

Aaron sat back. "Yeah, I damn near did, but the sar'major and colonel both *counselled* me on why that wasn't a good idea, and why they couldn't just let me go on emergency leave. Plus they both said if Jesse was awake and not in a coma, they'd have let me go. As it is, I'm back a week early, 'cause I came back with the admin pogues, but at least I'm on leave as of tomorrow morning, and I have thirty days authorized."

Matt said, "What's the plan now?"

"I'm gonna go dump this crap, get some food and sleep until morning. I'll call in at zero eight, and be out the door and on the road one minute after. Have you heard anything from Mr. Cronin on the fucks that hit the ranch?"

Matt shifted in his seat. "Nah, you know him; he's pretty closed mouth about anything over an open line. Matter of fact, I haven't heard from him in a couple of days. Felicia is talking to Angelina pretty much every day, so that's where I was getting the updates I was passing to you. I did talk to Trey once, and explained why you weren't there. You going to stay at the ranch, right?"

Aaron replied, "Yep, I'm supposed to check with Felix Ortega when I get there, and I guess he's kinda filling in for Francisco. I wonder what the situation is with him?"

"I don't know, other than they had to sedate him at the ranch. Oh yeah, Felicia will be at the apartment, and she's probably going to fall apart. Just a heads up."

Aaron looked at Matt. "So things are *progressing* between the two of y'all?"

Matt shrugged. "Yeah, I guess that's a good word. Oh yeah, your phone is in the console. Forgot to mention that earlier."

Aaron dug his phone out of the console, and the rest of the ride was spent in silence as Aaron caught up on the emails and voice mails sitting on his phone, including one from Jesse telling him how much she missed him.

As Matt turned into the parking space at the apartment, he saw that Aaron was playing one message over and over. Rather than say anything, he just sat quietly until Aaron looked up and saw they were home. They got out of the truck, with Matt grabbing the seabag and Aaron shouldering his pack. As Matt opened the front door, Felicia hit Aaron like a mini-tornado: hugging him, crying and telling him she was sorry for what had happened. Aaron gently disengaged her, and walked into his room. Dropping the pack on the bed, he went to retrieve his duffle bag and found Felicia and Matt in a confrontation, he heard Felicia say, "Well, did you tell him?"

Matt mumbled, "No, I didn't! That wasn't..."

Aaron broke in, "Tell me what?"

Felicia blurted, "Matt didn't tell you they tried to kill Jesse again?"

"*No!*" Turning on Matt he shouted, "Why am I just *now* finding out about this?"

Matt held up his hands. "What would you have done Aaron? You were six *thousand* miles away. It got handled, they never got to Jesse, and all three of them are dead."

Aaron started. "Dead? How? Did Mr. Cronin take them out?"

Matt answered, "Well, he was involved, but they took themselves out."

Aaron threw up his hands and turned away, picked up his seabag and took it back to his room. A half hour later, after Matt and Felicia had quiet words and cleared up their misunderstandings, Matt cautiously knocked on Aaron's door. "Hey man, you want dinner? I got steaks." Hearing what he took to be a mumbled acceptance, he and Felicia fixed steaks, potatoes and a salad. Over dinner, Matt and Felicia filled Aaron in on what had been going on, including what they'd gotten from Angelina, the sheriff, and Colonel Muir who was heading up the retired Marines guarding Jesse. Somewhat mollified, Aaron seemed to relax a bit, and told a couple of stories of what had gone on during the det. By the end of the meal, everybody was in a much better mood. Aaron finally said, "Okay, I'm going down for a few hours. I've got my bags packed, and I'm hitting the road as soon as I call in tomorrow morning. Y'all still planning to come out in two weeks?"

Matt and Felicia looked at each other. "Do you think Jesse is going to recover? And if so, is there still going to be a wedding?"

Aaron replied, "I have faith. I'm hoping she will, and will still want to marry me. So yes or no?"

A look passed between the two and Felicia replied, "Yes, *we* will be there, for you *and* for Jesse." With that, she came around the table and gave him a hug and a kiss on the cheek.

The next morning Matt got up and saw Aaron off, with the promise that if Aaron needed anything, he would bring it. Thirteen hours and two speeding tickets later, Aaron pulled into the hospital parking lot in Ft. Stockton. Getting out and stretching gave him a minute to get his mind together, he looked up and saw stars horizon to horizon and a full moon hanging low in the sky. He said a quick prayer as he walked toward the hospital entrance, and wondered if they would even let him in. Approaching the front entry, he saw a man step out of the shadows by the door. He was dressed in a blazer and khaki slacks with a radio in his hand. Aaron instinctually knew this was one of the retired Marines. Stopping in front of the retired Marine he said, "Staff Sergeant Miller here to see Miss Jesse Cronin."

The man replied, "Seen your picture, staff sergeant. Up the elevator, turn right, end of the hall. Angelina is expecting you." As Aaron turned away, he heard the man say, "Post three to one and base. Miller is on the way up."

Aaron paused. "Thanks. And thanks for keeping Jesse alive." The man just nodded back.

Aaron went slowly up the stairs to the second floor, then down the hall to the ICU, nodding to the two retired Marines, but not saying anything to them. He stopped at the door, now that he was here, not sure he was ready to see Jesse. Summoning his courage, he slowly opened the door and stepped into the ICU. Angelina came quickly around the desk and hugged him whispering, "I'm glad you're here, Aaron."

He asked, "Where is she?"

Angelina took his hand and led him back to the cubicle were Jesse was. Trey was updating the chart and didn't see or hear Aaron come in. Aaron took that moment to stop at the foot of the bed and look; his first thought was that Jesse looked like a combat casualty, then realized she literally *was* a combat casualty, albeit one that took place in the USA rather than overseas. Trey finally took his stethoscope off, hanging it around his neck and turned to put the chart back on the foot of the bed. He looked up and met Aaron's eyes, and Aaron saw both sympathy and worry in his expression. Trey just stuck out his hand and said, "I'm glad you're here."

Aaron shook his hand and blurted, "Trey, is she gonna make it?"

Trey answered, "Yeah, Baby Girl is gonna make it. She's too damn stubborn not to!"

"How bad is it? She doesn't look good..."

A voice behind Aaron answered, "She's recovering nicely, the swelling is almost completely reduced in her skull, and we've dropped the medications to the point that she's only on maintenance for pain. She's starting to move on her own, so I believe she is slowly coming out of the coma. Her shoulder and leg are coming along nicely, and I don't see any problems there. By the way, I'm Dr. Hoffman."

Aaron said, "Thanks, Doc. Is it okay if I sit with her a while?"

Hoffman replied, "Of course. But you need rest too. Please don't stay so long that you can't finish your drive in safety." Beckoning to Angelina and Trey, he backed out of the cubicle, leaving Aaron still standing at the foot of the bed.

Aaron stepped around to the side of the bed, taking Jesse's hand as he did so. It felt limp, and he unconsciously started rubbing it while telling Jesse he loved her and how much he missed her. Tears rolled unheeded down his cheeks as he continued to talk softly to her. Finally, he leaned over and kissed her cheek, lay her hand softly back on the bed and left the cubicle. Angelina looked up as Aaron stopped in front of her. "What time can I come back in the morning? And who was that doctor?"

Angelina said, "Visiting hours start at nine in the morning. And don't bring flowers, we have way too many in here now. Besides, we don't need Jesse getting an infection or lung problem from pollen. There'll be plenty of time for that when she's back with us. That's Dr. Hoffman, he was one of Trey's professors and he's a neurosurgeon. And yes, he's a tad strange, but most doctors are."

Aaron smiled at that, thanked her, and walked slowly back to his truck. He called Felix, met him at the ranch house and climbed into bed in a daze.

He rolled out the next morning, took a quick shower and remembered he hadn't called Matt. He did so, and hit a McDonald's on the way to the hospital. It finally hit him that he hadn't seen either the old man or Francisco, and when he walked back into the ICU, he asked Angelina. He was stunned to find that no one seemed to know where either of them were, and hadn't heard from them for almost a week. His next thought was that *something* was getting done, and done without him, which pissed him off.

The Shot

After eight hours of hard riding, they were just below the military crest of the ridge above Zapata's compound. The last two hours had been nerve-wracking, trying to move as quietly as possible, and constantly scanning for possible guards/lookout posts. They hadn't seen anyone, and now it was all about getting into the best position for the shot. The old man was belly down, glassing the compound when Francisco crawled up on his left. "Looks just like the picture, doesn't it?"

The old man squirmed back a few feet, laser rangefinder in hand. "Yep, I just lased the back roof over the patio, it's about eleven hundred yards. I think I need to get down and further right to get a good angle for the shot." Pointing down to a small knob he continued, "Somewhere right around that knob would give me a decent sight line, and it's probably three or four hundred yards closer. That way I can be damn sure I'm hitting the right guy."

Francisco took the binoculars and methodically swept the area. "I count eleven guards, six outside and five on the walls or inside. We going to try to take any of them?"

Looking at the sun, and the weather moving in behind them, the old man replied, "Not planning on it. I think one maybe two shots and haul ass outta here in a couple of hours. I'm not really interested in anybody but Zapata, and I know we kill him, they'll replace him, but I want to make sure the sumbitches *think* about what happened before they do."

Francisco nodded. "Yeah, but I'm not sure Guilfoile or Harrington, or the 'Yards are thinking that way. I think they want their pound of flesh too, and I know damn well I do!"

The old man looked over at Francisco. "I know what you're saying, Francisco, but taking just one shot and trying to get out *may* be the only thing that keeps us alive. I didn't plan this as a suicide mission."

Easing back down the slope, the old man and Francisco got up and walked back to the rest of the group. Scratching out a diagram in the dirt, the old man laid out his plan and what he wanted to do. Guilfoile immediately protested: he didn't want to be the horse holder, but Cronin convinced him he was the best option, and if he valued Dusty at all, he was probably the only one to hold them. The old man pointed to an overhang a few yards away. "It probably won't hold all the horses, but if you get them nose in, and feed them, it should keep them calm for a little while. I want to do this shot and be out of here in a couple of hours."

Grumbling, Guilfoile acquiesced. Meanwhile, Harrington and the 'Yards were deep in a discussion in Degar about whom would go where and how. They had all snuck looks and considered it a target rich environment, and wanted to avenge Toby in the worst way, especially Mikey and Deng, since they hadn't gotten in on the earlier killing of the bad guys. Harrington finally turned to the old man. "Well, looking at what you've drawn up, and the slope down there, we can fan out the four 'Yards down below your spot by about thirty yards, and cover most of the approaches from there. I don't think I can get down that far, or back up in a hurry, so I'll cover the back door up here, along with Guilfoile, and also cover the reverse side of the ridge if we get any visitors."

The old man nodded. "Okay, I want to be in position to make the shot if he comes out. We need to start easing into position in the next half hour or so. I want to shoot as soon as we get a good ID, and I'm counting on Francisco to spot for me. We're going to drop down to the west, then come around the ridge to that knob. It looks like there is a trail down there that the 'Yards could use too. As soon as I shoot, start pulling back up here, keeping under cover as best you can."

The old man went to Diablo, uncased the rifle and meticulously checked everything from scope to action to a clear barrel. Taking a silicon rag out of the case, he wiped the bolt, barrel and action down, then reached into his saddlebags and took out a box of ammo. He opened it and loaded the rifle with five rounds then started to put the box back, but ended up sticking it in his backpack instead. To Francisco he said, "You ready?"

Francisco looked up from taping two magazines together. "Yep, no use waiting any longer."

A half hour later the old man and Francisco were in position on the knob. The old man took a sandbag out of his backpack, fluffed it to his satisfaction and set the rifle in position on it, leaving the scope covers closed. Francisco stuck his head up long enough to lase the back doors and said, "Looks like five hundred sixty two yards John. Down angle is twelve degrees. Looks like an east to west wind, I'm guessing about ten miles an hour."

The old man rolled the rifle to get at the turret controls setting the parallax first, then mumbled, "Sixty-nine, down twelve loses two-ish... Call it sixty-seven and change, so eleven MOA plus a click, ten is sixteen on the wind, so two point five-ish MOA, so eight clicks and one left." He set both turret controls for windage and elevation, tapping them gently with the covers before putting the caps in his pocket.

He looked at Francisco. "If I get a shot, I'm not going for a head shot today. I'm going center of mass, twice just to make sure. Once we get a little closer to sunset, or he pops out, give me a quick recheck on the range and wind, and I'll just change the hold if it's different than calculated. I will try a second shot depending on what happens just to make sure."

Francisco sobbed, "Si. I wish I could take the shot, but you are much better at this range. And my anger would probably make me miss anyway. For my sake, John, and for Juanita's memory, kill that sonofabitch."

Ten minutes later the first patter of rain fell, accompanied by booming thunder and lightning in the distance, as the weather front moved over them. The old man just hunched down, thinking *well, I hope we still have horses to go back to. I really hope Guilfoile is as good as he thinks he is. And I wonder if Zapata will even step out.*

***

Down below, Ernesto 'Cuchillo' Zapata stepped out onto the back patio accompanied by Roberto and the young chica he had just finished with. Turning to her he said, "Drinks for Roberto and I, and make sure you clean up the bedroom before I return." Swatting her on the butt, he turned away as she scurried off. "Roberto, is Flores still here?"

Roberto spoke softly into his radio then said, "*Si, Jefe* he is in the pool room now."

"Have the guards invite him to join us! This sunset will be spectacular with the clouds that are forming! It would be a shame for him to miss it, afterward we can have dinner and more drinks while I make him understand I am taking care of the problems with the distribution so that he can go back to the Zetas tomorrow and satisfy them. I don't want to mention the loss of the money though. We will play that down."

"*Si, Jefe*." Speaking into his radio again, Roberto told the guards to bring Flores, and nodded to Zapata, "*Momento*."

199

Unbeknownst to any of the major protagonists, the 'Yards had found a path all the way down and were moving silently toward the walls of the compound. All had their dhas out and were picking out targets among the guards who were mounting a desultory guard, or slowly walking posts near the accesses to the compound.

***

On the knob, the old man flipped the scope covers up and settled in behind the gun as Francisco glassed the patio. "Definitely Zapata is the one on the left, and looks like Roberto is there too. I saw Roberto talking into his radio, but I don't see any changes in the guards."

"Concur. Wind check? I'm feeling it on my right cheek now."

Francisco took a quick look down. "Damn, the wind is now out of the west, I think it's about ten knots."

"Okay, I'll change the hold to four MOA right that should put the round on. I'm read…"

Francisco started cussing a blue streak, and started to get up raising his AR. The old man grabbed him, 'Francisco, what the fuck are you doing?"

"That *bastardo*, Flores, he was the one who killed my children. I'm going to kill him! Now!"

"Gahdammit, Francisco, get your head straight, I need you to call my shots and the primary is Zapata,

I'll try to get a shot on the other guy, but I need your help spotting me!"

Francisco lay back down. "I am sorry John, my emotions…"

"Okay, let me get a get a shot in here. Give me a lineup."

Francisco glassed the patio. "Zapata is in the center, Flores to his right, Roberto to his left and behind, and some young girl serving drinks. Hold fire."

"Target and holding for him to turn around."

"Zapata is passing out cigars, and Roberto is lighting them. Hold. Wind ten from the right."

"Holding."

"Girl is gone. Toasting, now walking away from Roberto. Wind ten from the right."

"Target."

Francisco sighed, "Send it."

BOOM.

The old man rode the recoil, knowing he had roughly ¾ of second before the round impacted and a couple of seconds for reaction time.

"Hit! I saw a splash of blood on his shirt! And he's down."

With a second round up, the old man said, "Target."

"Send it."

BOOM.

A second round hits Zapata making the body jump. Again riding the recoil he said, "Where is Flores?"

***

At the sound of the first round from the knob, the 'Yards each took out one of the guards they'd selected and Mikey and Deng, since they had one less body count than Fred and Elmer, moved toward two guards huddled under a little eave by an entry way. Mikey and Deng each got on one side of the eave and Mikey hit the wall hard with his dha, causing both of the guards to straighten up and grab their rifles off their shoulders. When they did, Mikey and Deng each sliced the throats of a guard, and followed up with a thrust to the chest. Deng's dha hung up on the battle pack of AK rounds, and he was cussing and kicking the body before he finally got it loose.

Mikey saw a roll of twine hanging on a nail, and grabbed it, along with the AK from the dead guard, and motioned for Deng to follow him.

***

"Flores is scrambling toward the house on all fours. Roberto has his pistol out, looking around and is on his radio."

"Target."

"Send it, please God kill the sonofabitch!"

BOOM.

"Missed him, he zigged as I shot."

Francisco jumped up and fired all twenty rounds in his magazine at the back patio, screaming as the old man calmly chambered another round. Flores, scrambling for his life, had reached the door and was opening it. Exhaling the old man punched one more round downrange. BOOM. Riding the recoil, he dropped back on target in time to see Flores sprawl across the threshold of the door. Quickly scoping the area, he saw Roberto grabbing his shoulder, and looking back up toward the ridge. He was puzzled until he realized Francisco's spray and pray had at least winged Roberto.

Getting to his knees, he realized he was hearing gunfire from below the knob and to the left side of the compound wall, but nothing from the right. Scoping quickly, he could barely see through the rain what he assumed were guards firing along ground level down the wall of the compound, but not up toward the knob. Rather than waste any rounds, he levered himself up and grabbed Francisco who was on his knees sobbing. "Come on, everybody and their damn brother down there knows where we are now. We've got to shit and git, if we want to survive this."

Thunder and lightning broke overhead, along with heavy rain, as the old man lifted Francisco to his feet. They slowly made their way back to the overhang where the horses were, and lo and behold, they were still there, along with Guilfoile and Harrington. Guilfoile looking harried and relieved asked, "Did you get him? I heard a lot of shots."

Harrington crowded in close as the old man said, "I hit him twice center mass, so he's toast, and also took out another guy for Francisco. Where are the 'Yards?"

Harrington kept scanning, "I don't know, I heard an AR, and a bunch of AKs, but I haven't seen hide nor hair of them yet."

Pulling a dry rag from his saddlebags, the old man methodically wiped down the rifle saying, "That was Francisco. Apparently the other guy is the one that killed his kids a number of years ago. Francisco. Francisco!" Putting the rifle back in the case, he re-strapped it on the back of Diablo's saddle.

Francisco dully looked around, "John, please tell me you got him? *Please?*"

The old man said patiently, "Yes, I got a round into him, and he was down at the threshold of the door. Now snap out of it dammit, we need you in the here and now." He patted Diablo on the flank and saw that his ears were back. "Head's up, somebody's coming."

Drawing his .45, he moved to clear Diablo as Harrington and Francisco spread out and brought their rifles up. Out of the rain came all four 'Yards, with all four now carrying AKs and wearing chest packs of magazines.

The old man shook his head, looked at Harrington and asked, "Did you know they were going all the way down to the compound?"

Harrington held up his hands. "No! I told 'em not to do that, but it's obvious they didn't listen. At least they're all back."

Holstering his pistol the old man asked Mikey in Degar, "What the hell did you do?"

Mikey smiled and told the old man and Harrington they had found a path all the way down to the bottom, and managed to cut up six of the guards on two sides of the compound. His comment was something to the effect that they weren't real guards, more like thugs with guns. He laughed when he explained how they'd found a roll of twine and tied one of the guard's AKs to a tree at the corner of the compound leading to the front gate, then they used the rest of the twine they'd found let them get back to the track up the ridge before they pulled the trigger, setting off the gunfight at the front of the compound.

The old man finally said, "Okay. Let's mount up and get out of here. They know we're here, so it's going to be a fight on the way out. Francisco on point, Harrington, Guilfoile, and I'll bring up the rear." Turning to the 'Yards he told them in Degar not to spread out too wide, and to move directly back down the trail, keeping within 100 yards of the trail.

On the Run

In the compound, Roberto was trying to marshal the guards while dragging both Zapata and Flores back inside. He could hear AK fire outside the compound, but couldn't get anyone to answer him with a coherent location for the shooters. He knew at least some of the rounds had come from the ridge line, and one of them had hit him in the arm. Rolling Zapata over, he saw immediately he was gone; two rounds had hit him in the upper chest, and one must have blown up his heart, because there was no pulse, and apparently not a lot of blood left.

Flores moaned, and then screamed as Roberto started to roll him over. Looking down, he could see blood welling from Flores lower back and upper shoulder. Going to the door, he yelled for the doctor to be brought to him, and went back to trying to organize the guards. Finally getting through to one of the guard leaders, he directed them to climb the ridge and kill anyone they found, while he directed that the Federales be notified of the attack and that they should start searching for the shooters. When asked how many, he stopped for a second, then said two shooters. He also told the team leader to call for ambulances, knowing there had to be at least a few people down.

When the doctor came in, he pointed him at Flores, and told him what he thought the injuries were. While the doctor worked on Flores, Roberto picked up the phone, surprised to find it still working. Dialing a number from memory, he waited for it to be answered then said, "This is Roberto we have been attacked. Cuchillo is dead and your number three is badly injured. I am going to find the shooters now." Hanging up, he turned back to watch the doctor, who said, "You're bleeding. Where were you hit?"

Roberto looked down at himself in surprise, then the top of his shoulder started stinging. He opened his shirt to discover a furrow across the top of his shoulder a half inch from his neck. Impatiently, he said, "It's not serious, it can wait." And stalked from the room, yelling into his radio.

At the front door, he was met by two of the three team leaders, Santos and Jose; the third appeared to be missing. So far they had found six bodies, apparently killed by knives or machetes, and had three more that were wounded by AK fire. Sporadic AK fire still sounded outside the compound, but he was sure it wasn't aimed at anything by now. Santos said he'd put four of his team in a truck with orders to get around the backside of the ridge and cut off any retreat to the north. He'd also sent another truck with three to the west in case they tried to break toward Highway 20.

**

After riding all night, the old man figured they'd made nineteen maybe twenty hard miles, and called a halt as the sun rose. He'd purposely ridden by the bowl they had camped in the previous night, not wanting to be predictable, and wanting as much distance as he could get between the compound and them. Looking around he saw a small fall of water, probably from the rains that had continued most of the night. Pointing, he said, "Okay, canteens and we'll take four-five hours here. Dry camp, split up the supplies if you will Guilfoile, give everybody a complete MRE. Nose bags and the last of the grain for the horses too. 'Yards go down first. The rest of us will take turns guarding in one hour shifts."

Guilfoile passed out the MREs as the old man and Francisco got nose bags on the horses and hobbled them at the back of the depression. Harrington seemed even worse than before, needing Mikey's help to keep from falling as they eased him to a flat place where he could lay down. He flipped the binoculars to Francisco saying, "Can you go check our back trail and see if anybody is trying to close us from either side? While you do that, I'll grab a bite, then take the watch."

Francisco caught them and took off up to the top of the ridge without a word. The old man leaned back against his saddle took the satphone out and turned it on, then picked up the MRE packet. Tuna was *not* his favorite, and he was tempted to switch with Francisco, but just sucked it up and ripped the pack open. He poured water and the instant coffee into the beverage bag, then walked over to the runoff, filling the heater bag and quickly stuffing it in the box. Sitting back down, he dug out a spoon and the little Tabasco bottle, dumped the Tabasco in and stirred it around as well as he could. Looking at his watch, he regretfully turned the satphone off and put in back in the saddlebags. Slowly eating the tuna, he used the crackers in the package to at least kill *some* of the tuna's taste. Finishing, he picked up the heater box and pulled out the instant coffee. Normally he wouldn't put anything in his coffee, but knowing he'd need the energy, if only for a little while, he dumped the sugar and creamer packets in and shook it up. He pulled his battered old coffee cup out of the saddlebag and poured the mixture in as Francisco returned.

Francisco squatted, handing the binoculars back. "Nothing to the east, doesn't appear to be anything on the back-trail, but there seems to be more traffic on twenty and I caught flashes off vehicles that were moving up some of the arroyos on the other side of the ridge. I didn't see anything that could get close to us. As far as I remember, unless they bring in horses or a helicopter, we should be okay until we get to where twenty cuts across."

The old man said, "Thanks. We've got to try to push hard up through here, and I want to be by most of the little ranchos before they start sending people out. The one that worries me is the Hacienda down in the flat that has the little strip on it. I'm hoping they can't or won't put a helo out there to search for us."

Francisco looked around. "Yeah, not much we can do about that one. Try to get by in the night is the best I think."

The old man stood up. "Eat and get some rest. I'll be back in two hours."

Francisco sat down, and started opening his MRE as the old man walked around the camp, noting that Harrington and all the 'Yards were down and out. Guilfoile was leaned back against his saddle, but the old man couldn't tell if he was awake or asleep. Moving over to the horses, he pulled the nosebags off, letting them graze on what grass was available. Folding the bags up, he put them back in the pack and surreptitiously counted the remaining MREs; they only had eight left.

***

Back in the compound, Roberto continued to drive the remaining guards, constantly on the radio and urging them to stay alert and find the shooters. The three men he'd sent up the mountain had come back bedraggled and frustrated, seeing only a few shell cases on the ground and having no idea where they'd gone as the rain had wiped out all traces of the shooters. They'd found the two guards that were normally stationed on the mountainside trail dead with their throats cut and radios and guns missing.

He'd locked the compound down, cut off the phones and told the guards to shoot anyone that tried to leave. Two of the peons had been killed last night trying to sneak out and they'd finally found the third team leader, shot in the back of the head and lying near the wall. Roberto called the local Federales, demanding they launch their helicopter, but was met with refusal until they got approval from *higher* headquarters. Personally, Roberto thought it was because they were afraid to fly in the weather.

As the sun rose, two SUVs came up the road toward the compound and Roberto walked down to the front gate to meet them. He sent a guard out to see who was there, and the guard reported back that it was people from the Zeta cartel. After getting the gate open, Roberto cleared the veranda in front of the house and directed the two SUVs to pull directly in front of the steps. Heavily armed men erupted from both vehicles, pushing Roberto up against the front wall until a soft voice told his captors to let him go. He recognized Carlos Montoya, the number two in the Zetas and the acknowledged power behind the throne. Roberto bowed to Montoya and said, "*Jefe,* I'm sorry but we've lost both Zapata and Flores. The doctor did his best, but Flores died in the hospital around midnight."

Montoya asked, "What happened, Roberto? How did you let anyone get this close?"

Roberto started sweating, "*Jefe*, I don't know how they got this close unless they flew a helicopter in or came overland. Both guards on the mountain trail were found dead with their throats cut by the searchers I sent up last night, and four more guards down here were also cut up. Somebody tied one of the rifles in a tree at the corner of the compound and tied a string to the trigger, that's what got people shooting last night. We found the gun after everything was over. Also, they only took two guns from the guards they killed."

Montoya probed, "And what about Zapata and Flores?"

Roberto hunched his shoulders. "*Jefe,* you know how he liked to go out on the patio and smoke?" Montoya nodded. "He does that even though I'd warned him time and again."

Montoya made a come on motion.

Roberto continued, "He did so again, and invited Flores to have a drink with him and watch the sunset and rain move in. He and Flores had their drinks and were smoking cigars when Zapata went down. I never heard the shot, and he was hit a second time. Then I heard an automatic rifle firing, but it wasn't an AK, it was something else. I was trying to get Flores to the door and under cover and he was hit as he fell through the door."

Montoya said, "Show me. Were you shot too?" Pointing to the blood on the shirt and what appeared to be a bandage poking out of the collar.

As Roberto led Montoya and his guards to the second floor bedroom he said, "I was burned by a round, I'm not sure when I got hit." Opening the door to the bedroom, he led them in. Zapata lay on the bed where Roberto had put him last night, and the blood from Flores still stained the floor along with the detritus of the doctor's attempt to patch him up.

Montoya walked around the bed, then stepped over the blood and looked out at the patio; motioning to his guards, he sent them out to secure the patio before he stepped out. Seeing the bullet hole through the glass door, he looked around until he found were it had hit the tile then squatted and looked out the door. Holding his arm at the angle he'd captured, he walked out the door shuffled around until he'd gotten himself in line with the hole in the door and the impact on the tile. Looking up at the mountainside, he asked, "From that knob up there? Was that where the shots came from? And where were your guards?"

Roberto picked up his radio. "May I?" Montoya nodded, and Roberto called to the replacements on the mountain side, they came out of concealment and waved, and Montoya nodded. Roberto then said, "The knob is where they found some shell cases, so that is where we believe the shots came from."

Turning around, Montoya noted the scattered damage around the area of the door. "Curious that at least three shots hit Zapata and Flores but these others are scattered. Two shooters?"

"Possible, *Jefe*. I have been trying to find them rather than worrying about what they shot."

Montoya nodded. "Continue, Roberto, you did what you were told. I cannot fault you if Zapata wouldn't listen, but Flores should have known better. Now we have to find another *Federale Commandante* to move in here that we can trust. I will need the books and everything else that Zapata was working on, and a list of all his mules and coyotes. For now, you will continue to work from here, but we may move you elsewhere."

Roberto bowed his head in relief. "*Si, Jefe*. May I go now?"

Montoya said, "The office first, then bring the accountant and the books and anything else. Then you can go."

Roberto nodded and led them to Zapata's office, then used his radio to get the accountant on the way, and as an afterthought, told the guards to bring Jesus up too.

Moving North

Francisco toed the old man's boot, bringing him out of a deep sleep. Looking around the old man realized everyone else was already up and the horses were saddled with the exception of Diablo. Groaning, he levered himself up and picked up the saddle and blanket. Going to Diablo he saddled him and looked around at the group. "Any major problems?" Everyone shook their heads and the old man continued, "Okay, we need to drive hard today, we need to be in position to sneak by that hacienda again on the way back north. Looks like we did about twenty-one miles last night, and that's damn good considering. Same line up as last night. We'll move a little slower today, I don't want to cross any ridge lines until we scout them first. So we'll get an occasional break for a few minutes. Questions? Comments? Okay, let's do it."

Mounting up he marveled yet again at the 'Yards' resilience as they stoically trotted out ahead of the horses and slid off to the sides of the trail. They had to be worn down, but you'd never know it. Forty years earlier, Sergeant Cronin had learned just how durable the Montagnards were when he was shot in the leg on a patrol near the Ho Chi Min trail and they'd carried him for two days back to the ville. And not a damn one of them had weighed over a hundred pounds if that. *He just wanted to get them all back home. Home… Did he really think they could make it?*

Ten hours later, they hunkered down behind the last ridge before the hacienda and its little runway. The old man groaned and rolled his shoulders as he eased back down the ridge. Turning to Francisco, he said, "I think we need to stay here until sunset, we've been lucky so far, and I'm not willing to push it right now. Might as well break out the rest of the MREs and split them up; we'll get some food into us, and the horses can graze for a few hours."

Francisco dropped back down into the arroyo where the rest of the group were resting as Guilfoile climb up beside the old man. He said, "Sheriff, I dunno what's wrong with Harrington, but he don't look good at all, and I can't understand what he's saying to them 'Yards; but I think they're concerned too. And I know we're about out of food so I was wonderin' can I try to hunt a bit while we're here?"

The old man replied, "Yeah, I've been watching him, and I'm concerned too. But we're too deep in this to do anything else right now. How are you planning to hunt?"

Guilfoile patted his little .22 rifle. "Betsy here don't miss, and she's pretty damn quiet. I been watching and I know I can find some rabbits, been seeing them all day. I can get at least a couple and I found a place I can put a hatful of fire and do some cookin' too. Hell, Sheriff, I ain't contributed a damn thing to this little trip, and I feel bad 'bout takin' your food. Figure I can at least earn a bit of respect this way."

The old man leaned back against the slope. "It's not about respect, you've earned ours already by pitching in, never complaining. And if you hadn't held the horses in that storm the other night, we'd all be stuck on that damn ridge right now. You're right about the food though. Are you sure you can plink a few rabbits and not get us caught?"

Guilfoile smiled grimly. "I've been putting food in the pot for a long time with this ol' girl. Don't you worry." With that, he rose and eased back down the slope.

The old man sighed and tried to get his thoughts in order. He knew he was tired, and so was everyone else. The horses were getting beaten down, they were running out of food, and still had a day and a half at best, two days at worst to the border. *And they still had to get back across Highway 20. He was pretty sure there would be a watch there, and he didn't know if people were on their back trail, coming in from Highway 20 and 22 or whether they were going to put up surveillance assets. He was tempted to call Billy, but knew there wasn't a damn thing he could do even if he did make the call. Harrington was another worry, something was seriously wrong there, and he didn't know what. He resolved to try to get Mikey to tell him what was up. Maybe Guilfoile could get some meat; they were going to need something...*

He pushed off and eased back down the slope to the temporary camp. As he walked in, Francisco handed him half an MRE and asked for the binoculars, saying he'd take the watch. The old man sat on a rock and finished the MRE, then saw Francisco had left him the coffee packet. With a smile, he poured water out of his canteen into the bag, mixed in the coffee, creamer and sugar and stuffed it in the heater bag. A few minutes later, he pulled the bag out and shook it a few times, before breaking the seal and cautiously sipping the mixture. Grimacing at the taste, he picked up the remnants of the MRE and walked down to where somebody had dug a hole and dropped the bags in the hole.

Stretching and rolling his shoulders to try to relax, he walked further down the arroyo, seeing a glint off to the side, he turned and found a broken piece of pottery. Picking it up, he wondered how old it was, and how it had found its way here. He turned it over in his hands, and decided it must have been a part of a fairly big pot at one time. Scuffing in the dirt with his boot, he didn't see anymore and dropped it back where he'd seen it. He looked down the arroyo and took in the rock walls, opening out into the flats below, and the peace and quiet. Nothing stirred but the wind, and the smell of sagebrush was strong. He thought there was something to be said for being out in the remote part of the country. No blare of TV, no honking horns, no ringing phones, no light pollution at night.

Three hours later, the old man led the group out of the arroyo, crested the ridge and led them around the hacienda down on the flat. Another four hours and Mikey came in, stopping Francisco, then everyone else. He came back to the old man saying there were lights and people over the next ridge. Francisco came back and told the old man to hold his horse. In a three way conversation, they were able to get across to Mikey that Francisco would go back with him and look over the ridge to see if he could figure out what was going on.

A half hour later, Francisco came back with Mikey and the other 'Yards in tow. Everyone crowded around as Francisco spelled out what he'd seen. "Looks like it's a truck full of guys with guns, and I think the truck is broke down. I could hear them cussing and trying to figure out why they didn't have any cell coverage or radio coverage. I heard one say something about Roberto, so I'm guessing they are looking for us. I saw at least four guys, but there may be more that were off in the dark. Mikey doesn't believe we can get around them, if I understand him right."

Mikey spit out a comment in Degar to the old man and Harrington, who translated. "He says no way around with the horses. Too many big cracks in the ground. They can kill them all now, and be done before they get help. Mikey thinks if we wait it would be bad. The others agree with him, and want to go now."

The old man hesitated and Francisco said, "John, I overheard enough to know they're hunting us. It's us or them…"

The old man said, "Okay, then it's gonna be them." Turning to Mikey he rattled off directions to the four 'Yards as to how he wanted them taken, and reached for his rifle case. Uncasing his sniper rifle, he continued, "I've told them to spread out, stay out of the lights and take them as close together as they can. I'm gonna back them up from the top of the ridge."

He turned to see Guilfoile starting up the slope with the 'Yards, now devoid of their rifles. "Where are you going?"

Guilfoile said, "If you need quiet, ol' Betsy here is quiet. And you saw where I shot those rabbits didn't you?"

Mystified the old man asked, "What? I didn't look close at them. Why is that important right now?"

Guilfoile answered, "I shot 'em all through the eye. Don't get shit for rabbit fur with holes in it. Out to a hunnert yards, I can pretty much hit anything I'm aiming at, remember?"

"Alright. Mike, you've got the horses. Francisco, ease down about fifty yards west of us in case we miss somebody or get a runner." With that he followed Guilfoile up the slope. Moving slowly down, he wiggled into a good shooting position, pulled three rounds out of his shirt pocket and loaded the rifle, snicking the bolt home. Down below, the guards continued to yell at each other, with one standing in front of the truck looking at something in the headlights. Not knowing where the 'Yards were, nor when they were going to attack kept the tension ramping up.

***

The 'Yards were sneaking slowly but surely into position, with Mikey deciding he would take the one in front of the truck. Deng and Elmer got within feet of the two arguing on the passenger's side of the truck; then both rose silently to their feet on hearing a trill from Mikey. Coming in high, they sliced through the two guards windpipes and stabbed them through the backs.

Fred had quickly cut the throat of the guard standing at the back of the truck taking a piss and lowered him to the ground quietly. Mikey was frustrated, since the one he'd tried to distract still hadn't moved so he trilled again louder. The guard reached for his AK this time.

***

As the minutes ticked by with no change in the situation below, and the old man concentrated on controlling his breathing and not looking directly into the bright lights, trying to maintain some semblance of his night vision; suddenly he heard a quiet *spang* next to him and Guilfoile say with satisfaction, "I got him!" The old man looked in time to see the one guard who'd been standing between the headlights let his carbine fall from his hands and crumple to the ground.

"What the…?"

"I guess he heard or saw something. I saw him grab the carbine, so I figured I'd better take him right then. Didn't have time to let you know. Sorry," Guilfoile answered in a matter of fact tone.

The old man heard scrambling from his left and saw Francisco coming along the ridge, when he got to them, the three of them walked down to the broken down truck and the body. Mikey and the other 'Yards came out of the dark, with Mikey cussing a blue streak in Degar. The old man started chuckling, and turned to Guilfoile. "He's pissed at you; he was trying to lure the one you shot out of the lights. Instead you took him out, so now Mikey has one less kill than the rest of them."

Rolling the body over with his foot, the old man looked at the dead man. "Where'd you hit him?"

Guilfoile toed the head over, point at the ear he said, "Right in the ear. Shoulda scrambled his brains."

The old man pulled out his tac light and clicked it on, sure enough a thin trickle of blood was running from the guard's ear. The old man turned to Guilfoile. "That was some damn good shooting!"

Guilfoile ducked his head. "Nah, not really. He wasn't movin' that fast. Not near as fast as them rabbits did."

Mikey asked the old man a question, and he grimaced. Dropping his head, he answered Mikey in Degar and Mikey passed orders to the other three 'Yards then drew his dha and chopped the guard's head off. Guilfoile turned and threw up as Mikey planted the head on the radiator bracket of the truck, soon joined by the heads of the other guards. With a smile, Mikey gently closed the hood on top of the heads.

The old man went to the driver's side, reached in and turned the lights off. Walking slowly back up the ridge, he listened to the 'Yards chattering happily, and was transported back many years. One of the long buried memories was about another set of 'Yards. *He'd been on a patrol near the Ho Chi Minh trail with the 'Yards when they'd surprised a 57mm anti-aircraft crew taking a piss break. They'd killed all of them and systematically beheaded them, placing the heads on the wheels of the gun and radar unit, then pounding the head of the officer down on the muzzle of the gun itself. He remembered the NVA had never put another gun anywhere near that site.*

Climbing back over the ridge, they mounted up and continued moving north. At first light, they holed up in an arroyo that had a small stream running down the center and some sparse grass for the horses. Guilfoile built a small smokeless fire after Francisco had glassed the area and confirmed there were no trails of smoke, or any indication of movement anywhere within range. Mikey and the other 'Yards had gathered round Harrington, gleefully retelling the adventure of taking out the guard patrol. The old man pulled out the satphone turned it on, and sat it on the rock next to him as he ate the haunch of rabbit Francisco handed him. As every day thus far, it never rang. The old man scrolled through the presets, looked at the number for Billy, and thought long and hard about dialing it.

Shaking his head, he instead turned the satphone off and stuffed it back in his saddlebags.

After a couple of hours, the old man toed Francisco awake, and asked him to take the watch for an hour. The old man got a quick nap, then he Francisco and Guilfoile checked the horses. Diablo was thinning down, but still had all the spunk the old man expected. Francisco and, Harrington's horses as well as the pack horse were wearing down quickly, and were moving listlessly cropping what little grass they could get. Guilfoile's horse, Dusty, was probably in the best shape of any, given the fact that Guilfoile was the lightest of the four riding. Mounting up, they had no sooner topped out on the ridge than they saw a monster Mule deer.

Before the old man could say a word, he heard a quiet *spang* and saw the buck drop in its tracks. Guilfoile reined over, slid off Dusty and pulled his strange little axe from his belt. In minutes he'd caped the hide, taken the best cuts of meat and the head and bundled them in the rolled up hide, now sitting on a very skittish pack horse. Remounting and picking up the lead rope he said, "Meat for dinner, and I can get a thousand bucks for that cape and horns. Not too many sixteen-pointers seen up in the states."

The old man asked bemusedly, "A thousand? For a damn deer head?

Guilfoile answered, "Sure, got a few folks that will pay that easy. They run deer leases and folks don't get a trophy, they can *buy* one."

The old man said, "Lemme guess, eye shot again?"

"Yep, that way they can shoot the hide with whatever caliber they want, and be able to *prove* they are great hunters. Just gotta remember to shake the twenty-two out before they complete the taxiing."

Francisco asked, "What was that little hatchet you used? I don't think I've seen one like that before."

Flipping open the bottom of the holster, Guilfoile pulled out what the old man suddenly recognized as a tomahawk, not a hand axe.

As he passed it to Francisco, the old man said, "Looks like an old pipe tomahawk I've got at the house. But this one's a lot shorter."

Guilfoile replied, "Yep, I'm not exactly tall, so this works well. Got it off'n a guy named Johnson up in Tennessee a few years ago." He glanced at Francisco, who was holding the knife. "It's sharp, watch yourself." Only to see Francisco sucking his thumb where he'd ran it over the edge of the blade.

Francisco handed it back saying, "It is, and I'm surprised gutting out that deer didn't dull it!"

Guilfoile laughed. "Actually, it is a bit dull, and I'll sharpen it the first chance I get. Since I can't *legally* carry a gun, being a felon and all, I carry this thing. Plus it's a damn good little chopper when I'm working on busting out cedar trees for folks. And nobody sees this as a weapon."

"Okay, let's get moving, we're wasting daylight, and I want to be at or across twenty by tonight," the old man said as he reined Diablo around.

Seven hours and a shift to the west to get away from a dry trail that wound between the ridge lines that had a dust trail from a vehicle on it, they were on a dirt track that ran just above Highway 20 . Due to their jog, they were further west than the old man wanted to be, and he sat debating what to do as he glassed the highway. He wasn't too worried about the sparse traffic, but what got his attention were pickup trucks and SUVs sitting about three quarters of a mile apart on the sides of the road.

Jesse

Aaron leaned his head against the mattress in the ICU as he held Jesse's hand, after two days he was hoarse and beginning to wonder if he'd done the right thing. Nothing he could do seemed to help, regardless of what the docs, Angelina and Trey said. He was worried too, both Cronin and Francisco were still missing but nobody seemed real concerned about it. He didn't know what else he could do, and he knew he was getting run down, sitting here eight, ten hours or more a day. He couldn't sleep, was jumping at every damn sound, and that old house had quite a few sounds. The wedding was supposed to be in two weeks. *Stop it, just stop it! You said you loved her now prove it asshole. For better or worse, and this sure as hell ain't better. Dear God, please bring Jesse back whole and complete. She's got so much to live for, and doesn't deserve this. Please God.*

Aaron drifted off to sleep sitting there, dreaming of Jesse in his arms, only to have somebody start yanking at his hand. *Yanking at his hand, wait, what?* Muzzily he raised his head and realized it was Jesse's hand and it was *moving*!

Lunging to his feet, Aaron looked down at Jesse, her eyes were still closed, but he could see her eyeballs moving back and forth under the lids, like she was trying to do something. Not knowing what else to do, he yelled, "Doc, Angelina, Trey, somebody? Help!"

Angelina and Trey hit the cube first, closely followed by both docs, all babbling, "What, what, what's the matter?"

"Jesse, she moved her hand! And look at her eyeballs moving!"

Doc Hoffman pushed past Trey and pulled a penlight from his smock, peeled an eyelid back, and shined the light in Jesse's eye, moving to the other eye, he repeated the procedure, and turned with a smile, "Equal and reacting! And I felt her try to pull back."

Trey rumbled a chuckle as Angelina clapped her hands, Doc Truesdale said, "She's close. She's real close."

"Mpjhg, wat..." came from Jesse. Angelina pushed doc out of the way and picked up a cup that Aaron had been sipping out of and dribbled a few drops in Jesse's mouth. They all watched as Jesse licked her lips and rolled her head to the side. Rolling back up, she said more clearly, "Water, dry."

Angelina pulled a straw out of the side table, put it in the cup and stuck the tip in Jesse's mouth. She took some water and smiled slowly. "Throat hurts, why?"

Doc Truesdale said, "Jesse it's because you have a feeding tube down your throat. I don't want to take it out right now, but if you stay with us, we'll get it out shortly. Are you hungry?"

Jesse mumbled, "Yes. Hungry. Eyes, hurt."

Angelina picked up a wipe from the container and gently rubbed both eyes, asking, "Better?"

Jesse nodded. "Why am I…? Hospital?"

That caused everyone to pause and look at each other, with shrugs and puzzled expressions all around. No one had thought of how to handle this, much less give her a quick answer. Trey finally said, "Jesse what do you remember?"

Jesse cracked her eyes open at hearing Trey's voice, then looked at each one in turn; settling on Aaron's face last. She smiled at him and gripped his hand, "Member turning round to chase asshole on sixty-seven… Speeding in the rain, stupid asshole. Did I wreck?"

Both docs stepped out of the cube, and a hurried conversation took place. Jesse looked at Aaron. "What are you doing here? You're supposed to be deployed."

Aaron put his other hand on her arm. "I'm back, came to see you, Jesse. We're supposed to.."

Jesse's eyes opened wide, "Wedding, oh shit. All the planning, we didn't miss it, did we?"

Aaron said, "No baby, we haven't missed it. Just waiting on you to come back to us, it's still a week and a half away."

Jesse looked down at her leg. "Oh crap, I broke my damn leg? My head hurts and my shoulder too. What did I do? Arrgghhh, the sheriff is going to kill me for wrecking the new car."

Doc Truesdale came back in, with Doc Hoffman following and frowning. "Jesse you weren't in a car wreck. You don't have any memory of what happened?"

Jesse, in a lost voice said, "No, what.. *why can't I remember?"* She wailed.

Doc Truesdale said, "Everybody out but Angelina, I need to examine Jesse. *Now!*"

Jesse looked around in bewilderment as everyone left, with Aaron leaning over and planting a quick kiss on her cheek as he squeezed her hand.

Outside the cube, Aaron leaned over to Trey, "What the hell are we going to tell her?"

Trey looked at him, "She's going to have to know the truth. She's a big girl, but it might be a good idea to have a preacher here. She's *not* going to be happy!"

Aaron said, "I know its *Padre* Lopez, he's one of them, but I can't remember the preacher's name. I think I've only talked to him one time."

Angelina came out in tears, looked at them both and sniffed, "This sucks! Doc slipped a sedative into her IV, but she's not going to be out long. How the hell do we tell her Juanita and Toby are dead? Much less that we don't know where John and Francisco are?"

Doc Truesdale came out and said, "Okay, she'll be out about six hours. We've got that long to get our act together. Ang, get on the phone, call the preacher, call the sheriff and try to get hold of John and or Francisco. Trey, you've got the watch till I get back."

The two docs walked out arguing in low tones, as Aaron looked around with a bewildered expression, "What am *I* supposed to do?"

Angelina and Trey answered in chorus, "Go sleep. Be back here in six hours, *go*!" Angelina finished.

They both got busy, leaving Aaron standing there, and he turned toward the door and slowly left the ICU. As he left he looked over and said, "Hey Morton, Jesse is kinda awake. But they sedated her. Let the guys know, will ya?

The retired Marine, smiled and immediately started talking into his cuff mic, as Aaron continued out of the hospital. At his truck he finally pulled out his phone, looked at the time and punched Matt's number and speaker. When Matt answered he said, "Jesse came out of the coma just now, but she's got no memory of what happened. Doc T sedated her. They're going to call in the preacher and she's supposed to wake back up in six hours."

"That's great news! Felicia, Jesse's come out of the coma! Have you talked to Mr. Cronin?" Matt asked.

Leaning against the truck, Aaron said, "No, nobody seems to know where he is, or what he's doing. And Francisco is gone too. They left right after Juanita's funeral. Matt what am I going to do if Jesse doesn't want to get married?"

Felicia answered in Matt's place, "Aaron Miller, you shut up. She loved you before, and she loves you now. Don't even start down that path, *do you hear me*?" Then Matt said, "Go to bed, sleep and get back there when she wakes up. And if she asks, tell her the truth."

Aaron pushed off the truck. "Yes, ma'am, yes sir. I be going boss."

Matt chuckled. "Go. We'll talk tomorrow."
Felicia piped up, "Night Aaron."

Aaron said, "Good night, talk to y'all tomorrow." Hanging up, he realized it *was* a good night, and he got in the truck and said a quick prayer of thanks. The drive back to the ranch passed quickly, and he fell into a dreamless sleep as soon as his head touched the pillow.

Fight's On

The old man glassed the road again, and slipped back from the ridge crest. "They're still sitting out there. I don't know that it's going to be any easier if we move back east, other than the draws are closer to each other if we could punch across the road." Harrington started coughing and finally turned spit and the old man saw bright red blood on the ground. "Mike, what the hell?"

Mike Harrington turned a harried face to the old man. "John, I'm dying. I didn't tell you before, I was afraid you wouldn't take me. Stomach cancer, inoperable; they gave me three months to live two months ago. I ain't done much to help you, but at least I saw justice done for Toby, so I can go in peace."

Mikey asked a question in Degar, and Harrington answered him, provoking sad faces on all the 'Yards. The old man turned to the 'Yards and told them in Degar they should honor Harrington for his strength and giving his life for Toby. He drove it home as a point of honor, and all the 'Yards nodded solemnly.

The old man said, "Mike, you're going to make it back. I'm *not* leaving you here. Not no, but hell no."

Harrington looked up. "John, I don't know if I can go on. I'm hurtin', hurtin' bad."

Francisco said, "John, this *might* be a way to get us across the highway. We're a hunting party, I'm the guide, you and Harrington are the hunters, and he fell off the horse that was spooked by a rattler and he's hurt inside. You keep your rifle on your horse, Eddie, you transfer your rifle to Harrington's horse, in the scabbard. All they'll see is a butt stock. And you're the packer and my assistant guide. Mike, you give your rifle to one of the 'Yards. They're pretty damn quiet and if we ride right to one of the trucks that will distract them long enough for the 'Yards to sneak across the road in the dark and we can meet up with them on the far side."

The old man said, "If we ride down in the open, they may just shoot our asses first and ask questions later."

Francisco replied, "No, they know hunters are down here on a regular basis for those big Mulies, and this one is pretty damn close to a record! I can say we're trying to get back to our camp in *Maderas del Carmen* Park and call for help."

The old man looked at the group. "Anybody got a better idea?" Hearing nothing, and seeing Guilfoile moving his rifle to Harrington's horse, he turned to the 'Yards and told them the plan and where they would meet on the opposite side of the road. Deng took Harrington's AR gingerly and making sure it was safed, slung it over his back.

Francisco broke down his AR, shoving the upper and lower into a saddle bag, and hoping they wouldn't pay any attention to the flash hider that unfortunately stuck out of the top of the bag. He pulled his shirt out, using it to cover his pistol, and scrunched his hat to the side, tousling his hair and trying to look as disreputable as possible. The old man told Harrington the next time he coughed to let the blood dribble down his shirt, making it look more convincing. Guilfoile had gotten down and was rolling in the dirt, making himself as slovenly as he could and smearing dirt on his face so as to look as much the dumb horse handler as possible.

As the sun began to set, they rode openly over the crest of the ridge, making directly for the *Policia* SUV sitting nearest the arroyo heading toward *Maderas del Carmen.* The four people who were with the vehicle got out and watched them come slowly down the ridge, and the old man winced to see one of them get on a portable radio, which had been his worst fear. In the distance they saw another SUV turn on its headlights and begin heading their way as they hit the flat by the highway.

***

Roberto listened to the radio call from the *Federale Sergento*, and directed him to hold the people until he could get there. Roberto called the closest shooters to the sergeant on a different radio and told them to go help the Federales. Throwing the mic down, he jumped into his SUV and headed toward the location, figuring he could make it in ten minutes. He quickly placed a call to Montoya saying, "*Jefe,* we have a possible hit on the shooters. There are a group including at least two *Norte*

Americanos coming down the ridge to the highway now. Do you want them brought in?"

Montoya answered, "If they are the ones, yes. If you have any question, or aren't sure just kill them. They should not be here anyway."

"*Si Jefe,*" Roberto said as he hung up.

***

Francisco took the lead, riding like he barely knew how to stay in the saddle, as he approached the *Federales.* As he got within shouting range, he began in rapid-fire Spanish asking for help, how one of the hunters was hurt and could they please help get him back to the park.

The fat *Federale* sergeant leaned negligently against the hood of the SUV, and waited until Francisco was closer to finally hold up his hand. "*Alto!*" Motioning to the other *Federales,* he said something they didn't hear, but they spread out and one of them nervously fingered his MP-5. Reaching into the SUV, he turned on the headlights, and directed everyone to come stand in the headlights. Francisco protested that he had a man hurt, whom he didn't want to get off the horse since he'd had so much trouble getting him mounted.

As this discussion continued, the other SUV pulled up and four cartel shooters jumped out. They swaggered over and took over from the Sergeant, yelling at Guilfoile and pointing their AKs at the four men. Harrington hung grimly to the cantle of his horse and seeming stared around in befuddlement, as the old man slouched with both hands resting on the cantle of his saddle. Guilfoile was working Dusty with his knees, making the guards stay back from him, and playing dumb. He also had the pack horse's lead rope looped around the cantle of that saddle, and the old man noticed that he now had his leg over the lead rope and the reins loosely in his left hand.

One of the *Federales* walked around behind the horses, and started trying to get the saddlebags off Harrington's horse. They were well strapped down, and he couldn't pull them loose so he cussed and moved behind Diablo reaching up for the old man's bags. Diablo didn't like that and kicked out, nailing the *Federale* in the chest and causing him to pull the trigger on his MP-5 inadvertently.

At the sound of the shot, the old man and Francisco both pulled pistols from under their shirts as Guilfoile bailed off Dusty directly into the four cartel shooters. The old man took out a second *Federale* with a shot to the head, as Francisco put two into the chest of the fat sergeant. Scanning right he saw Harrington was fighting for control of his horse and the old man turned punching out and shot the fourth *Federale* with a shot that went directly through his moustache. A random thought occurred to him*: Yep you really do tend to aim for distinctive features they just seem to draw one's eye.*

The old man scanned left, and saw Dusty and the pack horse but no Guilfoile, so he pulled Diablo back and left. Diablo took the opportunity to stomp the *Federale* he'd kicked one more time.

Guilfoile had jumped directly into the cartel shooters, pulling his tomahawk as he cleared Dusty. He'd taken the first shooter with a choked up shot directly into the face, splitting the shooters forehead and dropping him on the spot. Landing on the balls of his feet, he turned inside the shooter on his left, slicing him from shoulder to belt buckle, pushing the AK aside with his hand. Placing the tomahawk's handle on his leg, he slid his hand down to a full grip and pivoted back to his right, pivoting from the hips to drive the tomahawk into the third shooter's neck. The tomahawk stuck momentarily, and Guilfoile had to yank it free. Spinning around, he saw the fourth shooter frantically backing away, trying to bring his gun up. Guilfoile did the calculus of range, time and speed, and threw the tomahawk at the fourth shooter, hoping if nothing else to distract him. In the "it's better to be lucky than good" category, Guilfoile's tomahawk buried itself blade first in the fourth shooter's throat.

The old man put a round into the first shooter's chest as he moaned and rolled on the ground, figuring it was a mercy shot. He yelled at Guilfoile, "Mount up, we gotta ride!"

Guilfoile retrieved his tomahawk and scrambled back aboard Dusty. Fumbling with the lead rope he finally got unwrapped it from the cantle got it out from under his thigh as he kicked Dusty into motion. Francisco and Harrington were already making for the arroyo as Guilfoile and the old man brought up the rear. Weaving up the arroyo, they found a low slope and drove the horses up and over into another arroyo that went west toward the location where they told the 'Yards they would rendezvous.

**

Roberto heard the gunshots and mashed harder on the gas, cursing, he grabbed the mic and screamed, "Everybody converge on the *Federales* location. We've found our shooters."

Four minutes later, Roberto slid to a stop his headlights illuminating a scene of carnage with bodies scattered everywhere. Roberto stepped from his truck and pulled a flashlight out of the console, walking slowly among the bodies, he saw that four of the eight bodies had what looked like more knife or sword cuts. He shivered momentarily, remembering Zapata and his love of cutting people up. He walked back to where the *Federale* sergeant lay sprawled on his back with a look of surprise on his face. Kicking him in the side, Roberto spit on him muttering, *Bastardo*. Going behind the SUV, he saw tracks of multiple horses leading off into the blackness to the north of the highway.

Santos, one of Roberto's team leaders slid to a stop and jumped from his truck moments later. Roberto called to him, "Follow these horse tracks, these are the people that cut down our friends.

Santos jumped back into his truck and pulled around hitting his high beams; he proceeded to slowly follow the tracks as they rose and dipped toward the entrance to the arroyo. Roberto screamed into the night, "Faster you fools, they are getting away!"

Pulling out his cell phone, Roberto called Montoya once again, "*Jefe*, these must be the ones that killed Zapata. There are eight dead, four have been cut up here. We are chasing them into the hills north of twenty now."

Montoya was cold as he said, "What happened Roberto, I thought you had this under control."

"*Jefe*, I don't know. I was on my way, but heard gunfire before I could get here. There is no one left alive to ask."

"Find them. Kill them. They cannot be allowed to escape."

"*Si Jefe*." Roberto disconnected and started to throw the cell, but though better of it and shoved it back in his pocket.

Kicking the sergeant's body again, he waited for the next vehicle and sent them after the first group.

***

A half hour later the old man and the others were sitting at the base of the little tabletop mesa they'd told the 'Yards was the rendezvous. Harrington had been helped off his horse and lay back on the ground asking, "What the fuck happened back there? I thought that damn horse was going to pitch me into the middle of next week!"

The old man said, "Well, Diablo started it, and we had to finish it. I can't believe we got out of there without a single injury! That is absolutely amazing. Guess the old man upstairs was looking out for us."

Rio Grande

Francisco pulled up short of the bluff at the river and the rest gathered round quietly. The old man looked at the group in the moonlight, seeing tired faces and noting all of the horses were standing heads down. The old man said quietly, "Okay, same as the way we crossed coming down, every 'Yard grabs a stirrup and we ease back across. I know everybody's tired, but this is the last push. I want to be across the river before sunrise. He looked down at Mikey and told the 'Yards in Degar to pick a stirrup and hang on, and to drop their rifles in the water halfway across the river. Mikey protested, but the old man was unyielding, they could not take the rifles back. Grumbling the 'Yards agreed.

Glancing at Francisco he said, "Okay, let's go home."

"Two more miles, just two more miles and we're done. I never believed we'd make it!" Harrington said, smiling for the first time in days. Francisco smiled tiredly, his teeth showing white under his moustache, and nodded. Turning away, he led off down the bluff to the river, followed by Harrington and Guilfoile with the old man bringing up the rear. At the edge of the water, Francisco stopped momentarily for one of the 'Yards to grab his stirrup.

He chucked the horse and stepped into the water, and gunfire erupted from both sides of the trail.

The old man slapped Diablo as he jerked his head left, drawing his 1911 and shooting at the muzzle flashes. Out of the corner of his eyes, he saw Harrington breaking to the right. Guilfoile was off Dusty, and a corner of the old man's mind wondered if he'd been shot off or not. Charging the muzzle flashes he heard and felt the passing of the bullets, as he continued pulling the trigger until he'd emptied the 1911 and slammed a new magazine in. Diablo jumped a half seen log nearly unseating the old man and he registered two people lying behind the log. Turning Diablo, he charged back, shooting four more times into the bodies. Diablo jumped back over the log and cantered back to where Francisco and Guilfoile's horses were standing. Leaping down, the old man saw two shapes in the water, and rushed to them. Guilfoile was holding Francisco in his arms, and as the old man slid to his knees, he heard Francisco say, "*Si Juanita, si. Estoy yendo a casa mi amor.*" Francisco stiffened, then collapsed in Guilfoile's arms. The old man bowed his head, tears coming to his eyes, and reached down and touched Francisco's face, now with a slight smile on it.

Guilfoile asked quietly, "What did he say?"

The old man answered, "He said 'yes Juanita, yes, I'm coming home my love.'" The old man looked around and didn't see Harrington, so he got up and walked slowly toward the right side of the ambush where Harrington' horse stood, reins trailing. He found all the 'Yards staring at

Harrington's body, lying face up with a stitching of bullet holes running up his chest. He saw another log and walked over looked and saw what was left of two bodies after the 'Yards had gotten through with them. He sat slowly on the log, putting his head in his hands and thinking, *Why God, why let us get this close? Why did you take them now? Please don't let them have died in vain.*

He slowly stood and told the 'Yards in Degar, "Pick up the body"; adding softly in Degar, "We need to go on. We'll put Harrington over the horse along with Francisco and make the last miles." The Montagnards picked up Harrington and reverently carried his body to the horse, which shied at the smell of blood, but they were able to get the body over the saddle. The old man tied the body on, then went to Francisco and, with Guilfoile's help, got Francisco over his horse. He tied Francisco on, handed Guilfoile the reins and picked up Francisco and Harrington's rifles. Tying then to the pack horse with piggin strings, he remounted Diablo. Picking up the slack reins from Harrington's horse, he turned mechanically and started into the river, telling the 'Yards to grab on to his and Guilfoile's horses.

Wading silently across the river, he turned and looked to make sure the 'Yards had dropped their rifles. They had, and he turned back to the front. Half an hour later, they walked into the old Harris place just as the sun broke the eastern horizon.

The old man and Guilfoile let the horses into the barn and dished out the baits of grain that had been left in the bin for them. Francisco's and

Harrington's bodies had been laid in the shade, and the 'Yards huddled disconsolately next to Harrington. The old man said, "Eddie, you better head for home. You don't need to be anywhere near the shit that is about to hit the fan. You saved us a couple of times, and I owe you for that, but I want you to make tracks. Keep the pack horse, he's not a bad saddle horse either. I'll get you a bill of sale for it in the next few days. If Clay asks, you went hunting, trying to make some money, you don't know shit about us, you haven't seen us, and you sure as hell weren't in Mexico. Understood?"

Guilfoile hung his head. "Yeah, Mr. Sheriff, I understand, but I don't understand what happened back there. I mean did they know we were coming? Or was that just random chance? We wuz so close…"

"I don't know, and we'll probably never know. I just know I've got two dead friends I have to deal with. Go home. Forget you ever were involved in this. Sell that damn Mulie and try to make a clean start, okay?"

Guilfoile nodded, walking over to the 'Yards, he shook hands with each of them, then led Dusty and the pack horse out of the barn. Mounting up, he turned and rode out of the ranch yard without a backward glance.

The old man stepped out of the barn and pulled the satphone from his saddlebags, thumbing it on. He dialed Felix's number and when Felix answered, told him they were back, and to bring the trucks. Disconnecting, he thought for a minute, then dialed

Billy Moore's satphone. As he listened to it ring, he tried to make up his mind what to say.

Billy finally answered after what seemed a long time, "John?"

"Yeah, Billy, it's me. We're back but things went to shit. Francisco and Mike are both down."

"Down?"

"Yeah, down as in dead. All the 'Yards are back okay, but Francisco and Mike were killed at the river," the old man said.

"Aw fuck. Have you called anybody else?" Billy asked.

"Yeah, I called Felix to bring the truck. Billy, what the hell do I do now? I can't, hell I *won't* dump them in a hole in the ground and just walk off and leave them. Both of them deserve better."

Billy thought for a minute. "Call Clay, call him right now. Tell him Francisco and Mike were killed at the river. Give him the circumstances *at the river*, but don't say another damn word. Do you hear me? I'll fly into Alpine as soon as I can get there."

The old man slumped against the barn door. "Okay, I'll call him. Don't know if he'll pick up since he doesn't know this number. Damn, damn, damn…"

Billy said, "If he doesn't answer call me back and I'll call him. I know he's got my cell phone programmed."

"Okay." The old man hung up before Billy could give him the news that Jesse had awakened from the coma and was asking for him.

The old man fished out his wheel book, found Clay's number and dialed. After six rings, it went to voice mail and the old man left a message for Clay to call him.

Mikey came out of the barn and asked if there was anything that could be done, but the old man just shook his head and continued to pace the barnyard. He finally gave up and called Billy back, "Billy, no joy with Clay. He didn't answer and I haven't gotten a call back from him."

Bill replied, "I'm on the way to the airport and I've got him on the cell now. Where are you? The old Harris place?"

The old man said, "Yeah, the old Harris place in the barn."

"And Jesse is awake, she's asking for you."

It took a few seconds for the news to sink in. As it did, the old man broke into tears. "She's awake? Is she all there?"

"Yep, she's been awake for two days. Aaron is with her, and the docs put her skull back together yesterday afternoon. The only problem is, she doesn't remember a damn thing about the shootout John. Well, and a bit of a balance problem too."

"Thank you, God! Did you give Clay this number? Or should I try him again, or what?" The old man asked.

"He's at the airport, he's going to fire up the Loach and fly down there. He said to mark out a landing zone for him."

"Okay, what about the 'Yards?"

Billy said, "I told him they were there. Had to John. Okay, Clay just hung up with me. Figure you'll see him in about fifteen. I'll be there, well Alpine, as soon as I can."

"Roger all, thanks. I'll go figure out someplace for Clay to land," the old man said. Hanging up and powering off the satphone, he called to Mikey and the other 'Yards. Looking around the old ranch, the pasture in front of the house was the best choice. With the 'Yards help, they flattened an X in the grass and picked up and cleared out as many limbs and rocks as they could from the pasture, just as they were tamping down the last of the grass, the old man heard the flutter of helicopter blades and saw the Loach coming in from the north. Hurriedly clearing the 'Yards out of the pasture, he gave the old military hand gestures to land and stepped away, turning his back on the expected rotor blast.

Clay landed the helo gently on the marks in the pasture and completed the shutdown as the old man waited patiently with the 'Yards arrayed behind him. Finally, Clay climbed from the helo and walked over, "John, what the fuck happened?" Nodding to the 'Yards he said, "Gentlemen."

The old man said, "You want to Mirandize me now or later Clay? Bottom line, Francisco and Mike Harrington are both laying in the barn dead because of me."

Clay waved his hand. "Stop that shit! Just tell me what happened and show me the bodies."

The old man turned and started for the barn saying, "We were crossing the river when what I think were some cartel types opened fire on us at the low bluff crossing in that little oxbow bend. There were four of them, two on each side, apparently hunkered down behind some driftwood piles. All four of them shot at Francisco, blowing him off his horse immediately."

They walked into the barn, and Clay bent to look at Francisco, then Harrington's bodies, "Continue."

"I turned left and managed to take out the two on that side. Dunno how I kept from being hit. Mike went to the right, and they stitched him from the groin to the head."

"I know Francisco, who's the other gent?"

The old man rubbed his eyes for a second, "Master Sergeant Michael P. Harrington, US Army retired, he lives… lived in Fayetteville, North Carolina."

"Lemme guess, you knew him when, right? And these gents?"

Chewing this lip the old man thought for a minute. "Mike was Toby's grandfather. The four Montagnards are from Toby's tribe back in North Carolina."

Clay walked over to the old man's saddle thrown over the tack rail; squinting, he rubbed his hand over the cantle and looked back at the old man. "You were flat-ass lucky John, they hit the cantle and a round scored your jeans on the right leg. So if I go look, I'm going to find four bodies down at the river?"

The old man said, "Yep, unless the cartel has moved them."

"Okay, I'll be back in a few. You got anybody coming to get you?" Clay asked.

"Yeah, Felix is on the way with the Suburban and a trailer."

Clay looked around the barn, noting the three horses in the stalls, the tack removed, and the fact that they were eating grain out of the feeding troughs. He lifted the lid on the feed bin and saw it was half full, then headed back to the helo. Powering it back up, he lifted off and flew to the south. The old man could see the helo dip and it was then lost to sight, until a few minutes later Clay returned and sat it back on the pasture, just about the time an ambulance turned into the ranch yard.

The medic climbed out of the ambulance and said, "Morning, captain, don't normally see you this far south. I understand you have two bodies that need to be transported to Fort Stockton coroner, is that correct?"

The old man looked over at Clay who was coming up behind the medics. Clay nodded and the old man said, "Yes and they're both friends, so…

The medic said, "Understood. Ranger, is there anything you or the captain need before we transport?"

Clay replied, "Nope. Just take it easy and treat them gently. Doc Truesdale will be waiting at the hospital for you."

The medics bagged both bodies, and put them on stretchers in the back of the ambulance, prompting a discussion in Degar with Mikey and Deng, who both wanted to accompany Harrington's body. It took quite a bit of discussion before they understood that would not be allowed, and that the old man trusted the people who were going to handle the body. Once that was resolved and the ambulance departed, the old man turned back to Clay, "Anymore questions?"

Clay leaned against the pole fence, propping a boot on the lower pole. "Nope, looks like a pretty open and shut case. You were attacked and defended yourselves. I saw the four bodies, and the two on my left were, well they looked like they'd been hacked to pieces. Saw a truck pulling up on the south side, so I left."

The old man said, "Blame that on me, Clay. Mikey and the rest of the 'Yards went after those two. I was too far away to stop 'em."

"What the hell did they use on them? Machetes?"

The old man turned to Mikey and told him in Degar to get his dha. Mikey stepped behind the feed bin and brought it out, handing it in the scabbard to Clay. Clay looked at the scabbard and asked, "May I?"

Mikey made a pulling gesture to Clay, and nodded okay. Clay withdrew the blade almost completely from the scabbard and whistled. "Damn, that is one wicked blade! And all four of them got in on taking those two down?"

The old man asked Mikey, who nodded in the affirmative. Clay slid the dha home and handed the scabbard back to Mikey.

"It's my fault, Clay. They aren't to blame. And don't deserve to do anything other than go free," the old man said.

Clay replied, "Looks to me like y'all were attacked, and defended yourselves trying to cross the river to go hunting. And I think you mixed up your directions, I think you went right instead of left. I guess I need to go notify the Federales that it looks like the cartel guys jumped the wrong folks this morning." Looking around Clay continued, "Apropos of nothing whatsoever, I bet Dusty will be back in his pasture when I get back home this morning; guess I don't have to go search for him anymore. I guess you'll be wanting to go see Jesse, now that she's rejoined us. Tell her Ronni and I will drop by in the next couple of days." Kicking off the pole, Clay added, "And John, you're going to file a report with Jose, right? Or do you just want to append mine as the investigating officer to yours?"

The old man looked at Clay. "Append I guess. Clay…"

"Shut up, John, just shut up. Don't dig a hole. Lemme know when Francisco's funeral is. I'd be proud to be a pallbearer for him."

The old man just nodded, and Clay returned to the helo fired it up, and departed leaving the old man and the 'Yards sitting in the barn with the horses. The 'Yards all dropped off to sleep again, but the old man's thoughts wouldn't let him. *How am I going to explain to Jesse that I got Francisco killed? And do I dare tell her about Zapata… No, I've got to tell her, promised not to hide stuff anymore. And she needs to have her mind at ease. I wonder if she'll go through with the wedding. If she goes to California with Aaron, and takes his name, then that only leaves me as a target. Yeah, that works. Can't let her stay here…*

His thoughts were interrupted by Felix driving into the ranch yard with trailer in tow, backing up to the barn door, Felix came forward with a smile that slowly turned into a look of horror when neither Francisco nor Harrington stepped through the door. "Francisco? *Senor* Harrington?" Felix asked.

The old man said bluntly, "Dead, by cartel shooters as we crossed the river this morning. Their bodies are on the way to Doc Truesdale now. We'll need another grave in the cemetery and another headstone. Do you want to arrange the funeral or have me do it, or have the ladies do it?"

Felix shook his head sadly. "I think the women. They would not be happy if we did it. Senor Harrington too?"

"No, his body will go back with Mikey and be buried in a plot in North Carolina. Let's load up and get back up to the ranch. Did you by chance bring my cell phone?"

"*Si*, it's on charge on the console."

The old man walked around to the side door and picked up his cell, flipping it open, he saw twenty messages and decided they could wait. Slipping the phone onto his belt, he helped Felix load the horses and tack in the trailer and the weapons into the back of the Suburban. The 'Yards crowded into the back seat, and the old man motioned to Felix to drive as he headed for the passenger side. Felix eased the SUV back out of the ranch yard, and turned north toward Alpine. About half way there, the old man was jolted out of a half sleep by his cell phone. He looked at the number, and answered, "Yeah, Billy?"

"Don't go to the Alpine airport, come straight to the ranch. I'll meet you there," Billy said.

"Alright, I need to clean up before I go see Jesse anyway. And I need to file a report with Jose also."

"You haven't called the sheriff yet?" Billy asked.

"No, I figured to wait till I could…"

"Call him now. Tell him the bare bones, tell him Clay has been down and investigated. Tell him to officially notify Doc Truesdale about the bodies. Don't say anything else till you and I talk. Understood?"

Testily the old man answered, "Yes sir. WILCO[21], roger out." Hanging up the phone, he turned to Felix and said, "I guess straight to the ranch."

***

Roberto stood at the river, looking at the four bodies that had been brought back to the truck. Two had gunshot wounds, and the other two had what he thought had to be machete cuts. Regardless, all four were dead, but at least these were Sinaloa dead, not his. Smiling grimly, he broke out the satphone and called Montoya. "*Jefe*, they have escaped us, they are back across the border in the US, and I have been

---

[21] WIL1 COmply

watched by a US military chopper. They also killed four Sinaloa cartel types and again some were hacked with machetes. I can't help but wonder if the Indians have taken a hand here."

Montoya was not pleased, but when questioned Roberto could not follow any further, with only one truck and the inability to cross at this location without going on foot, so he ordered Roberto to return to the compound, remove all incriminating evidence, and burn it to the ground before reporting back to him in Cozumel. Roberto told the guards to throw the bodies in the river and they drove slowly back into the dawn as he contemplated his future.

The Ranch

The old man nodded off all the way back to the ranch, finally coming awake as they pulled in by the corral. He helped Felix and Ricky get the horses out of the trailer and the tack put away, then pointed the 'Yards at the bunkhouse and told them to clean up and sleep. With some trepidation, he walked back to the new house and stepped in the back door. Just inside he stopped in amazement, Felix and the folks he'd brought in had completely redone the kitchen cabinets, the center island and all the appliances. Felix came in behind him and said, "I hope you're happy, *Senor*. We did the best we could. We are still looking for dishes, glasses and pots and pans to replace those that were broken. We've also patched the holes in the wall, and replaced wiring and piping where bullets cut them. Thankfully the leaks were small and didn't impact the walls."

The old man replied, "Thank you, I couldn't have asked for better, nor did I expect it to be done so soon. I guess with Jesse now back with us, I'll move back in here, but I'm not going to do that until tomorrow. Speaking of that, we need to arrange to get food for the 'Yards tonight."

Felix replied, "Olivia has already arranged for dinner. Its barbecue, and rice and she's making a couple of gallons of iced tea."

"Thanks, I'm going to go take a shower and go see Jesse as soon as Billy gets here. Ah hell, I might as well move my stuff back over here while I'm waiting."

"Do you need any help?" Felix asked. "Olivia has washed all the linens over here too. And cleaned the house."

"No, I can get it," the old man said, and walked gingerly through the house. Felix didn't follow him, instead going back to make sure the 'Yards were taken care of. The old man carried the few items from the old house back to his bedroom, took a shower and lay down on the bed for a minute.

A half hour later, he heard somebody pounding on the front door. Groaning, he rolled off the bed and staggered to the front door yelling, "I'm coming, I'm coming."

Taking a quick look out the window, he verified it was Billy and he opened the door. "Sorry, I must have fallen asleep."

"Yeah, you look like shit. Gimme the rundown and let's figure out where we go from here. Have you seen Jesse yet?"

"Nope, I was waiting on you." An hour later, the old man finished detailing the last ten days, ending with his conversation with Clay at the old Harris spread.

Billy shoved his ever-present yellow pad away and leaned back. "You're damn lucky to be alive, and before you ask, no I didn't know about Mike's condition. As soon as Truesdale releases the body,

I'll fly it and the 'Yards back. Have you called Deng and told her Mike's dead?"

"Shit… No I haven't. *Dammit*, this is a call I really don't want to make, Billy."

"I'll…"

"No, I got him killed, I'll make the call."

"Okay, while you're doing that, I'm going to call Mattson and have him give the SFA[22] guys a heads up. Mike wanted to be buried at Fort Bragg after he's cremated," Billy said.

The old man looked at him in surprise, and Billy said, "I was his lawyer too."

The old man got up from the table, took out his cell and dialed Deng, wondering how to break the news that she now had to bury her dad two weeks after she buried her son. A few minutes later he flopped back down at the table, shoved his phone away and rubbed his eyes. "God, *that* did *not* go well."

Billy nodded in sympathy. "Yeah, it never gets easy. I got hold of Mattson, he'll handle Mike's body, the cremation and get the funeral set up. There was a provision for Deng to see the body before its cremated, so I'm going to have to get a different airplane to take him back. The casket won't fit through the door on mine. Also, I told him you and I would be pallbearers. Mattson wants all of us in uniform, and he'll be buried in the Veterans' Cemetery at Fort Bragg."

---

[22] Special Forces Association

"I don't have a uniform anymore. I guess I'll just have to be the odd man out," the old man said.

Billy pulled his note pad to him. "Gimme your sizes. I know your green beanie is here. It's sitting in the office on the shelf. I think your awards are the same as mine, right?"

After a few minutes of back and forth, the old man finally said, "I need to go see Jesse," and got up.

Billy looked up asking, "Mind if I tag along?"

Jesse

The old man walked into Jesse's ICU cube by himself and stood quietly at the foot of the bed, just watching Jesse and Aaron for a moment. Aaron saw him first, and a look of relief came over his face. Jesse looked up, saw him and broke down in tears, mumbling, "I'm sorry Papa, I'm sorry."

Without realizing how he did it, the old man was standing at Jesse's side, taking her in his arms while Aaron held her other hand. He whispered, "You don't have anything to be sorry for Jesse. You did everything you could. I'm just thankful you survived."

"But I got Juanita and Toby killed, Papa!" She sobbed.

"*No*! You didn't get them killed, between the three of you, you took out three of them, and the other three are gone too, so *none of them lived*! That's not your fault, none of this is your fault", he said.

Jesse pushed away, suddenly changing moods. "Where have you been Papa? Why weren't you here when I woke up? Aaron was here, where were you?"

The old man didn't react, saying softly, "I was taking care of business, just taking care of business, and I didn't find out until this morning you'd regained consciousness."

Jesse cocked her head. "What *kind* of business, Papa? What was more important than me?"

Glancing at Aaron, he turned back to Jesse. "Killing the man that ordered the shootings, Jesse. He'll never bother you again. And as a bonus, we also took out the guy that killed Francisco's children too. Only thing is Francisco were killed as we came back across the river."

Jesse looked at him in shock. "Francisco? No!" A sob escaped her throat as she cried. She managed to pull herself together a few seconds later.

"Mike Harrington was also shot and killed," the old man said.

"Mike Harrington?" she sniffed. "Who's he?"

"Mike was Toby's grandfather. He Billy and I were all in service together. Neither Mike nor Francisco ever felt a thing. They were shot down by cartel types thinking we were running drugs."

Jesse sobbed, "When Papa?"

The old man replied, "About six hours ago, hon."

Doc Truesdale interrupted them. "John, can I talk to you a minute please? Jesse do you mind?"

Jesse shook her head, and the old man slipped her off his lap and back on the bed, noting she'd never let go of Aaron's hand. Nodding to Aaron, he got up and followed Truesdale out.

At the nurse's station, doc turned. "John, she's got no memory of what happened. Maybe I did the wrong thing, but I told her to the best of my knowledge what she and Juanita did. Clay's also been in and talked to her. Problem is, not only is her memory flaky right now, she's getting some pretty significant mood swings, and her balance is not real good. And she really doesn't need a lot more stress right now."

"What would you have me do, lie to her?"

"No, but you could be a little gentler, that beeping you were ignoring was her blood pressure going sky high, and I really don't want her stroking out on us. The other thing is, I've finished the autopsies on Francisco and the other gent, Harrington?"

The old man said, "Mike Harrington, a friend of mine and Billy's, and Toby's grandfather."

"Oh shit..."

"Yeah, exactly."

Doc continued, "I've released the bodies to the funeral home, and was wondering how to get Harrington taken care of."

The old man said, "Billy is taking care of that, matter of fact he's out in the hallway now. How much longer will Jessc need to be here?"

Doc answered, "I'd like at least another week. I want to keep a close eye on the skull fracture and the patch, and I want her to get some initial physical thcrapy where I can maintain monitoring on her. Aaron and the retired Marines are covering security, and Aaron's practically been living here. Can you give me that, John? And be a little less blunt? Please?"

The old man looked up. "Alright, Doc, I'll do my damnedest. I've got some things that I need to do, and we need to bury Francisco…"

Doc said, "Jesse can't go. Nope, not going to stress her like that; I don't want her seeing that. You've got to understand how *fragile* she is right now."

"Mentally or physically?" the old man asked.

"Both. If she falls, it could kill her, plain and simple. She can't even go to the bathroom by herself. I'm having her escorted and helped by the nurses. Her mood swings are playing hob with her BP, and I'm trying *not* to use addictive drugs to moderate her. Thankfully, Aaron has been doing a good job by being here and strong for her," Doc said.

"Understood," the old man said, pushing off the nurse's station.

The old man went out and found Billy deep in discussion with Gilbert, one of the retired Marines standing guard about what had gone on during the attempt on Jesse's life. The old man listened quietly, and waited until they'd finished before nodding to Billy to step further down the hall. "Doc doesn't want Jesse to attend Francisco's funeral, and he's pissed at me for telling her. He's concerned she might have a stroke, and is having some mood swing problems, in addition to memory loss and balance issues. I want to get Francisco buried next to Juanita, and do what needs to be taken care of, but I don't know what they had for personal stuff."

Billy replied, "I'm pretty sure I know who was handling their affairs, lawyer named Garza here in town. I'll take care of that. Are you going to have the funeral home coordinate the funeral?"

Nodding, the old man said, "Well them, the *padre* and Jose. I'd rather have the Hispanic community take the lead than me do it. Francisco and Juanita were well-respected and I think it's only appropriate to do it that way. I'll pick up the tab, but I don't want to make a big thing out of it."

Billy said, "Okay, we can make that happen. By the way, I talked to Muir and McMurtrie, and they appreciate your covering the hotel bills and food for the MCL[23] folks. I gather they haven't been able to pay for much of anything in town. I had the sheriff put out the word their money was no good and I've been paying the bills out of the operating account; so if you have a problem, it's on me."

"Nah, that's fine. I was thinking about that the other day, but if you've got it handled, so much the better."

"Okay, are we done with business?" Billy asked. "I want to go see Jesse before they kick us out and we need to have a little chat."

Turning back, they trooped back into the ICU and into Jesse's cube. Jesse and Aaron were once again huddled and oblivious to those around them, until Billy laughed out loud. "Boy, y'all are a pair!"

Aaron looked up with a dazed expression and Jesse said, "What, you've never seen lovebirds before, Uncle Billy?"

---

[23] Marine Corps League

Billy laughed again, "No Jesse, it's not that; it's that Aaron is dead on his feet and his SA is in the toilet. I know he loves you, but he needs some real sleep and some real food, not the crap they serve downstairs. After you and I have our little girl to girl chat, we're going to disappear him and put some real food in him, then put his ass down for at least twelve hours."

The old man snickered. "Girl to girl?"

Billy puffed up. "Yeah, we're both short and have pigtails! Or at least *I* do now."

Everyone laughed and both the old man and Aaron kissed Jesse's cheek, and stepped out to the nurse's station as Billy drug up a chair. "Jesse, we do need to talk. But now isn't the time or the place. Once you're out of here and off the medication, we need to sit down and discuss some legal stuff that needs to be changed.

Jesse cocked her head. "I don't understand?"

"Like I said, once you're off the drugs and coherent, we'll revisit this. I just want you better and out of here right now," Billy said.

Jesse raised the bed a bit further. "Okay, when I have a clear head, but now I'm worried, Uncle Billy."

Billy replied, "Okay, now I'm gonna take my butt out of here and let you get some rest girl."

He patted Jesse's hand and rose to leave, but Jesse grabbed his hand and pulled him close saying softly, "Thank you, Uncle Billy, for everything."

Billy choked up, and simply nodded as he disengaged. Walking out to the nurse's station he turned to Trey. "You take care of that girl in there."

Trey looked at Billy and saw the look in his eyes. "Will do, sir, will do."

Turning away, Billy said to the old man and Aaron, "Food me. I need sustenance to keep my girlish figure intact and my brain working to its full potential."

The old man muttered under his breath, "God forbid," as he followed Aaron and Billy out of the ICU.

After a good steak dinner, Aaron was literally too tired to drive, and Billy drove his truck back to the ranch.

After Aaron staggered off to the old house, Billy and the old man sat in the kitchen over a cup of coffee. "John, I fucked up. As your lawyer I need to tell you both your and Jesse's wills have to be changed."

"I don't understand. What is wrong? I've got everything going to Jesse, less the codicil for Francisco and Juanita. Yeah, we do need to fix that now."

Billy sighed. "That's not all of it John, I'd never imagined the situation we were almost in. If you and Jesse had both died, your wills would have counteracted each other, because you both left everything to the other person and unless some distant relative of yours came forward, everything would escheat to the state of Texas. That is what I need to talk to Jesse about, and I also want her to think about a pre-nup."

The old man replied, "Shit, I never thought of that either. Nope, she'll never go for that stuff either. The only *family* I've got left are Aunt Bea's kids, but I haven't seen them in at least twenty years. Hell, I don't even know how to get hold of them."

"Well, we need to come up with something in case Jesse pre-deceases you. We can write in codicils that only take place in the case of a pre-dec, but you need to figure that out. Anything to keep the money out of the state's hands. Sometime over the next couple of days you need to sit down and figure this out," Billy said.

The old man leaned back. "Dammit, I shouldn't even have to be worrying about this shit! This kinda crap shouldn't be happening to Jesse either. She should be looking forward to a wedding and making a family, *not* looking over her damn shoulder for the next shooter that wants to kill her!"

Billy finished his coffee, got up and washed the cup, sitting it in the dish strainer. "I know, none of us *should* have to worry, but we're here now, and it's gotta be done. I'm going to bed, I'll get up with Garza tomorrow and get Francisco's stuff taken care of. Funeral in two days?"

The old man said, "Probably. We'll have to go to the truck stop to get breakfast, I don't have any food in the house yet."

More Funerals

Felix and Olivia came over to the old man just before the services started. "*Senor*, would you please be one of the pallbearers? I know you've taken a backseat during this whole funeral, but the community believes you should be one of those that carries Francisco to his final rest."

The old man replied, "I'd be honored."

Felix looked intently at the old man. "Please tell me his death was not in vain."

Startled the old man said, "No, it wasn't. Trust me, he avenged a very old debt in addition to avenging a much more current one."

Felix and Olivia both nodded and turned back as the organist started playing. The old man slipped into an outside pew with the rest of the pallbearers as the *padre* started intoning the funeral service.

The old man's thoughts slipped back in time twenty-nine years. *They were getting ready to hit a cocaine lab up in the mountains above Medellin based on a lead that Fabio Vazquez might be there. He was the team leader and as they were getting ready to brief up, the attaché brought this young Mexican officer into the conference room saying he was now on the team.*

Agent Cronin had stepped out into the passageway with the attaché and raised holy hell about the last minute add he knew nothing about, but the attaché had told him to shut up and carry on, that it had been approved from on high. They'd done the raid and missed Vazquez by minutes, but took out over a ton of pure cocaine that night along with two of the lab specialists.

A year and a half later, he'd shaken hands with that young Mexican officer and turned over the lead of the team to him.

Almost nine years later, Lupe Montoya had knocked frantically on the ranch house door, a bleeding Carlos Montoya laying in the back seat and dying. She had pleaded for help, and Sergeant Cronin had called Doc Truesdale who'd rushed over and patched up Carlos on the kitchen table while Lupe poured out the tale of horror that had happened in Piedras Negras that morning.

The cartel killers had come for them, not knowing Carlos had come home late the night before. When they kicked in the door, they'd shot young Francisco and Juanita as they slept on the couch in the living room, and come charging down the hallway. Carlos had met them in the hall with his father's old Obregon pistol in hand. He'd taken out all three of the shooters, but they'd gotten plenty of lead into him. Lupe had gotten Carlos to the car somehow, covered him with a serape and driven across the border at Eagle Pass just before dawn after a last look at her dead children. Less than four hours later, she'd banged on his door.

Amazingly, Carlos had survived being shot six times, and recovered slowly while Sergeant Cronin

*had gone in and had a little closed door meeting
with the sheriff after he'd called some folks at the
DEA in Washington. Four days later, a package had
arrived from Washington with green cards for
Francisco and Juanita Cortez.*

*He'd hired them then and there, and
Carlos/Francisco had taken to ranching like a duck
to water. He often wondered if Lupe/Juanita had
ever told him what she'd seen in the living room.*

The *padre* was finishing the service and
everyone stood for the final benediction jostling the
old man out of his revere. He stood with the others,
then moved with the other pallbearers to carry
Francisco out the doors of the church for the final
time.

Pulling into the pasture by the cemetery, the old
man noted that Ricky and his friends had everything
well in hand. He got out, put his hat on and moved
over to the hearse with the other pallbearers.
Moving Francisco quietly to the gravesite next to
Juanita, he stood for a moment thinking about how
many years they had been together, how they were
for all practical purposes family, and what the last
six months had wrought. Shaking his head in
sadness, he went to move to the back of the crowd
when Dorothy and Olivia pulled him up the front
row with Felix and the sheriff.

The old man did a double take when he realized
the flag on Francisco's casket was the Mexican
Army flag. He looked quickly at Felix, who just
smiled at him. The *padre* gave a short but moving
service, and four of the men in the community the

old man knew had been in the military stepped forward and folded the flag, handing it to the *padre*, who said, in English,

"This will hang in a place of honor in the church for the many things Francisco has contributed to this community over these last twenty years. And we know he did not die in vain. Go in peace Francisco, Juanita is waiting for you." A short prayer ended the service and everyone started leaving.

The old man pulled Felix to the side. "Did you know…?"

Felix nodded. "Carlos and Lupe, we've known for years. And we've known for years what you did to help."

The old man didn't say a word, just left quietly; he couldn't help but wonder what else Felix and the others knew.

***

The next morning Billy picked the old man up at the airport, and they flew to Fayetteville, North Carolina for Harrington's burial.

As they were changing into their uniforms, the old man said to Billy, "I wonder if this will ever end?"

Grunting as he bent to blouse his trousers Billy answered, "I dunno, but I *do* know we can't give up. We didn't give up in Nam, and I'm sure as hell not ready to give up here. They can play all the political games they want up in DC, but it's still the little people like us that will make the difference in the long run. *We* are America, not those shits sitting inside the beltway."

Command Sergeant Major Burke knocked then came into the room. "Y'all bout ready?"

They both nodded and followed him out the door, "Okay standard military funeral, and we've got quite a crowd of 'Yards in the chapel, probably the most I've ever seen here. Y'all spent some time with them, right?"

The old man said, "Yeah, Mike, Billy and I all did tours on the trail with this particular tribe of 'Yards. And they were and still are loyal to us. Although I can't figure out why, the way they got treated."

Burke shrugged. "They know y'all and you were there with them. You're not some faceless bureaucrat sitting in some office somewhere. And y'all actually cared for them; medicine, weapons, shared their lifestyle. That counts for a lot in some cultures."

Billy replied, "Yeah, and some of us still support them as much as we can."

"I've heard how *some* folks help out. Not that I *know* any of them or anything."

They all chuckled at that, and moved into the chapel proper. The old man looked quickly out over the crowd, picking out Mikey, Fred and Elmer the 'Yards that had accompanied them. He nodded to them and received nods in return before he took his place on the front pew. The chaplain officiating gave a brief prayer and led them through a hymn, then turned the ceremony over to the retired Special Forces chaplain from the local chapter for the remainder of the ceremony.

At the graveside, after they placed Harrington's casket on the lowering device, the old man and others stood at attention until the service was completed. After the three volleys were fired by seven current Green Berets, and three rounds collected to be included in the folded flag. They managed to fold the flag without any major problems, and the CSM presented the folded flag to Harrington's wife, who sat in a daze.

The old man and Billy hung back until most of the people had given their condolences, then approached Mrs. Harrington. Billy said, "Mrs. Harrington, I'm…"

She looked sharply at him, the daze falling away. "I know who you are Billy Moore, and you John Cronin. I've heard about you two for years. I just want to know one thing; did Mike die for a good reason?"

The old man replied, "Yes, ma'am, he did. He avenged his grandson's death, and he was a big help to me. He probably saved my life at the river where he was killed."

"Good, he knew he didn't have long, and was fretting about dying in front of me and how I'd take it. I've been prepared for this since I married him in sixty-four, and I never thought we'd get forty plus years together, so I can't complain."

Billy said, "I have some paperwork…"

"Billy, you've taken care of Mike for damn near thirty years. Whatever I need to sign, just give it to me and handle the rest okay? Mike trusted you, and if you were good enough for him, I'm not about to question it."

One of the ladies came forward and whispered in her ear, and led her off, leaving the old man and Billy standing there.

A couple of hours later, changed and with Billy now in possession of the newly signed paperwork by Mrs. Harrington they sat in the car in the parking lot. They looked at each other with Billy asking, "Club for a drink or airplane?"

"Airplane, I want to get back to Jesse. I'm a little hinky about being gone just now."

Billy turned toward the airport saying, "Airplane it is."

Fallout

The old man came from the hospital after checking on Jesse to find Bucky sitting in his office with his feet up on the desk. The old man swept Bucky's feet off the desk saying, "Damn, were you born in a barn or what?"

Bucky chuckled. "I was trying to catch a nap. Us old folks you know…"

The old man hung his hat on the rack, rolled his shoulders, and picked up two coffee cups, "Black?"

"Sure. Unless it's older than a day, then cream and sugar."

The old man came back a couple of minutes later with two cups of black coffee handing one to Bucky as he eased behind his desk. "Well, is there any *good* news or are you here to cause more trouble?"

"Well, in the good news category, there is apparently a *lot* of confusion down in Mexico right now among the cartel types. Seems somebody offed one Ernesto Zapata and the local *Federale Commandante* and got away clean. And carved up a few guards and cartel types from the Zetas along the way including four minus their heads, which were set on the radiator of their broke down truck up in the Sierras. And person or persons unknown chopped up more cartel types from the Zetas and some more *Federales* up on twenty, then chopped up some more cartel types from Sinaloa up on the border. And nobody has a clue!" Bucky smiled as he finished.

The old man leaned back sipping his coffee. "You know who we lost, right?"

Bucky said sadly, "Yeah, I heard. I'm sorry I didn't make Francisco's funeral, but I was up at headquarters getting my ass chewed for not being on top of what was going on."

"You in any trouble?"

Bucky waved it off. "Nah, not really. They just like to gnaw on me anytime they can. And lately we've been doing good, so they had to come after me for something."

"What do you mean by confusion?"

Bucky laughed. "Well, they've never had one of the honchos get taken out without *somebody* claiming credit, and both cartels are scared the Tarahumera are on the warpath because of the folks being chopped up, and every single chopper disappearing. And both cartels are accusing the others of perpetrating the ramp up in violence. The Zetas have also pulled in their horns with the *Federale Commandante,* who by the way, was also the number three man in the Zetas, being capped."

"The Tarahumera?" The old man asked. "I didn't think they were involved in drugs."

"Well, they aren't, but they are being pushed out by the cartels and illegal forestry. They live up in the hills and aren't real friendly. They are long distance travelers and runners, and can live off the land too, and don't deal with either cartel that we're aware of," Bucky replied, as he leaned forward. "How's Jesse, and is she still being guarded? I've stopped by a couple of times to check on her, but Doc wouldn't let me in. Apparently he's trying to limit folks that see her."

The old man replied, "Yeah, he wouldn't even let her go to Francisco's funeral, he says she's too *fragile* both mentally and physically right now."

Jesse? *Fragile*? That is *not* a word I'd associate with her."

The old man sipped his coffee then said, "Yeah, she's got no memory of what happened, and she's got some mood problems and balance problems, plus a plate in her head now. Fragile."

"Shit. Is she gonna make it back John?"

"I hope…no, I *think* so. She's a lot stronger than Doc gives her credit for. Aaron is here now, her fiancé; I think you met him, he was in the shootout at the Alton place, remember?"

Bucky nodded. "Yeah, Marine and a good kid as far as I can see. So is the wedding still on?"

"Yeah, Jesse is already trying to figure out how to get down the aisle with her cast on, and Beverly was there when I left this morning; they were going over wedding books. I swear this damn wedding is worse than anything I ever put up with in the military or law enforcement," the old man said.

Bucky snickered. "Be glad you only got to do this once. I've got three damn girls, and in about ten years, I'm just gonna go be a hermit till they're all gone. I'm assuming they will go to California?"

"Yeah, I want to get her out of here. A name change and getting as far away from here as possible right now seems like a pretty good idea. Doc isn't happy, he wants to see her through the physical therapy, but frankly, she can probably get as good or better at Pendleton. I don't know what the real fallout is going to be, but I know we were targeted, and anything I can do to get her out of the line of fire, I'm going to do it," the old man said.

Bucky nodded somberly. "Yeah, we really don't know what's going to happen. Point of fact, you were targeted and survived, are they gonna come after you again? I have no fucking clue. I doubt they've put together the real circumstances, since nobody ever actually *saw* y'all. But if they start digging through, they might find the info, or one of the lieutenants will tell whomever takes over about it. I know Jose and the papers have managed to keep y'all's involvement out of the papers and off TV which is good, but sooner or later somebody's gonna come sniffing around. Problem is, you may never know who that is."

The old man replied, "Even more reason to get Jesse out of here sooner rather than later."

"Have you told her yet?"

"Nah, I figure that can wait until after the wedding. 'Sides, it's going to take her a week or so to get mobile enough to travel safely and I want to see at least some of her PT to see how she's coming along."

The sheriff knocked on the door. "John, Bucky? Got a minute?"

"Sure, here or your office?"

"Here's fine. John, I'm concerned about Jesse's wellbeing if she stays around here, but I know she'll be visiting on a regular basis, so I want to carry her as a regular deputy. This will allow her to carry all the time and not have to worry about the forty hours a month requirement. I'll pay her some nominal salary, just to keep it legal; if that's alright with you."

The old man said, "Fine by me! We were just sitting here cussing the possibilities. Did you ever figure out how the kid knew Jesse was in the hospital?"

The sheriff hung his head. "You're not going to like this, but we showed pictures around and it appears they were eating at the truck stop when a couple of troopers and DEA snipers went in to get some coffee the morning we buried Juanita. One of the troopers vaguely remembered they were talking among themselves about how Jesse was doing while they were waiting on their coffee."

"Shit!"

Bucky chimed in, "Loose lips sink ships and all that."

The sheriff replied, "Yeah, and they feel like shit about it, but its water under the bridge. But I'm pretty sure their captain got a chunk of their asses if they owned up to it. How much longer is Jesse going to be here, John?"

Leaning back he replied, "Figure a max of two weeks, gotta get her some therapy and get her married, then Aaron's leave runs out six days later.

Dunno if she's going to be able to drive with him, or whether putting her on an airplane is the better option."

Bucky chimed in, "You can bet she's going to fight to ride with Aaron. First days married, she's not going to want to be separated, and probably neither is he."

The old man threw up his hands. "Crap! Whatever happened to gahdamn common sense? Guess we'll find out if she or Aaron has any left by the wedding. Billy's already offered to fly her out, but I don't think she even remembers that conversation."

The sheriff looked at the old man. "You ready to go back on the schedule?"

The old man looked hard at the sheriff. "Are you sure you want me back?"

"Don't be stupid, you went on vacation, came back and you're now back at work. Of course I want you back. Bucky, don't you want John back in the saddle?"

"Damn straight I do. I need his expertise now more than ever," Bucky replied.

At the door, the sheriff paused. "Oh yeah, we had the troopers do the final on the attack on Jesse, seems both those military kids were UA or AWOL[24] or something from Fort Bliss, and the one, Marquez had gang ties going back to about age ten. Somehow he hooked up with the Coyotes and apparently they'd done one killing over in Phoenix for Sinaloa,

---

[24] Absent WithOut Leave

and were trying to branch out. Apparently he'd recruited four other young soldiers to be shooters, turns out *all* of them were in treatment for severe PTSD[25] coming back from Iraq. One of the others that was in on the Phoenix deal, but not this one. He dropped a dime and turned states' evidence. So they've got a pretty good paper trail and hopefully are going to roll up some of the recruiters from Sinaloa." Chuckling he continued, "Bucky, sounds like your counterpart over in San Diego is gonna be busy!"

"Bout damn time he got off his ass and did something." Bucky grinned as he picked up his hat. "I'm gonna go see Jesse and head back to Laredo. Gotta go stir up a few hornet's nests to look like I'm doing something productive!"

The sheriff stuck his head back around the door. "Ah, John are you carrying a rifle in the car?"

The old man answered, "I've got the MRAD[26] locked down in the trunk, plus a hundred rounds. I figure if I need a big gun, I'm gonna *need* a big gun and lots of ammo. Besides, the Mongrel is my personal weapon. Why?"

The sheriff shrugged. "With all the shit going on lately, I want everybody carrying heavy. And ready to respond to anything that comes up. You know as well as I do, we got off lucky when those three ended up killing themselves trying to get on ten. That could have gone the other way real quick."

---

[25] Post-Traumatic Stress Disorder
[26] Multi-Role Adaptive Design

Bucky and the old man both nodded somberly. Bucky got up grabbed his hat and said, "For what it's worth, welcome back."

The old man shook his hand and said, "We'll see. Have fun stirring up the hornets, just remember not to get stung."

The old man walked back down to the coffee pot, filled another cup and wandered into dispatch. Nodding to the ladies there, he walked over to the board and moved his puck from vacation to in. Lisa piped up, "You back on your regular schedule, captain?"

The old man answered, "As regular as it ever is, Lisa."

Lisa laughed then asked, "How's Jesse this morning?"

"Starting physical therapy today, so she's going to be hurting before the day's over. But she's coming back pretty well. The big problem is going to be the full leg cast. She's not going to be really mobile for probably four months at the least."

Lisa winced. "Oh, she is *not* going to like that. And she's going to be bitching about the eight gain. My dad went through that, and he's never lost the thirty pounds he gained."

The old man nodded. "I'm *not* going to tell her that, you can if you want to Lisa."

Lisa smiled. "Nope, I may just be a dumb dispatcher, but I *know* not to talk to another woman about weight gain. Nope, not gonna happen."

The old man smiled back and wandered out of dispatch toward his office. Sitting at his desk, he quickly read through the latest intel updates and got caught back up on what was going on with the deputies on patrol. It looked like the normal number of tickets, domestics and the usual suspects doing the usual things.

Since there wasn't anything hanging that needed his attention, he decided to get out on the road and get back into the swing of patrolling.

Rehab

Jesse eased her leg off the bed and it thumped to the floor. "Well, damn, that ain't good," she said to Trey. "I don't have shit for control. I knew I'd be weak, but this is ridiculous." Propping herself up with her arm, she tried to re-arrange the hospital gown without success. "Ah crap, I guess my ass is going to be hanging out too, and me with no underwear. Oh well, good thing I don't have much modesty."

Trey rumbled a laugh. "Girl, you know there ain't no modesty in a hospital. Ain't no time for it."

"Shut up and help me into the damn chair. I've got a week to get my ass together before the wedding. Speaking of which, is Beverly coming down tomorrow?"

"Actually, she's coming down tonight. I'm taking the night off, and we're going to get a little *personal* time," Trey replied.

Jesse smiled. "I hope to hell the old man has earplugs handy! He's gonna need 'em if you're gonna get *personal* with Beverly." Grunting with effort, Jesse stood wavering for a moment until Trey grabbed her arm and steadied her. "Damn, talk about a head rush! My balance really sucks right now. What happens if I fall?"

Trey, shaking his head, eased Jesse down into the wheelchair. "Doc thinks you're gonna break all to pieces if you fall, but I think you just need to get back on that horse so to speak. We're gonna see how bad you are today, and Doc and the therapist are gonna work out a plan for you. Of course, with a busted leg, broken ribs *again* and a hole in your shoulder, I don't see you doing much for a while. This isn't going to be an overnight fix, Jesse. Just sayin'."

Jesse smile up at Trey. "I've got a week, so let's get going. Time's a wasting."

Trey laughed and pushed Jesse from the ICU down to physical therapy, accompanied by Gilbert and Morrow from the retired Marine contingent. Once they were in the PT area, Gilbert called into the base, informing them of the location change, and Colonel Muir wished Jesse well in PT.

Tina, the cute, petite little physical therapist looked up over the top of her glasses. "Well, who do we have here?" Trey passed her chart across the desk, and Tina flipped efficiently through it, noting Doc Truesdale's orders and suggestions. Tina looked up a couple of times, as if measuring Jesse. Finally, she turned and pulled what looked like a football helmet, minus the face guard, from a shelf behind the desk saying, "Okay, roll Miss Jesse over to the mats and let's see what we've got to work with, looking up at Trey she asked, "You see these LOCF[27] scores?"

---

[27] Rancho Los Amigos Levels of Cognitive

As Trey positioned Jesse and helped her on with the helmet he replied, "Yeah, she's been running seven, eight, nine since she came out of the coma. Seeing a bit of improvement, but she's not a ten yet, at least in my opinion."

"You know her before?" Tina asked, reaching out to help Jesse up.

"Yeah, we were in college together, so about five years. We studied together and tutored each other in a few courses."

Jesse, standing and wobbling, said, "*Hey*, I'm right here. I can *hear* y'all."

Tina turned and looked up at Trey. "Yep, nine right there." Turning to Jesse, she continued, "Don't worry about it, we do this to *all* the patients. Now I'm gonna let go of you if you think you can stand on your own. Do you think you can do that?"

Jesse bared her teeth. "Of course I can! Just let me..." And slumped back to be caught by Trey. "Oh shit, head rush again."

Tina noted something on a clipboard, then said, "Okay, that didn't go real well, did it? You said head rush, like a dizzy head rush, or like a drunk head rush?" She and Trey helped Jesse over to a low set of parallel bars.

"Dizzy, *definitely* dizzy. Wow, that sucks," Jesse said. She put her hands on the parallel bars, wincing slightly from the pain in the ribs and shoulder. "Lemme try this again." Tina and Trey eased their grips and finally let go. Jesse was able to stand for

Functioning Scale

about thirty seconds before the trembling in her arms gave her away. Trey pushed the wheelchair over to Jesse, and Tina eased her down into it.

"Okay, you haven't been out of bed for almost three weeks, so a lot of that is normal," Tina said reaching for a dynamometer. "Let's see how your grip strength is Miss Jesse. I want you to hold the handle like this and squeeze as hard as you can." Tina handed her the instrument and asked, "Are you ready? Okay, squeeze as hard as you can. Harder! Harder! Relax. Now the other hand." After three cycles, Tina took the instrument back and looked at Jesse. "Left handed?"

Jesse said, "Yeah, why? And how's my grip strength?"

"Your grip is almost perfectly equal between right and left hands, so that is indicative of a left handed dominance. Strangely enough, right-handers almost always have a ten percent greater grip strength in their right hands. Oh, and your grip strength is a bit low, but some exercises should bring that back up with no problem. Now comes the fun part."

Jesse asked peevishly, "Fun? I don't call *any* of this fun."

Tina shrugged. "No, it's really not, but it *is* necessary to figure out where you are, and where you need to be in your recovery process. Now I know you've got busted ribs, and they are going to be stiff and sore, but I need to get some measurements on your shoulder and see if we have any rotational issues there."

Jesse shrugged and winced. "I know this is gonna hurt, so let's get it done."

Fifteen minutes later, with Jesse leaking tears, Tina had completed the measurements she needed. Nodding to Trey, she said, "Okay, that's all the damage we can do today, but plan on being back down here tomorrow and we'll get your started on your rehab Miss Jesse. For what it's worth, I think you're a lot further along than anyone expected, especially the docs."

As Gilbert held the door, he said to Trey, "Damn that hurt just standing here watching it."

Gilbert reported they were on the move as Trey wheeled Jesse out and said, "Oh, you ain't seen nothing yet. And she's not in bad shape. Hell, I hate PT, always those chirpy little personalities, hiding the sadist underneath."

Gilbert chuckled. "Oh hell, be glad you didn't rehab in a military hospital, ain't *no* chirpy personalities there, more like DIs[28]. And they're *all* assholes. I think they train 'em in brigs to give 'em the attitude they need."

Trey shook with laughter, until Jesse said, "Hey you two, shut up, you're *not* helping." Prompting all of them to laugh. Back up in the ICU, Jesse was finally maneuvered back into the bed, prompting more grumbling from Jesse as she was reattached to all the monitors and IVs.

Aaron came in during visiting hours and was sitting with Jesse as she described the PT session,

---

[28] Drill Instructors

when Doc Truesdale and the old man came in, closely followed by Angelina.

The old man leaned up against the cube wall as Doc and Angelina moved in on each side of Jesse, poking prodding and taking notes while discussing her as if she wasn't there. She finally reached out and poked Angelina in the ribs. "Hey, I'm awake down here. It was bad enough when Trey and what's-her-name, Tina were doing that to me earlier. Would you at least tell me what the hell is going on?"

Doc looked down in surprise. "You wouldn't understand half of what we're talking about, and we're just trying to get the case notes caught up. I'm a little concerned Tina wants to push you as hard as she does, considering your situation."

"My fragility you mean? Which is why I wasn't allowed to attend Francisco's funeral, why I'm never without a keeper? Why I can't even go pee? *That fragility?*"

The old man coughed to cover a chuckle, prompting a glare from Jesse as she lay back on the bed. Doc glanced at Angelina who only shrugged, then focused his attention on Jesse. "I've worked too damn hard to keep your ungrateful butt alive to let *you* do something stupid like fall down, go boom, and *not* wake up. *You* are not bulletproof, contrary to your..."

"Well no shit, I've got the holes to *prove* that," Jesse said, prompting Aaron to start coughing and earning him glares from both Jesse and Angelina. "I never thought I was after the shootout at the Alton's.

I'm getting *married* in seven damn days. I am *not* going to do that strapped in a chair, wearing a football helmet for God's sake! A girl's gotta have a little pride, Doc."

Doc looked over at the old man who said, "Doc, you're on your own here. I'm just a fly on the wall for this one."

Doc harrumphed and started again. "Jesse, it's not… Ah hell, all you damn women are gonna gang up on me anyway. Just try not to kill yourself while you're still in my care." He glanced at Aaron. "Son, I think you're gonna have your hands full with this one." Gathering up the tatters of his dignity, he stomped out of the cubicle mumbling to himself.

Jesse and Angelina smiled at each other, and Angelina stepped out, bringing back Jesse's dinner on a tray. "Only the best in rubber chicken and limp lettuce followed by the finest green Jello for you tonight, my dear. I'll leave you alone to enjoy this fine repast." She burst out laughing. "Sorry, I'm not that good a bullshitter." Slapping a hand over her mouth, she looked at Aaron and the old man. "You two and your buddies are the reason my language has gone to crap." Everyone laughed at that and Jesse raised the cover on the tray in trepidation.

Sighing, she said, "Oh I would just about kill for a Big Mac and fries. Do you know how bad that is?"

"I can fix that baby," Aaron said, looking at Angelina.

"Bring two, and you're on, Aaron," Angelina replied. Aaron glanced at the old man, who shook his head.

Aaron left and the old man sat in the chair bringing Jesse up to speed on the ranch and what he was doing to get the bills and other things paid, as she desultorily played with the Jello, taking a small bite every now and then. Jesse finally asked how things were going at work, and the old man regaled her with Bucky's recital of the uproar south of the border. This finally brought a smile to Jesse's face.

Aaron returned in about twenty minutes, bags in hand, and that reminded the old man he was hungry. Leaving the kids to dinner, he kissed Jesse on the cheek and headed for the truck stop to get his own food.

***

A week later Jesse stood leaning on the bar in the PT room looking at Tina. "Okay, I know I'm not perfect, but this *is* an improvement, right?"

Tina cocked her head. "Let's see you walk the length of the bar, turn around and walk back without having to grab onto anything, then we'll talk."

Jesse sighed, pushed off the bar and stumped, for lack of a better word, down to the end of the bar. Swinging the cast around, she almost stumbled, but saved it at the last second. Stumping back to the other end of the bar, she stepped out the end and bowed, almost going over on her nose. "Okay, *now* can I get rid of this damn helmet? It's making my head itch like crazy!"

Tina relented. "Fine, but you still need to be careful, especially on uneven surfaces, and I don't even want to think of your trying to go up or down stairs yet."

Jesse took the helmet off, flipped it to Aaron and vigorously rubbed the parts of her head she could get to around the bandages, much to Aaron and Morrow's amusement. She glared at both of them then said to Tina, "Okay, what's next?"

"Range of motion on the shoulder, and strength reps. Your shoulder is coming along pretty good, but I still don't recommend you use crutches just yet. And some core work to help those ribs heal."

Jesse limped over to the Nautilus machine and flopped down, then maneuvered the leg cast to a semi-comfortable position while Tina set up the resistance and motion limits she wanted Jesse working within. "Okay, you're ready to go girl, ten reps times three, then we'll change positions." Jesse rolled her eyes, but dutifully started on the exercise. By the time she was finished, sweat was rolling down her face, and tears were in her eyes, but she'd completed all thirty reps.

Resetting the machine, Tina said, "Okay, strength reps, ten times three and you're done for the day." Jesse assumed the position and cranked them out but could only get twenty-eight reps before she stopped. "I can't do anymore. My shoulder's burning and it feels like my head is going to pop."

Tina said, "Good enough. You *are* a bit red in the face, and you're still forgetting to breathe at the end. Without a good breathing pattern, that's going to happen every time. Oxygen *is* your friend, remember?"

Jesse sat up with Aaron's help. "Yeah, yeah, I know. God what I wouldn't give for a shower right now!"

Aaron smiled. "Yeah that would be nice." Prompting Jesse to take a shot at his ribs, and Tina and Morrow to both laugh. Aaron helped Jesse back into the wheel chair and pushed her out the door.

Morrow stopped for a minute and asked, "How's she doing?"

Tina answered, "Pretty good considering, she was in pretty good shape before, and she's got a lot of frustrations to get out, so I'm kinda using those to motivate her."

Morrow laughed. "You're as bad as some of the instructors I had in the Corps. Lemme go catch up with them before they get lost and I get in trouble."

Tina held out a hand. "Is she really in that much danger? I mean, this is a hospital, but seeing you guys always around carrying guns is not the norm, if you know what I mean."

"Yes, ma'am, folks that count and have the intel think so. They've already made one try at killing her in here and we don't want a repeat. And we try not to be too obvious."

Tina replied, "Well it's just… I dunno… You're all so *military* it's like y'all are cookie cutter versions of each other."

Laughing, Morrow reached for the door. "Well, ma'am, a career in the Marine Corps *does* give one a certain mindset and a certain bearing. Thanks for your honest appraisal." With that, he was out the door and hurrying to catch Jesse and Aaron at the elevator. Tina stood hip-shot staring at the closed door and thinking about what he'd said.

Wedding Prep

Matt, Aaron, Jerry, Al and Toad walked slowly from the bunkhouse toward the main house, wearing mostly workout gear, and running shoes. They'd decided they needed to get a run in to blow the cobwebs away from the beer last night, but they all wanted coffee before they started. Knocking on the back door, Matt heard the old man calling for them to come in. He led the crew into the kitchen and the old man pointed to the large percolator chugging away on the end of the counter. "Coffee's close enough, use those Styrofoam cups if you want a large cup, otherwise the regular cups are in the last cabinet on the end. You need milk or sugar, it's on the center island."

During the round of good mornings, Trey came slowly into the kitchen dressed in a pair of shorts and sandals on his feet. Toad looked over and said with a grin, "Damn, the man mountain is alive!"

Trey walked silently to the percolator, drew a cup of coffee and turned on Toad. "You want to live through the day, knock that shit off you little sawed off runt." Then he smiled, "Otherwise, I'm gonna make you even shorter than you already are."

Toad backed off with a smile, saying, "Hey I was just joking. Any shorter and they'll kick me out of the Corps."

Jerry looked at Trey's leg. "Damn, what happened to your leg, Trey?"

Trey glanced down. "Ah hell, Sarge, just a little bit of surgery. I blew the knee out playing football a few years ago."

"Guess you don't run a lot now do you?" Jerry asked.

"Nope, don't need to, but if I have to I can still move pretty good."

Beverly and Jesse came in headed toward the coffee, and Beverly said, "Only when *he* wants to move. If *I* want him to do something, forget it. Here Jesse, lemme get that." Picking up both cups, she carried them to the table and Jesse stumped over to the table on her crutches.

Sitting carefully down on the edge of the chair, Jesse looked up at Aaron. "You better be worth all the shit I'm going to go through today. Just want to remind you of that. *Dear.*"

All the men laughed as Aaron blushed, and they trooped out to the front porch, leaving the old man leaning on the counter and Jesse and Beverly sitting at the table. The old man asked, "Butterflies or second thoughts?"

"Nope, Papa, but today is *not* going to be fun. I still don't know how I'm going to get down the aisle with this," she said, rapping on the cast. "And I'm not sure what it's going to look like with the dress, or if I can even wear the dress. And my shoulder is sore from just the last two days of trying to move around with crutches, but I hate that damn wheelchair. I keep running into shit with my foot!"

Beverly sipped her coffee, then said, "Don't worry, we'll get you in that dress, come hell or high water girl. And Mindy or was it Cindy is doing your wig for the wedding. We'll make it work or the men will *pay!*"

"Cindy, bless her heart, I hated to drop that on her, but I really don't want to get married looking like this," Jesse said ruefully as she scrubbed her very short hair.

The old man said, "I think it's flat enough that we can put you in the wheel chair and roll you to the altar without any problem…"

Jesse bristled. "I am *not* getting married sitting in a damn wheel chair. I *will* stand next to Aaron."

Holding up his hands in a defensive gesture as Beverly snickered, he said, "Okay, fine. I'll put your walker up there right by the altar. Aaron and I can lift you and stand you up."

Trey rumbled from the door way, "Ah hell, just throw her over your shoulder, nobody'll care."

Beverly said, "You, shut up."

Jesse just glared, and Trey broke out in a huge smile. "The boys have gone for a run. They said they'd be back in about an hour. Maybe by then the rest of the coven will be up."

Jesse turned on the old man, "*Papa,* why did you ever have to start that?"

The old man replied innocently, "I only said something *once.*"

"Sure, sure," Jesse said, realizing she was rubbing a finger over one of the bullet gouges that Felix and the folks hadn't been able to sand out of the table. "I just wish Francisco, Juanita and Toby could be here today. And I wish Rex was still underfoot all the time."

The old man replied, "So do I, hon, so do I."

A knock on the back door broke the mood, and the old man yelled, "Come in, it's open."

Felicia came in, followed by Mindy, Cindy and Lupe, the other bridesmaids. Cindy looked around and said, "Oh… Coffee! I need coffee!" Prompting laughter from the others in the kitchen.

Jesse was humming something under her breath, when she suddenly said, "Sixpence! Papa, I need a sixpence."

The old man started. "A *what*?"

Bobbing back and forth Jesse sang, "Something old, something new, something borrowed, something blue, *and a sixpence in my shoe!* That sixpence! That's the only thing I'm missing."

The old man looked at her skeptically. "A *sixpence*? Really? Hon, this is Texas, not England."

Jesse demanded, "Papa, go check your jar. I'm betting you have one in there."

Rolling his eyes and grumbling, the old man disappeared into the office, and Jesse followed him slowly. She leaned on the side of the door as the old man dumped his jar of coins on the desk and started digging through them.

"Papa? Am I doing the right thing?"

The old man stopped, turned and said, "Jesse, I can't answer that. You know your own heart, and while I don't want you to go, at the same time I want you to be happy. And I've seen you happier with

Aaron than anyone before. Your life and your dreams have to be your own, not mine. Do you understand that?"

Jesse limped over and hugged the old man. "Yes, I do Papa, but at the same time, I'm scared. This is a huge step for me. And what's happened to me has to make Aaron wonder doesn't it?"

Hugging her back he said, "Why? You've shown more resilience that I had at your age. Damn girl, three weeks ago you were as good as dead lying on the kitchen floor! I can't see why Aaron wouldn't want you to be his wife. Hell, you've proven you've got guts, and you're smart, you're not a clinger, you're a woman to stand on her own two feet, and be a partner. There ain't much more a man can ask."

"Are you sure?"

"Arrghhh, I'm as sure as I can be. Now do you want that sixpence or not?"

Jesse let go of the old man saying, "I do, thank you for raising me, Papa, and know that I love you."

"I love you too, Jesse, now go get off that leg."

"Yes, sir! Jesse said and stumped back to the kitchen. A few minutes later the old man came back into the kitchen, slapping one slightly used sixpence down on the table. "Any more damn last minute requests?"

Jesse smiled. "No, Papa, that'll do it for now. Thank you."

The old man hooked his head toward the back door, and Trey nodded, then went back to the guest room and grabbed a shirt. Going out the back door, he found the old man firing off the grills and asked what he could do. Mentally counting off in his head, the old man said, "Well, we've gotta feed fifteen maybe sixteen people, so I'm figuring I'd start cooking bacon and some sausage now, and get some water heating for the hot pans. We're going to have to eat out here, not enough room in the house. Felix and Olivia are doing biscuits, and I've got to put more in pretty quick in this oven. Olivia said she'd also do some pancakes. But I figure bacon and eggs for most, and I can make some sausage gravy too." Hauling out a sheet of expanded diamond plate, he flipped that onto one grill, and disappeared back into the house. Coming to the door, he handed Trey four dozen eggs, then four pounds of bacon. Finally he came back with two of the biggest cast iron pans Trey had ever seen.

"Damn, Mister C, how big are those pans?"

"Eighteen inches by three inches deep, and they're well over a hundred years old. According to family history, these made a few trail drives along with some dutch ovens and other stuff we've got around here."

Flipping open his Benchmade, he opened the packages of bacon, grabbing a couple of pieces he threw those in the two pans, then said, "If you want to help, you can lay the bacon and sausage out on the grill and I'll get the biscuits going."

Trey picked up a package of bacon and proceeded to start laying them out as the old man went back into the house, coming back a few minutes later with two refills on the coffee and packages of sausage. "I put Beverly to work, since she says she knows how to make sausage gravy."

Trey smacked his head. "Dammit, I should have told you, she does some great gravy!"

The old man smiled. "She said she could and you'd probably forget. You want to crack eggs or cook?"

"Hell, Mister C, I can't cook for shit. I'll crack eggs as soon as I get the sausage on."

The old man disappeared back into the house and came back a few minutes later with a large bowl. "Okay, start cracking. I'm going to start flipping bacon and sausages."

Felicia and Lupe came out carrying plates and two kettles of hot water that went into the hot pans and Felicia lit the heaters under each one of them. Felicia asked, "More coffee?"

The old man said, "Sure, and tell the girls about fifteen minutes till breakfast. The boys should be back by then too."

She nodded and returned with more coffee, and two gallons of orange juice. Jesse stumped down the steps and flopped in a chair, cussing under her breath prompting a raised eyebrow from the old man. "Papa, I *still* don't know what to do. I sure as hell can't walk down the aisle, and what am I going to do after we're married?"

The old man chuckled. "Two choices: either Aaron pushes you, or he could pick you up and carry you. I know, maybe I'll suggest that to him!"

"*Papa!* Don't you dare!"

The old man just laughed as he shoveled bacon and sausages onto a plate and handed it to Trey. "Okay, lay the last of the bacon out. I'm going to start on the eggs."

Mindy stuck her head out the door. "Hey, there's a buzzer going off, what's that for?"

Jesse just rolled her eyes. "Tell Beverly it's the biscuits please." Mindy ducked back into the kitchen and Jesse said, "Not *all* the ditsy ones are blonde." Prompting laughter from everyone.

Thirty minutes later it looked like a cloud of locusts had descended on the food, Trey was disconsolately shuffling through the various hot pans, but every single thing was gone, except for half a biscuit. Shrugging, he picked it up and looked over at the two tables thinking, *I can't believe this is actually happening. Three weeks ago Jesse was in a coma, damn near dead. And now, she's getting married. And Beverly and I are in the wedding party. Lotta my homies would think we're just kissing up to the man, but what they don't understand is these folks are as much family as mom, dad and the in-laws are. Why can't folks just accept others for who they are, not what they are? Regardless, I wouldn't be here today if it weren't for Jesse and her help at school, and I'd never have met Beverly. Damn those drug dealers!*

Trey was jerked from his thoughts by the old man. "Okay folks, we've got a little over two hours till the ceremony. That means we need to start herding the cats. Ladies, you too, Jesse, y'all have the old house. Marines to the bunkhouse, lady guests to the new house. Beverly, you get the first shower while we clean up out here."

Felix, Olivia and Trey helped clean up and lay out the table covers for the reception as Ricky went around and opened the front pasture gate, and got ready to park the early arrivals.

Thankfully, the Ramos brothers had extra coolers, as it seemed many of those who were coming in had brought something in the way of food, dessert or drinks. The wedding presents were accumulating on the table closest to the house, and threatened to topple over at any minute as more were piled haphazardly on top.

It appeared a lot of folks came early just to socialize. As Angelina and her hubby came in with their kids and parents, Felicia ran over for a tearful reunion with the family. Matt stayed away until Felicia forcefully drug him over to them and everyone laughed when little Pedro grabbed Matt's leg and started growling at him, remembering Christmas last year.

The old man stood by the back porch, nodding to himself. *Yep, that's another one that's going to bite the dust, whether Matt knows it or not. But it should be interesting, considering that Matt is damn near a foot taller than anyone in Felicia and Angelina's family.*

Billy scruffily dressed in jeans and an old polo shirt eased out the back door and came to stand by the old man, "You going to at least put on a coat and tie?" The old man asked.

Billy nodded. "You giving Jesse away in your uniform?"

"Nah, this is her time, mine and yours is long past. Jack should be doing this while I sit in the shade doddering in my rocking chair."

"Yeah, in the best of all worlds… Speaking of which, did you ever go see Bill about whatever the hell the Fibbies wanted with you?" Billy asked.

The old man chuckled. "I called Milty up at Quantico first, found out it was a come-around from the little dust up I had in Bangkok with that idiot from State. State wanted me held and or questioned about how I got there, who paid, and all the other crap. Apparently, I really did upset their applecart, especially since the Chinese guy was sentenced to life in prison. *Rumor* has it, they were trying to cook a deal to get him declared PNG[29] and sent back to China rather than go to trial, in addition to trying to get the Thais to release the ship. I think based on the conviction, they kept the ship *and* the cargo, and threw his ass under the jail too."

Billy laughed. "Yeah, you stirred it up again didn't you?"

The old man continued, "So once I got the rundown from Milty, including the fact that apparently State is pissed at the Legate office in Bangkok for not finding me, I called Bill and explained what was going on and why. At that point Bill apologized again, and said he's got a new ASAC reporting in a couple of weeks. He's *still* pissed the

---

[29] Persona Non Grata

old one didn't talk to him first. I think the first one got sent some place in North Dakota. Anyway, I'm not going to talk to him, and he's already sent a flamer back up to State telling them to do their own damn dirty work."

The old man flipped the last of his coffee on the ground, and said, "I get the shower before you do, you take too damn long with that pony tail of yours. Gimme about fifteen."

Billy replied with a smile, "Go ahead, I'm just going to stand here and enjoy all the pretty girls in their pretty dresses!"

***

In Cozumel, Roberto stepped quietly into Montoya's office. "You called, *Jefe*?"

"*Si,* Roberto, I have talked to my equal with Sinaloa, and they swear they didn't put a hit on Zapata. We are at a dead end, unless the *Norte Americanos* slipped a team in and did it," picking up a file he asked, "Do we know what happened to the hit team sent against this sheriff, Cronin? Up in Texas?"

Roberto fidgeted, "*Jefe*, as best we can determine, they hit the ranch and killed two women and a boy, but missed the sheriff. Eduardo told me they were going to make one more try, but somehow they ended up dead. According to the papers, they shot each other; but I don't believe that. I think the *Federales* up there shot them down somehow and lied about it."

305

Montoya laid the file back down. "Is there any possibility that this Cronin could have killed Zapata?"

Roberto rocked back on his heels thinking. "Probably not, *Jefe* that was more than one man could have done. We haven't found any Tamahumara that admitted to being in that part of the state, but Cronin is a shooter, not a cutter. Somebody cut up a lot of our people. I think it might have been a DEA team with some *cochiloco* peons from one of the vigilante groups that wanted revenge. There were at least two rifles fired from that knob, one was shooting US military sniper ammunition and the other US Military M-16 ammunition."

Montoya tapped the file thoughtfully. "So probably not him, but does he still need killing?"

Roberto replied, "*Jefe,* that is not my call. I recommended against it to start with; but *Cuchillo,* well, he was always wanting to solve everything with violence."

Montoya held up a hand. "Enough. For now we'll let him live and worry. You may go, Roberto.

The Ceremony

An hour later, the old man was sitting in the office, buffing his boots and heard a knock on the screen door, rather than get up he just yelled, "Come in, dammit. It's open!"

Laughter followed, and the sheriff, his wife Dorothy, Ranger Boone and his wife Ronni, followed by Eddie Guilfoile and his wife Iris came trooping in. The old man got up shook hands with everyone and gave Guilfoile a quick hug saying softly, "I'm glad you could make it, Eddie."

Guilfoile stepped back and said, "Thanks, we rode up with Mr. Clay. Is there anything we can do to help?"

The old man looked at Iris, noting her almost trembling and said, "Iris, would you and Ronni mind helping in the kitchen? I know y'all are both good cooks, and I don't want anything to get missed today. Is that okay?"

Iris visibly relaxed, and with Ronni leading, headed for the kitchen. Dorothy left with them, mumbling something about the "old boys club" as she went out.

The sheriff asked, "Where are the preacher and the *padre*? I figured they'd be in here bugging the devil out of everybody."

The old man laughed. "They're out in the barn trying to get their act together. They're both giving the vows, and are trying to smooth out any differences." Looking at his watch, he said, "Guess it's about that time. We better mosey on out."

Stepping out the back door, the old man went over to Esteban Ramos. "You ready to go?"

He replied, "Any time you're ready Mr. Cronin, we've got everything set, just waiting for the ceremony to be over, and it'll be time to eat. We did plenty so you'll have some extra to feed the folks that are staying here. Where are Jesse and her new hubby going to honeymoon?"

The old man laughed. "For now, right here. Jesse's still got some therapy to go through, and next week they'll drive back to California if she thinks she can ride that far. Otherwise, Aaron's going to drive, and Jesse will have to fly. It's a toss-up right now, but knowing her, she's going to ride in that truck come hell or high water."

Esteban said, "Gotta admit, I don't think I've ever seen a wedding layout like this one." Sweeping his hand over the area between the old and new houses. "It looks more like the fandango setup..."

The old man said, "Hell, it *is* the fandango setup. Rather than a dance floor, we made that the aisle so Jesse can be wheeled to the altar. With roughly two hundred folks here, there was no way in hell to do any different. I know Jesse and Aaron wanted a small wedding, but it kinda got out of hand."

Esteban asked, "Where are you putting the groom's parents?"

The old man sighed. "They aren't here, claimed it was too expensive for them to come out, even after I offered to pay for their plane tickets. I don't think Aaron has a real good relationship with them, if at all."

Bucky came over, obviously not comfortable in a suit and tie and grumbled, "I wouldn't do this for anybody *but* Jesse. For what it's worth, ain't heard shit out of San Buenaventura lately. Sounds like they pulled in their horns, or they're dropping back to running shit via the normal cartel routes."

The old man said, "Good. Heard anything about Roberto?"

Bucky replied, "Nope, he's like smoke on the water. Just disappeared, again."

Billy Moore snuck up behind the old man, saying, "Is this shit over, yet? I'm hungry! Hey Esteban, can you slip me a plate before this kicks off? I'm dyin' over here."

The old man turned and shook hands with Billy saying, "About damn time. I was wondering if you were going to make it."

"Wouldn't miss it for the world. She's the only good one *in* this family," he said with a grin, as he shook hands with Bucky who was laughing.

Eduardo, running the sound system looked over at the old man and nodded, then cued the prelude music. Those still standing quickly found seats as the preacher, *padre* and Aaron, resplendent in his dress uniform marched slowly down the aisle. After they arrived and everyone was positioned, Eduardo changed the music to the processional as the bridesmaids and groomsmen lined up by the old house. Trey and Beverly stepped off first, followed by Al and Lupe, then Jerry and Mindy, and surprisingly Toad and Cindy. All the Marines were in their dress uniforms, and the ladies were in similar gowns but of different colors that accentuated their complexions.

Next came Matt and Felicia, and the old man couldn't help but wonder when those two would tie the knot. It was obvious they were in love, whether or not they wanted to admit it, and if he could see it, he was pretty sure everyone else there could, too.

Angelina shooed little Jose forward, and he solemnly stepped carefully down the aisle carrying the rings, followed by his sister Angelica who was scattering rose petals enthusiastically. Jesse had eased out of the old house and was seated in her wheelchair, and as Eduardo segued into Here Comes the Bride, the old man pushed her wheelchair slowly down the aisle.

Getting her up and standing braced with the walker was easier than he had thought, and Felicia helpfully straightened Jesse's dress for her.

The preacher started off with the words, "Dearly beloved, we are gathered here today," then handed off to the *padre*, for the opening homilies. The preacher presided over the giving of the bride from the old man to Aaron. The *padre* gave the acknowledgements, and Rita and Jenn sang an *a capella* version of the love song, that Jesse had chosen. The preacher stepped up and gave the charge to the couple, reminding them of the sacredness of the vows they were about to exchange, and the duties of a marriage.

Then he and the *padre* both stepped forward to administer the vows, first telling them to face one another. They spoke the vows first and Aaron repeated them, his voice strong and determined.

"I, Aaron Miller, take you, Jesse Cronin, to be my lawfully wedded wife, to have and to hold, from this day forward, for better, for worse, for richer, for poorer, in sickness and in health, until death do us part."

Jesse's eyes never left Aaron's face. Tears glistened in them, as she started her vows.
"I, Jesse Cronin, take you, Aaron Miller, to be my lawfully wedded husband, to have and to hold, from this day forward, for better, for worse, for richer, for poorer, in sickness and in health, until death do us part."

Little Jose seemed to be lost in space, and finally the *padre* had to call him, "Jose, the rings please." Jose brought the rings and presented them to Aaron, then scampered back to Angelina, prompting laughter from everyone there. The preacher took the rings, and handed Jesse's to Aaron, who placed it on her finger with the words, "With this ring I thee wed, Jesse."

Handing Aaron's ring to Jesse, she took a moment to get her balance, then put Aaron's ring on his finger saying, "With this ring I thee wed, Aaron."

Both the preacher and *padre* said in chorus, "We now pronounce you man and wife, you may kiss the bride."

Aaron took Jesse in his arms and kissed her tenderly saying, "I love you Jesse. I love you." Jesse didn't say anything, just kissed Aaron more deeply.

The *padre*, gave a short blessing and closed the ceremony. Aaron helped Jesse back into the wheelchair and started pushing her back down the aisle as Rita and Jenn broke into an *a capella* version of a song they had picked for the couple.

The old man noted that Felicia was looking at Matt like a cat looking at a plate of cream, and he had to cough to hide his smile. It wasn't until the old man looked at Aaron's medals that he noticed both a Silver Star and Bronze Star resting on this tunic, along with a Purple Heart and what he thought of as the standard fruit salad. He also noted that Matt had the same top two, and multiple Purple Hearts. Curious now, he watched the other Marines and saw that each of them had Bronze Stars and Purple Hearts. These kids— no *men*— were warriors too. Aaron had pushed Jesse over to the table, and helped her into a chair so the old man walked over and bent to her, "Congratulations, Mrs. Miller. Now, you're Aaron's problem." And kissed her on the cheek.

Jesse stuck her tongue out at him, and slipped an arm around his waist, hanging into the holster of his 1911. "Dammit, Papa, if you made me break a nail…"

He chuckled. "It's Aaron's problem." And walked off.

Jesse was soon surrounded by well-wishers, and he noted the bridesmaids and groomsmen had taken over the adjacent table, and were still paired off.

Eduardo and Rosa stood in front of the crowd at the altar and Eduardo said loudly, "Since there will be no dancing due to Jesse's *condition*," prompting a laugh from everyone, "Rosa and I will do the Hat Dance in their honor. This is for you Mr. and Mrs. Miller." As the music started, everyone stopped and watched as they progressed through the dance, with Aaron and Jesse quietly holding hands and glancing back and forth between each other and the dance. At the end, everyone stood and applauded, including Jesse, who thanked them as soon as they came by the table.

After the cake cutting, pictures and more pictures, everyone lined up and went through the serving line the Ramos brothers had set up. The BBQ was a hit with everyone, and nobody went away hungry.

The old man smiled to himself, happy with the way the ceremony and reception had gone. *Couldn't have asked for a better day, and I hope Jesse remembers this for a long time. She's lucky to even be here today, and thank you for that, God. I hope Francisco, Juanita and Toby are happy for her too.*

Family and Friends

As the reception wound down and folks started leaving, the retired Marines, led by Colonel Muir and Gunner McMurtrie, approached the table. Aaron and the other Marines stood and Aaron helped Jesse to her feet. Gunner said, "I think we're done here, and we just wanted to stop by and congratulate y'all on your wedding. We're outta here since you're now home Mrs. Miller, and you've got a Marine watching over you."

Jesse hugged the Gunner surprising him and said, "Thank you, I know if it weren't for y'all I wouldn't be here today." Turning to Colonel Muir she hugged him asking, "Is there any way I can repay you for what y'all did?"

Muir replied, "Just be a good Marine wife."

Toad broke in, "Colonel Muir?"

Muir nodded and Toad said, "Don't go away, I got something for you." Hopping up from the table he trotted toward the bunkhouse as Jesse hugged the remaining retired Marines, thanking each of them in turn.

Jesse excused herself and with Mindy and Cindy's help stumped back to the old house. They quickly changed clothes and helped Jesse out of her wedding dress, chatting about how well it had gone and how pretty Jesse was. As they came back out, Mindy sighed. "Oh, Jerry is so cute in that uniform, he looks like a recruiting poster. I just wish I could get him away from the rest of them."

Jesse looked sharply at her. "Mindy, he's not a boy-toy, like the ones you play with up in Dallas.

Cindy quoted softly, "I went into a public-'ouse to get a pint o'beer, the publican 'e up an' sez, 'We serve no red-coats here.' The girls be'ind the bar they laughed an' giggled fit to die, O makin' mock o' uniforms that guard you while you sleep Is cheaper than them uniforms, an' they're starvation cheap; An' hustlin' drunken sodgers when they're goin' large a bit is five times better business than paradin' in full kit."

Mindy looked at her. "What was that? I know I've heard or read that before?"
Jesse smiled. " 'Tommy' by Rudyard Kipling. Remember the quote about 'people sleep peaceably in their beds at night only because rough men stand ready to do violence on their behalf'?"

Mindy said, "Yeah, why?"

Jesse said, "Because you're looking at two generations of very rough men standing there. They came home, but a lot of their friends didn't. You see those medals? They jokingly call that fruit salad, but that really is a resume they carry around anytime they are in uniform."

Mindy replied, "Oh, they do look pretty, but they're all different aren't they? I mean they all look pretty except for the one that they call Toad, he does kinda look like one."

315

Jesse said, "Mindy! Every one of those Marines has been in combat, and all of them have medals for valor. And Toad? He's one of the sweetest guys I've ever met. He's almost finished with a Masters in Physics, and he's an expert in weapons. He maintains all the special rifles the Marines use."

Cindy looked speculatively at Toad, remembering some of their earlier conversation, and decided to spend a little more time looking beyond the uniform and the looks to the person underneath.

Jesse said, "Come on, let's get back over there before they get too deep into the beer. Aaron and I may not be able to do much tonight, but he snores *bad* when he's had too much beer!"

Laughing the girls made their way slowly back to the table. The old man, Billy Moore and Clay and Ronni had joined the group, and all of them had a Shiners in hand. As they came back, Lupe ran and joined them.

The girls were handed beers, and Billy said, "A toast to the newlyweds! A health to you, a wealth to you, and the best that life can give to you. May fortune still be kind to you, and happiness be true to you, and life be long and good to you. This is the toast of all your friends to you!"

A clinking of bottles followed with *Salut, Prosit, Amen* and *Hell, Yeah* being heard from various quarters as everyone drank.

Billy turned to the old man and said, "Dammit John, I always knew you were a cheap bastard, but you don't even have a bottle of bubbly for the bride and groom? You're making them drink beer? How gauche!"

They all burst out laughing at Billy's comment and Trey leaned over and whispered to Beverly, who disappeared back into the house. Cindy turned to Toad asking, "What did you have to go get? I saw you go back to the bunkhouse."

Toad said, "Oh, I had to go get the colonel his pistol. It was a debt that had to get paid, and since I did the work, I got to deliver it."

Cindy asked, "Is that legal? I mean for you to just *give* him a pistol?"

Toad replied, "You're in law school, right?"

Cindy nodded. "Well, we did a legal transfer of ownership. I verified he has a concealed handgun permit, which means he's legal in the state of Texas, and he signed the paperwork I have from Colonel Ortega, so under Texas law, that is considered a legal exchange, even though it was a gift."

Cindy said, "We were told all gun sales had to go through some kind of check and something or other..."

Toad said, "NICS, National Instant Criminal Background Check System, it's run by the FBI and if you're a FFL, that's a person that has a federal firearms license like a dealer, you're supposed to run the person through that before you sell them a gun. Since Colonel Muir already has a concealed handgun permit, that means he's already had all those checks. 'Sides, I'm not about to get between two colonels over something like this!"

Cindy laughed. "I guess I need to learn the difference between what's in the book and reality don't I?"

They were interrupted by Beverly coming back with a wrapped gift, and Trey and Beverly standing in front of Jesse. Trey rumbled, "Jesse, we're giving this to you, not to Aaron, so hopefully it will be drunk at the appropriate time, and not by a bunch of lushes at your wedding!" Smiling, Beverly handed the gift to Jesse and whispered, "its good stuff, trust me."

Jesse smiled. "Thank you, and I'll take the chance now. Besides if anybody wants to fight for it, I can beat 'em off with my crutches. Aaron would you do the honors?"

Aaron took the gift and fought with the tape and bows for a minute, finally reaching into his pocket a pulling out his knife, and cutting the wrapping away. He pulled out a blue box and asked, "Pol Roger?"

Colonel Muir asked, "Does it say Winston Churchill?"

Aaron turned the box. "Yes, sir."

Colonel Muir said, "That's good stuff. That was the blend that Churchill preferred."

Gunner said with a smile. "Figures, the colonels can afford that stuff, we can't."

Everybody broke up laughing at that, and Jesse held out her hand. "Gimme, we're going to save that for later," She said, prompting another round of laughter.

After the retired Marines departed, Aaron, Matt and the other Marines decided to get out of their dress uniforms and get comfortable. The Ramos brothers had torn down the serving line and packed the left overs for the old man and put them in the house. Felix and Ricky, along with a couple of Ricky's friends were tearing down the tables and putting them back in the barn, as the last few guests departed.

Rather than move back inside, the old man, Billy and the others drug chairs around the two biggest tables and sat chatting. Billy turned to Cindy and asked, "Well Miss Parker, how are you liking law school?"

Cindy looked at Billy in shock. "How… er… How did you know…"

Billy laughed. "You didn't really think you'd be here if we hadn't checked you out do you? With what is going on?" Waving his hand at Jesse, who was chatting with the sheriff's wife and Ronni.

Cindy bristled. "That's…"

Billy, now deadly serious said, "No, it's *not* illegal. And believe me, every single person here today was vetted one way or another. There are people who would love nothing more than to kill John, Jesse and every law enforcement person here. Contrary to what you may be hearing in law school, there is some bad shit going on down here and on the border. And I'll be damned if *I* was going to let anybody spoil Jesse's day. Now back to my original question, how are you liking law school?"

Cindy sat back. "I like it okay, but I'm not sure what I want to do. I don't think I want to go into corporate law, or anything along that line. I think

I'm more interested in the criminal side, but I just finished Con Law II, and I'm dual tracking for law and public affairs."

Billy leaned forward. "You figured out where you want to intern yet?"

Cindy shook her head. "I don't know if I want to take the summer off, or just keep going to school. I know I need to make a decision pretty soon, Momma is wanting me to come home for the summer though."

Billy said, "Well if you want, since you live in Bellaire, I'll offer you an internship with my office. Guarantee you won't be doing shit work, and you'll get a pretty wide set of experiences. What I'd recommend is you point to at least starting in the DA's office rather than private practice if you're really interested in the constitutional and public policy side. Working for the DA, you'll get a breadth of cases, and spend a lot of time in the books, and probably no two cases will be the same."

Cindy sucked in her breath. "Do I have to give you an answer right now?"

Billy shook his head. "Nope, just give me a call before the end of the school year," and handed her a business card with his direct number on it.

As the Marines came back from the bunkhouse, now casually dressed, the old man, Billy, Bucky, and the sheriff and Clay and their wives moved inside, leaving the younger ones to the beer and last bits of cake. Sitting in the kitchen coffee cups in hand, they discussed the situation as they knew it, and Bucky said, "Well, after the last couple of weeks, it looks like the mules coming up through Big Bend has dropped to a trickle, and EPIC hasn't heard anything about any movements of anymore hit teams across the border, nor have any of our CIs heard anything. Looks like what I told you a couple of weeks ago was right, both the Zetas and Sinaloa have pulled in their horns at least for now."

Clay said, "Yep, pretty much agrees with what I'm seeing and hearing. Did a flight yesterday down along the border, and I didn't see any smokes south of the river and CBP hasn't had a single hit in Big Bend in the last two weeks."

The sheriff said, "Yeah, it's been quiet on ten too. Maybe too quiet." Turning to the old man he asked, "How are you going to do security for Jesse now that the retired Marines are gone?"

The old man replied, "Well, she's outpatient now, so she'll be stayin' here, at least for the next week. Doc Truesdale has agreed to vary the PT hours so we're not on a set schedule for taking her into the hospital and he's got it set up for us to park right by the ER door. Whoever takes her in will be carrying, and will stay out of the area and keep a lookout. Once she gets to Pendleton, I'm hoping with the name change, she'll be able to drop off the radar, but if not, Jose are you still willing to keep her on the rolls as a deputy?"

The sheriff said, "Hell that was my plan all along. Far as I'm concerned this is her permanent place of residence. And until she tells me different, she's one of my deputies, as long as I stay the sheriff."

"Thanks. I can't ask for more than that. Which reminds me, I need to run by the hotel and make sure I settle up any remaining bills from the Marines."

The sheriff laughed. "Yeah, Hazel is hating seeing them leave, she said the whole time they were there, all the other guests were quiet as mice. Guess seeing a bunch of folks with guns and attitudes is enough to make 'em walk the straight and narrow. And she couldn't say enough about how neat all those guys were."

The old man rolled his coffee cup in his hands. "Yeah, I owe them a debt I'll never be able to repay."

Billy said, "Ah hell, John, I gave 'em all my card and told 'em I'd represent them for free. What I didn't tell them was I'd bill *you* for the services."

That set off a round of laughter that broke the tension in the room. Ronni looked at Clay, and he said, "I think I'm getting the polite hook here guys, I guess it's time for us to hit the road."

Dorothy looked at the sheriff who said, "Yep, me too."

Bucky said, "I just want out of this damn monkey suit, and I probably should be checking in. I'm going to bail too."

The old man looked around the room saying, "I can't thank you enough for everything y'all have done." Jokingly, he continued, "Now get the hell outta my house. My tired old ass needs some sleep!"

Laughter followed, as everyone piled out the back door to give Aaron and Jesse one last congratulation before they left.

Finally, Aaron and Jesse made it back into the house, Jesse looking a little tired, and as she stumped through the kitchen leaning on Aaron she said, "We're done. Y'all hold the damn noise down out here okay?" With a wan smile on her face, she and Aaron continued on to her room.

The old man got up and went out the back door, making one more check before killing the lights, he noted Cindy and Toad deep in conversation at one table, and Lupe and Al deep in conversation at a different table. Mindy and Jerry were nowhere to be seen, but that wasn't his problem. Clearing his throat loudly, he said, "Lights are going off in five minutes, y'all are on your own. Good night." He got a chorus of good nights in return, and figured setting up a pot of coffee would take five minutes, then he'd kill the lights. Finished with the coffee, he flipped off the lights and sat back down at the table.

After a couple of minutes of conversation, Trey looked at Beverly asking, "You about ready? All of a sudden I'm tired."

Beverly laughed. "After the past couple of weeks, I'm surprised you're still upright, much less awake. See you in the morning Mister Cronin."

"Night, Trey, Beverly. Coffee will be on by five in the morning." Trey just groaned as they went down the hall. The old man thought for a minute, then flipped off the light and followed them.

In Jesse's room, Aaron and Jesse were curled in bed: Jesse, trying to get comfortable, went to roll over and hit Aaron's leg. "I'm sorry honey, I didn't mean to do that. I just can't find a comfortable spot."

Aaron replied, "Oh yeah, I know the feeling, when they had my leg in a cast after the shooting, I couldn't do shit. Couldn't get comfortable, couldn't sleep, couldn't do shit. You want me to get you a pill?"

"*No*! For better or worse, well worse in this case, this the one and only wedding night I'm planning on having, and drugging myself to sleep through it is *not* going to happen," Jesse said, then started crying. "I wanted this night to be special, and here I lay, like a lump... No, like a damn log..."

Burying her head in Aaron's shoulder, she continued to cry as Aaron held her; until he finally said, "Hey, Mrs. Miller, Gawd that sounds strange... We're going to have a lot more nights where we *can* have some fun, and it's not like we haven't already cos... con..."

Jesse raised her head with a hiccupping laugh. "Consummated. That the word you're trying to say? And, yes, we *have* consummated this union once or twice, haven't we Mr. Miller."

Aaron grinned at her in the dark. "Yes, we have and I love you Jesse Miller. Oh God, I love you. I was so scared..."

Jesse hugged him back. "I love you too Aaron, and right now I don't know which one scares me more, being shot at or being married."

"Why?"

"Well, getting shot at is over pretty quick, getting married, not so much. Now shut up and hold me," Jesse demanded.

"Yes, dear."

"You're learning," Jesse mumbled as she nodded off to sleep.

On the Range

Jesse came out of her room with her spare Python in the holster thrown over her shoulder and stumped into the kitchen. "Papa, I want *my* damn gun back, what is the hold up?"

The old man looked up from his coffee. "I'll check with the sheriff tomorrow. Honestly, I hadn't thought about it. Where do you think you're going?"

"It's Sunday, so that's range day, right? Besides, I want to shoot something; I need to get rid of some frustrations and you always said shooting was like Zen, to shoot well one actually has to concentrate and all that right?" Jesse asked with an arched eyebrow.

Aaron coughed to cover his laugh as the old man shook his head. "Er… Okay fine. But you'll need the cross draw holster, 'cause that one is going to bang into the top of the cast, and dig into your ribs. Did you think about that?"

Aaron got up. "I'll get it. Where is it, hon?"

Jesse thought for a minute then said, "Um… Top of the closet, big box on the right I think. Oh hell, just bring the box and I'll find it."

The old man said, "You're not going to walk, so we'll have to take you down the back way in the back of the Gator. I think there are some blankets in the barn I can throw in the back so you're not sitting flat on the bed." Curious, he asked, "Anything else you want to shoot?"

Jesse looked up from clearing the Python and set it on the table pointing away from everyone. "I think I can shoot the AR, not sure I want to try the thirty-thirty right now. Maybe some IPDA targets and if I can hit those, maybe a run or two on the calliope. I know I'm gonna suck," she said with a sigh.

Aaron came back with a big cardboard box, and plopped it on the table. "Damn girl, you've got more holsters than Carter's got liver pills in there. What did you do, buy one of everything in every catalog?"

Jesse shuffled through the box saying, "Well, it's not *easy* to find a holster that actually works for a woman. Unless you go to a custom maker, you end up with a box of cast offs, but for all the money spent, I can't afford to throw them away... Ah ha... There you are you little sucker." She smiled as she extracted a cross draw holster from the box, holding it up in triumph.

Diving back into the box again, she mumbled, "Belt, belt, I know it's in here somewhere."

Aaron and the old man both laughed, and left her to her devices. Aaron went to get his pistol and holster, and the old man heading toward the office and the safe. The old man slung his gunbelt on, spun the dial on the safe and pulled out two of the ARs from the front of the rack. Making sure they were safe, he leaned them against the desk and rummaged in the file cabinet for some boxes of ammo. He yelled down the hall, "Aaron, you've got a G seventeen, right?"

Aaron yelled back an affirmative, and the old man pulled a backpack out of the top drawer, checked that the blowout kit was still in the top pocket and started loading it up with boxes. Slinging the backpack on one shoulder, he closed the cabinet, locked the safe and picked up the two rifles. Lugging them back into the kitchen, he saw Jesse had finally found her belt and was in the process of transferring the speed loader pouches from one belt to the other. Setting the holster, she finally pointed the Python at the floor, reloaded it and snugged it into the holster.

Aaron came back with his G-17 strapped on his belt, and two mags on the offside in a double carrier. He proceeded to strip the mags, setting the bullets on the paper sitting on the side of the table saying, "I can't afford to shoot all my self-defense ammo, remind me when we get down there to swap mags and save the loaded mag of ammo please."

Jesse said, "I will." As the old man stripped the hollow points out of his two spare mags too. Jesse finally said, "Well, doh!" and pulled both speed loaders out their pouches and dumped the shells out of them. "I *really* want all of my memory back. This missing little shit stuff is getting old."

The old man said, "It's just going to take a while, just means you'll have to work a little harder up front. Y'all can stay here while I go get the Gator and find the blankets. Aaron, if you would, could you throw together a thermos of coffee?"

"Will do, sir," Aaron replied, rummaging through the cabinet for the thermos until Jesse said,

"Bottom left. And throw some of the sugar packets in your pocket will you?"

The old man went into the barn and found Ricky repairing a bridle on the tack room bench. "Problem, Ricky?" the old man asked, looking down at the bridle.

Ricky looked up with a start. "No, sir, just trying to stay ahead of the work. A couple of the holes were rounding out, and I figured better to replace the whole strap rather than try to cobble it together."

The old man nodded. "That's good. Are you doing okay? Are you happy living out here? I know all your friends are in town and living out here isn't conducive to a teenager's life. The truck's not a convertible, but at least you're not locked down out here."

Ricky scuffed a boot on the floor. "Actually, Senor, it's not bad. I mean I have a TV, there's air conditioning, and mama isn't yelling at me to pick up my clothes all the time. I just have to remember to wash my stuff before I run out."

The old man said, "Yeah, I can believe that," sensing things unsaid he asked, "Things okay with your dad?"

Ricky sighed. "Actually, he's probably happy I'm out here. He's been saying I was falling in with the wrong crowd, and I think the work he keeps loading me with is to run my ass in the ground so I won't have time or feel like going to town. What he doesn't realize, is I'm finally seeing what he was saying now that I'm away from them. And this is the first time I've ever really had responsibility without him or mama over my shoulder telling me what to do. I've been reading some of the husbanding books and range maintenance books that you left in the bunkhouse, and I'm starting to see how it all makes sense, and why we have to keep moving the cows around. I didn't realize how fragile the grazing is, and how hard you have to work to maintain the balance, much less all the real work that goes into just equipment maintenance," he said, holding up the bridle.

"Yeah, it's an all day, every day seven day a week job. If it's too much I can look at bringing somebody else on to help you. I keep forgetting you're not Toby, he really didn't want to go anywhere else; and really didn't have much of a life, now that I think of it."

Ricky smiled ruefully. "Oh, it's not that Mister Cronin. I'm saving money out here, and dad and I get the work done, no problem."

The old man nodded. "Okay, we're going to go down to the pump house and shoot, you want to join us?"

"No sir, I'll stay up here. What channel on the radio?"

The old man said, "We'll be up on five."

Ricky picked up the bridle and hung it back on the wall. "Okay, I'll be monitoring," he said as he headed back to the bunkhouse to get a radio.

The old man grabbed three of the cleaner horse blankets and lugged them out to the Gator, flopped them in the back and drove back to the house after he opened the gate. He opened the back door. "Okay, mount up," he said, as he stepped in and picked up the rifles, backpack and a radio from the rack by the door. Getting a radio check with Ricky, he dumped the backpack on the seat and lay the rifles on the far side of the Gator's bed.

Jesse stumped out the back door and Aaron carried her down the steps and set her in the back of the Gator with a smile. "Don't get used to that."

Jesse stuck her tongue out at Aaron. "Well, you were *supposed* to do that on our wedding night, but…"

Aaron said, "I would have but your cast wouldn't fit through the door." Prompting a coughing spell from the old man. Aaron said, "Go ahead, I'll follow and close the gates as we go."

The old man eased through both gates as Aaron opened then closed them behind him, then jumped into the front seat as the old man started down the old wagon track to the creek. "Are those wagon ruts?" Aaron asked, pointing to the sharp depressions in the track.

The old man nodded. "For years, a wagon was how they got water up from the creek, before the pump house was put in. Also there used to be a little bridge across the creek there too, so lots of wagons went this way for probably thirty-forty years. If you go further west, there are still wagon ruts in the prairie from the Conestoga's wheels on the Santa Fe trail."

At the pump house, Aaron helped Jesse out of the Gator and over to the picnic table, then went to help the old man set targets. The old man brought the spotting scope out and set it up behind the line while Aaron loaded his mags with practice ammo. While the old man was loading his mags and Jesse's speed loaders he said, "Okay, eyes and ears." Looking at Jesse, he asked, "You want to shoot standing or sitting?"

Jesse said, "Standing. I need to know if I can keep my balance. Aaron, if you'll guard me, I'd like to start at seven and try to work out from there." She put the two speed loaders in their pouches and loaded the Python with six rounds, then with Aaron's help, stood up and stumped over to the seven yard line.

The old man looked around making sure the area was clear and everybody had eye protection and hearing protection. Raising his voice, he said, "Range is hot, ready on the right, ready on the left, ready on the firing line. You may fire when ready."

Jesse, with Aaron behind her, drew her Python, assumed her grip and the old man could see her take a couple of deep breaths. Raising the pistol she brought it on target, her finger slipped into the trigger guard and her first round went downrange. The old man glanced through the spotting scope, noting a center mass hit. The second and third shots followed closely and were within an inch of the first. He saw Jesse drop the pistol back to a low ready, and got up, preparing to shoot on the target next to hers.

Stepping up, the old man drew his 1911 and put three downrange in short order. All were head shots and he smiled at that, then realized he hadn't heard

Jesse shoot again. Looking over, he saw Jesse in Aaron's arms, and immediately holstered his pistol.

"What happened? Are you hurt?"

Jesse shook her head. "No but I went to do a head shot, and your shot went off and… and… Papa I saw a *face* on the target," she sobbed.

"A face? What kind of face?" He asked.

Bewildered she answered, "I dunno, not somebody I ever remember knowing. He had a bushy mustache, and dark heavy eyebrows…"

The old man asked, "And long hair parted in the middle?"

Jesse look at him incredulously, "How… Yes, long black hair."

"Could you tell what he was wearing?"

"No, I just saw that face."

"Okay, I want you to turn around and try shooting a head shot again," the old man said. "I think I might know, but just humor me."

Jesse turned around and with Aaron right behind her, fired four rounds into the head. Turning she said, "Okay no face that time. What the hell, Papa?"

"Reload and let's try it with me shooting next to you. Then I'll tell you what I think happened."

Jesse dumped the spent shells, used one of the speed loaders and stepped back onto the line. Drawing a deep breath she said, "Okay, go ahead."

The old man fired four rapid shots, did a quick mag change and fired another seven rounds down range as Jesse finished her six rounds. He looked over and she shook her head. "No face that time."

Both reloaded and the old man said, "Okay, cold range. Let's go sit."

Pouring cups of coffee for everyone, the old man took a sip as Jesse shook a packet of sugar into hers, "What I *think* happened is your subconscious took over there for a minute. Once we get back to the house I'll show you a picture, but I believe the face you saw was the killer that you shot in the moustache."

"Oh lovely," Jesse muttered, "*another* damn nightmare waiting to happen."

Aaron asked, "What has your counsellor said?"

"That it's doubtful I'll ever remember anything; she goes back and forth between post-traumatic amnesia, and dissociative amnesia. With the other *little* stuff I keep forgetting, or not remembering I guess is the better term," Jesse said. "She thinks the short term stuff will get better once my head heals completely."

Finishing her coffee, Jesse said, "Okay, I came here to shoot, so let's shoot!" Reloading her speed loaders, she stepped back to ten yards, and waited while the old man and Aaron caught up. The old man gave the range commands, and she fired all three loads into the head without a miss. After a couple of more rounds of pistol against the calliope, they moved back to the table and shot ARs for a half hour, until Jesse finally admitted her shoulder was starting to hurt. The old man and Aaron tore everything down and put the gear back up as Jesse sat drinking the last of the coffee.

Aaron loaded Jesse in the back of the Gator and they made their way back slowly up to the house. Unloading everything, the old man took the Gator back to the barn, and walked slowly back to the house, trying to decide which pictures to show Jesse. He finally thought of one that was actually pretty clean, taken just before the autopsy. When he got back to the house, Jesse and Aaron were busy cleaning pistols and chatting happily.

Walking through, the old man went to the office pulled the file and came back to the kitchen. "Okay, Jesse," handing her the picture face down. "When you're ready, you can look at it."

Jesse flipped the picture over and put a hand to her mouth. "Oh, that is him. How can I possibly see him?" Jesse asked.

The old man took the picture back, "Dunno, but you obviously have some stuff stuck in your subconscious. Matter of fact, Trey told me you were actually pulling a trigger when the shots were fired at the hospital, even though you were in a coma."

Jesse looked down at her hands. "So the subconscious was willing and the body was willing, but I wasn't there huh?"

The old man replied, "Depends on what your definition of there is. Consciously you might not have been aware, but your body was. It is always that core strength that people don't understand, and a lot of that comes from the subconscious. It is the will to live, just like the competitiveness we all seem to have. Honestly, I'm just thankful you inherited that; if you hadn't we probably wouldn't be having this conversation today."

Jesse said, "Well, for better or worse, I'm still here. And Aaron has to put up with me from now on."

A Gift

A little after noon, the chime sounded indicating someone had come in the front gate of the ranch. The old man moved to the front window and saw a small motor home built on a truck chassis pull into the driveway. He hurried back to the office and flipped his gunbelt on grabbing his hat, and yelling down the hall to Jesse and Aaron to standby and cover. Walking onto the porch, he realized there was lettering on the side of the motor home, and it was some kennel. He stayed on the porch, not realizing the picture of malice he was radiating to the couple in the vehicle. The female in the passenger's seat got out and stood by the door until the man driving came around the front of the vehicle. Holding hands, the walked very tentatively to the base of the steps, with the female saying, "Excuse me sir, we're looking for Miss Cronin?"

Bluntly the old man asked, "Why do you want to see her?" He heard dogs yapping in the motor home, and was starting to wonder what the hell was going on.

"Sir, we heard through the LEO grapevine that… Well, her dog was killed by… Well, the people that attacked her. We raise dogs over in New Mexico primarily for law enforcement and guard service…"

Jesse interrupted from the door. *"Papa, stop that*! Miss Dreeson?"

The woman looked up. "Yes, I'm Amber Dreeson and this is my husband, Mike."

Jesse stumped out on the porch. "Just ignore the grumpy old man here and please come in. I'm sorry for the reception you've received."

Bewildered, the old man stepped to the side as the couple sidled up the steps, staying well clear of him. Jesse hissed, "I *told* you they were coming today, I talked to her and gave her directions. You be nice, dammit."

The old man followed the rest of them back into the living room and flopped down in his chair, wincing as the 1911 poked him in the ribs. Leaning forward he rubbed his ribs and said, "Okay, I'm sorry, but I'm a bit touchy about who comes to the ranch right now."

Mrs. Dreeson replied, "That's understandable…"

"Now, how did you hear about the shooting?" he interrupted.

"Well, we do K-nines for a number of law enforcement organizations in Texas, New Mexico and other places, and the word filtered out there had been an attack on your ranch, and your dog was killed trying to protect Jesse and the lady that died. We also heard the threat wasn't over, and we decided to donate a protection dog to her while she recovers and going forward."

Jesse burst into tears, and collapsed in Aaron's arms hearing this, much to the Dreeson's consternation. Finally, the old man said, "She's still having some problems with mood swings, and she doesn't remember a damn thing about what actually happened here that day. In addition to Rex being murdered, my ranch hand Toby was also murdered by the killers, and the only reason I wasn't here was I was in Bangkok testifying in a trial over there. I do appreciate what you're doing, and I can't thank you enough, but how were you going to select a dog for her?"

Dreeson replied, "We can bring the dogs in, if that is alright with you, or she can go out to the motor home and look at them there."

Jesse got up and stumped over giving both Dreesons a hug and kiss. "Oh, thank you, I really don't know what to say. Can you bring the dogs in here? I'm not getting around real good yet."

As Mike Dreeson left to bring in the dogs after a potty break; Felix's wife Olivia, came into the living room. "If anyone would like a sandwich, I can make them and bring them out to you. I'm sorry I'm late getting back Jesse."

"Oh, Olivia, I just appreciate the help, you know Papa can't cook worth a damn, neither can Aaron, and I'm afraid I'd fry or burn myself right now. If you'll leave the stuff on the island, we can get it ourselves, thank you," Jesse said.

Minutes later, Dreeson opened the front door cautiously. "Are you sure you want all these dogs in at once?"

The old man shrugged. "Why not? If we can't see them together, how will we know how well they interact, much less how can Jesse get a sense of the different personalities?"

Dreeson opened the door and said, "In," and nine Belgian Malinois of various ages came through the door in a scramble.

"We brought the ones we think would be most compatible, all of these dogs are direct Belgian bloodlines and range in age from about eighteen weeks to right around six months of age. These were all specifically picked from indicators they will have or are developing strong protection drives. Now saying that, these are family-oriented dogs, rather than individual oriented in most cases. They're socialized, and pretty good with kids," Amber said, and proceeded to give each of the dogs to Jesse by name.

Jesse oh'd and ah'd over the pups and tried to play with each a little bit and get a feel for how they acted. The old man, tired of watching, went into the kitchen with Mike Dreeson, "Sandwich?" He asked, pointing to the spread Olivia had put out. "It ain't much, but it'll fill a hole." Aaron walked in and the old man added, "And you better get what you want ahead of the Marine, this whole thing is just an appetizer for him."

Aaron hung his head. "Mr. Cronin, you know that isn't fair…"

The old man laughed. "Aaron, you know life ain't fair, but leave a bit for Mrs. Dreeson and your wife, that is, if you know what's good for you." Handing a plate to Mike, he motioned for him to go ahead.

As Dreeson built his sandwich he said, "We only brought nine dogs, figuring these were the best choices; if none of these workout, I can probably bring some more next weekend."

Aaron replied, "Well, we're leaving for California tomorrow, so I guess it's today or not at all. I can't tell you how much *I* appreciate this. Being an active duty Marine, I spend a lot of time on the road, and this will definite ease my mind when I'm not home. One question, we'll be living with a friend in an apartment, how big an issue is that, and what about the dog's reactions to visitors?"

Dreeson set his plate down. "Good question. The dog *should* adapt your friend as part of the family unit, and others that visit on a regular basis. They do like to run and play, and most of them have either a tug or ball… Almost *fetish* is the best word I can think of. What they won't tolerate is any kind of violence or perceived threat to their family unit. So you might warn your friends against horsing around."

Aaron nodded. "Good point, and I can do that. I run pretty much every morning, usually three to five miles, is that good for the dogs?"

"As long as when you leave the dog gets at least some exercise. If nothing else one of those ball throwers, and a football, soccer or baseball field would work fine."

The old man left them talking and wandered back into the living room, easing down in his chair, he was surprised to hear Jesse say, "Papa, you're being followed." The old man looked down, seeing a four or five month old pup sitting patiently at his feet. Jesse continued, "He followed you out to the kitchen, and followed you back."

"Nah, he just wants food." Leaning over, he looked at the pup and said, "No, people food," and watched the pup drop down on his belly.

Picking up his sandwich, he bit into it contentedly as he continued to watch Jesse play with several of the puppies. As she went to pick up one young female, it had an accident and dribbled on the floor, much to Amber's horror. Aaron jumped up and grabbed some paper towels from the kitchen as the Dreeson's tried to apologize, and Jesse laughingly put the puppy back down, saying, "Oh Boo-Boo… You had a boo-boo didn't you." The pup cocked her head and looked up at Jesse, then walked over to Jesse's good leg and put a paw on her knee. While the old man was watching that and chuckling, the pup at his feet had quietly gotten up and was nibbling on the sandwich now held limply in the old man's hand.

Amber Dreeson looked over, gasped, and said forcefully, "*No!*" The pup looked over at her, sat down and licked his chops as Aaron and Jesse burst out laughing. Amber quickly picked up the puppy and moved him away from the old man, apologizing all the while and offered to make him a new sandwich.

Jesse, the female puppy now firmly ensconced on her lap, finally gasped out, "Oh Papa, I've got Boo-Boo and you've got Yogi!"

The old man growled, "I don't *need* a dog, don't have time to take care of one."

Aaron looked mystified, "Boo-Boo? Yogi?"

Jesse sighed, petting the pup, "Yogi and Boo-Boo were cartoon bears in Jellystone Park. They were always looking for a pic-i-nik basket. I grew up watching them on Saturday morning cartoons. Didn't you ever watch cartoons?"

Aaron shook his head. "Very seldom. TV wasn't high on my parent's list."

Amber brought the old man another sandwich and handed the plate to him, apologizing again. He waved the apology off, and set the plate in his lap, only to look down and see the same puppy sitting at his feet, looking up at him with an ear cocked. Jesse laughed. "Papa, Yogi is after that pic-i-nik basket..." Prompting another gasp from Amber and a dash for the pup by Mike Dreeson. He picked up the pup, who looked dolefully back at the old man as he was hauled off.

Jesse, Aaron, Mike and Amber continued discussing the various puppies as the old man finished his sandwich, and he picked up the other's plates, carried them back into the kitchen and washed the plates and silverware. He started to turn and stopped, looking down he saw the same puppy sitting patiently by his leg. He said, "No," cleaned up the rest of the sandwich materials and wandered down to the office.

Hanging up his gunbelt, he sat down at the computer and starting working on the ranch and royalty books; occasionally checking his email and listening to the county radio chatter. Leaning back and not even thinking he dropped his hand over the side of the chair to where Rex used to lay, and recoiled when he felt a dog there.

Surprised, he looked over the side of the chair, and there was that damn pup again. Laying there just like Rex did, which damn near brought a tear to the old man's eyes. He reached down almost unwillingly and stroked the pup's head and ruffled the scruff of his neck, thinking of all the times he'd done that with Rex.

He decided he'd done enough book work and turned the monitor off, got up and wandered back into the living room. The four were still deep in discussion of the various puppies, and he just continued on out the front door finally sitting down in the rocker and just looking out over the pasture. He finally realized he was hearing scratching, and looked over at the screen door, there sat the same puppy, scratching at the door, and when he saw the old man look, the puppy whined softly.

Cussing himself, the old man got up and opened the screen door, and the pup followed him back and sat down by the arm of the rocker. He sat back down, and the pup just looked up at him with an ear cocked, then turned and looked out across the pasture just like the old man had done.

The old man petted him a couple of times, then just sat and relaxed. Finally, he heard Jesse say loudly, "Aaron, check the porch, Papa probably went out there, and maybe Yogi followed him." Getting up, he headed back in the house, looking down he saw the dog following him without any command.

He walked back into the living room and Amber rushed to take the puppy, but he told her, "Nah, he's alright," looking over at Jesse he asked, "Well, did you make a decision?"

Jesse held up the puppy on her lap. "Yep, Boo-Boo is the puppy of choice. I like her, and she likes me and Aaron both. Did *you* make a decision Papa?"

"I dunno. Seems like I can't get rid of this one."

The Dreesons looked at each other with a panicked expression and Mike said, "Uh, we were only going to give…"

The old man interrupted, "No, I'll pay for the pup, if I decide… Still thinking on it."

Amber said, "But Mr. Cronin, our dogs…"

"Probably aren't cheap, right?" The old man finished.

"No sir, they aren't. They are all from very good blood lines, and you won't…"

The old man stopped her and said, "Yogi, heel." The pup immediately came over and stood at his left leg, looking up expectantly. "I'm guessing this one isn't one of your prize dogs, right? A little problem with finding the right owner maybe?"

Mike replied, "It appears he's found one now."

The old man motioned to Mike, "Come on, I'll write you a check," and started for the office, with Yogi at heel. Jesse, Aaron and Amber just looked on in amazement.

Any Units

The old man eased north on Highway 18, looking forward to a quiet evening with Jesse and Aaron before they left in the morning. Suddenly, his reverie was interrupted by a broadcast on common, "Any units, any units, officer needs assistance; I-ten east, mile marker two-two-six. Shots fired, shots fired. White Ford van, Texas plates, at least two Hispanic males, they shot the officer making the stop and are running east."

The old man debated whether or not to respond, since he was *officially* off duty and this was Jesse and Aaron's last night here. But the Pavlovian response to a call for assistance kicked in. Realizing he was passing under I-10, he turned on to ten west and lit up code three. Hopefully it would be a short call, and maybe Jesse was monitoring the radio at the ranch. As he picked up the mic to report in, he heard a choppy voice over the radio, "This is Ranger Boone, I'm trailing the subject vehicle in my helo. They've slowed back down to the speed limit. Recommend setting up a roadblock somewhere west of Fort Stockton with available units. These guys need to be stopped before they get into a metro area."

The old man keyed up, "County car four, ten west at two-five-six, code three."

The sheriff came on, "County car one, ten west at two-four-eight."

A couple of troopers and various other sheriff's department vehicles chimed in with locations and the sheriff finally said, "All units, we'll set a road block at two-four-five. Ranger, can you tell how much clear space they have in front of them?"

Moments later, Clay answered, "Looks like about two miles clear in front of them and they're maintaining speed of about seventy-five. If you're going for a block, I'd shut down westbound as soon as possible."

The sheriff keyed the radio, "Car two-one-five, as soon as you get to two-four-six, get a block going. Car four, meet me in the median two-four-five. Troopers, respond to two-four-five also please. Cars two-oh-four and two-oh-six, get off on the access roads at two-four-six, block and standby."

Five minutes later, the old man pulled off in the median at mile marker two-four-five, meeting the sheriff and trooper sergeant. As he clicked on the external speaker, he heard Clay report the suspect vehicle was at mile marker two-three-six. The sheriff looked quickly around, "Okay, here's the plan. As soon as the cars in front of the suspects go by, we pull out and completely block the road. Let's see if they will try to shoot their way through us, or turn around and run the other way. Sarge, you've got guys coming in behind them, right?"

The sergeant replied, "Yeah, I've got two cars coming hard. Maybe slow them down and have them ready if the suspects decide to jump the median and head west?"

"Sounds like a plan. Reeves County has four cars coming also, and two at the original scene with the wounded trooper; they're sneaking through traffic behind the suspects, backing cars off," the sheriff said. Two more cars slid in. One was Deputy Hart, the other a trooper car with two officers. Looking at the old man the sheriff said, "John, I need you to be the shooter, we'll leave your car where it is, and you can go over my hood if you need to."

"Roger, be right back," the old man replied, heading to the trunk of his car. Removing the MRAD from its hard case, he loaded two magazines with ammo, pulled out the laser range finder, and walked calmly back to the front of his car stuffing earplugs into his ears. Holding the rifle against his hip, he just stood waiting as Clay came over the radio, "I can see y'all, maybe thirty seconds until the two ahead of the suspects are past y'all. You better get ready."

All the officers jumped back into their respective cars except the old man and one trooper who came over carrying an M-16. He remarked, "Just like the old days, I got a damn poodle shooter and nothing to do unless it gets up close and personal. What caliber is that monster?"

The old man chuckled. "Three-three-eight Lapua. I don't plan on it getting up close and personal if I can help it!"

Two cars zipped by and the sheriff and others pulled onto the interstate, blocking it shoulder to shoulder. The old man quickly set up across the hood of the sheriff's car, and took a sight picture just as Clay reported, "Looks like the suspects have stopped. I see one out with some kind of long rifle in his hand, looking at y'all. I'm guessing they're about a half mile from you, maybe a little less."

The trooper with the M-16 pointed to the laser range finder and asked, "Need a range?"

The old man glanced over. "Sure, appreciate that. And make damn sure you're not to the side of this sucker if I have to shoot. And I hope you've got ears!"

The trooper dug into his pocket and shoved a pair of foam earplugs in quickly, then laid out to get a good range. "Twelve-seventy-six it looks like."

The old man dialed 1276 into the BORS[30] on top of the MRADs scope and settled in again, mumbling quietly under his breath as he did so. Clay came over the radio again, "Looks like they're gonna run somewhere. Can anybody disable them?"

The sheriff ran over. "John, can you take out the engine?"

The old man shifted aim slightly. "Just tell me when."

The sheriff and trooper sergeant held a hurried conversation, then the sheriff came back saying formally, "You are authorized to disable their vehicle. You may fire when ready."

The old man immediately said, "Target."
BOOM!

---

[30] Barrett Optical Ranging System

He rode the scope as everyone around him cussed, and saw pieces of the grill and apparently the radiator fly off as the one suspect outside the vehicle jumped. He was able to see what looked like liquid dripping from under the hood, and said, "Good hit, at least radiator and unless I miss my guess, dead center of the engine block behind it."

Clay suddenly yelled into the radio. "Shots fired, shots fired! They're shooting at y'all!"

Everyone except the old man ducked. He just shifted aim slightly. "I've got the shooter lined up. Your call, sheriff."

Clay came on the radio again. "More shooters unloading from the rear, now three with weapons sighted. Ah shit, one finally noticed me. I'm gonna move off a ways."

The sheriff and trooper sergeant were in another consultation, and finally the sheriff came over. "John, can you just take the one shooting out?"

"Yeah, he's *hiding* behind the passenger's door, and it's clear behind him. I'll be shooting out into the waste area and Riley road is probably another mile beyond that. Have Clay check me clear on Riley and the service road if you would."

Bullets continued to occasionally ping down around the vehicles or skip off the road with little to no accuracy, so the old man waited patiently, finally the sheriff said, "You're clear, shoot when ready."

"Target."

BOOM!

He rode the scope as everyone cussed again, and saw pieces of the window glass erupt from the door as the shooter crumpled to the ground, his rifle flying off to the left side of the truck saying, "Good hit, one down, no movement."

Clay came over the radio saying, "Looks like that got their attention, people are throwing guns down and holding their hands up, and the driver is climbing out of the van, looks like he's wounded."

The sheriff sent Deputy Hart and the one of the troopers down to handle the situation, as the other trooper turned to the old man. "That was some pretty damn good shooting for bit over a half mile! What is that on top of the scope, and what were you mumbling, I couldn't hear you with the foamies in."

The old man stayed on the scope till the two cars arrived, then lifted the rifle, popped the magazine out and cleared it, then sat it on the top of the sheriff's car pointed off to the south. "It's called a BORS, it's a mini-calculator you pre-program with the ballistics of the round, and when you plug in the distance, it automatically computes the correct drop and other environmental stuff. Probably what I was mumbling was drop calculations, I still do that in case things go south."

"How far did that bullet drop?" The trooper asked. "I don't think the M-16 could have even gotten on that far unless it was bouncing down the concrete."

The old man looked up, noting the reddish tint to the clouds as the sun continued setting in the west. "About five hundred eighteen inches, give or take a couple. Bit of wind, kinda quartering right to left, so I was holding on the driver's side mirror for the first shot, and the center of the windshield for the second shot…"

Deputy Hart came over the radio, "Scene is secure; one signal seven, three in custody. One with injuries; request ambulance at this time. Oh yeah, and a big load of drugs in the back of the van."

Clay landed his helicopter behind the van and climbed out as the old man and the sheriff rolled up. Clay walked up to the back of the van and whistled. "Yeah, that's a shit ton of dope, probably cocaine, and I'm betting it's uncut too!" He came over to the body where the sheriff and the old man were standing.

The trooper sergeant walked over. "Center mass on both the engine and the shooter. Helluva nice job there, captain. You probably saved some lives today."

The old man nodded. "Yeah, maybe, but I hate like hell that I had to shoot that guy. It's another one that will haunt me." He paused a moment, pointing to the western sky. "But it's a good day for us *not* to die. How do you want to handle the reporting?"

"Well, it was initially our scene at two-two-nine, so we're just going to call this a continuation, unless you have a problem with it?"

"Nope, just tell me what you need, and I'll get it done. I would like to get out of here as soon as I can, my granddaughter and her new hubby are at the ranch and leaving tomorrow for California, so I would like to spend a bit of time with them. You want the rifle for ballistics checks?" The old man asked.

"Nah, if we could have a sample round…"

The old man handed the sergeant one out of his shirt pocket and asked, "When do you need the full report?"

"I'll take a quick and dirty tonight, and a full report in the next couple of days," the sergeant replied.

The old man went back to his car, pulled his clipboard and a blank report form out and sat in the driver's seat filling it out in detail, as the other two troopers pulled random packages of drugs and tested them, coming up with bright blue on every package. The trooper who had not been spotting said, "That old man is just plain cold, or crazy. I just don't know which one. Sumbitch never even flinched when that thug started firing, and he took him out like it was nothing more than target practice on a range. And making those shots at that range? How the fuck do you do that? It's like he's not human."

The second trooper turned to him, "You weren't ever in the military were you?"

"No, why?"

The second trooper said, "That old man has probably been in more shit than I ever saw in Iraq and Afghanistan, and he's just like most snipers I worked with in the Army. They don't think or act like us. They're on a different plane of existence. Most of 'em are old country boy hunters and fishermen, and they grew up outside. Nothing really gets them upset; hell, most of 'em have fantastic vision too, you see that old man isn't wearing glasses, either to drive or fill out paperwork? I'm betting he's still got twenty-twenty or better. And those shots? Right around thirteen hundred yards. You're not going to do that without being steady as hell, which means controlling heart rate, breathing, and a hundred other little things. Like reading the wind, he said he was holding on the center of the windshield to take that shooter down. That's damn near six feet from where the bullet hit. But it was a one shot kill to the chest."

"But he didn't react to killing that guy, even after it was over, he never reacted," the first trooper said.

"Nope, not that we'll ever see. But I'm betting he'll deal with it later and in his own private way. I'm just thankful he's on *our* side. Let's wrap this up, looks like about a hundred keys of pure coke based on our testing," the second trooper said. When they walked around from the back of the van, they noted the old man was already gone.

A half hour later, the old man pulled into the ranch yard, listening to the yelps of the puppies coming from the front door. Shaking his head, he wondered what ever prompted him to get another damn dog, especially right now.

One More Dinner

As soon as the old man hit the door, Yogi and Boo-Boo greeted him, with Boo-Boo wandering off to find Jesse. He hung his hat on the rack, dumped his gunbelt on the desk, rolled his shoulders and tried to shake some of the tension from the last couple of hours without success.

He walked into the kitchen to find Jesse and Aaron playing cards, and Jesse asked, "Bad one? We couldn't tell much from the radio traffic."

The old man continued on to the coffee pot, poured a cup and finally sat down. "Had to put one down. Stupid, *really* stupid, trying to shoot us from a half mile with a damn AK. And the dumbass wouldn't stop…" Yogi slipped his head onto the old man's leg, and he unconsciously started petting him, just as he'd done many times with Rex.

Aaron goggled. "A half a frikkin *mile*? Damn even the idiots downrange know better!"

In the interest of keeping Jesse up to speed as he'd vowed to do, he laid out the entire event as it went down, prompting a number of head shakes in disbelief, and concern about the ramping up of the violence that the cartels were willing to participate in. Finally the old man wound down, and neither Jesse nor Aaron could think of any more questions.

Jesse finally said, "Well, you feel like dinner? It wasn't going to be a big one anyway."

The old man nodded. "Yeah, are the potatoes totally dead, or did you salvage them? And is the grill started?"

"Potatoes are saved. I did a quick salad, all we need is the steak and I can heat the French bread up by the time the steaks are done."

The old man heaved himself up with a groan. "Okay, I'll get on them. Medium, medium and damn near raw, right?" He noticed the two T-bones and a fillet setting awfully close to the edge of the counter and added, "Not tempting fate or anything were you?"

Jesse grinned, holding up a yellow plastic pistol. "Nope, water pistols! Yogi or Boo-Boo got close or inquisitive, they got told 'no.' If they left it, they got a treat; if not, they got wet!"

Aaron just looked at Jesse and shook his head mumbling something about kids and new toys and followed the old man out to the grill. With Aaron's help, the steaks were seasoned and soon on the grill. "Are you ready to go? And is Jesse still trying to convince you to let her ride with you?"

"No, sir, I think I finally beat that one down last night, and she's going to take the pup too. It'll be a lot easier for her and for me. She'll be there and able to rest long before I get home. And the nice thing is I won't be having to stop every hour to let the pup out to pee. I'm scared as hell he'd haul ass on me, and if that happened I might as well *not* show up."

The old man laughed. "Yeah, never get between a woman and her kids *or* her damn pets. I figure we'll have breakfast at the normal time, get you on the road, and I'll take her to meet Billy at eleven at the airport. Billy can drop her at Carlsbad before he goes up to LA for whatever meeting he's got up there." Testing the steaks, he quickly flipped Aaron's over. "You know it's gonna be damn strange to be in this house alone. I don't think I ever remember a time when it was totally empty."

Aaron said, "I can't imagine *not* being alone. This whole marriage thing is totally strange to me, and I'm afraid my folks weren't real good role models on that. At least with Matt and... Ah hell with Matt and Felicia there most of the time too, at least I can watch them for clues. I really don't want to fuck this up," he said almost to himself.

The old man flipped the other two steaks, and took a quick peek at Aaron's. "Close. You want to grab me a clean plate and let Jesse know five minutes?"

"Will do, sir," Aaron said and trotted back into the house.

The old man looked around as the sun set slowly, checking that the sodium lights came on everywhere, and he absorbed the history of the ranch for a couple of minutes. Aaron's return with a clean plate caused him to start, and he quickly dished up the steaks, ran a brush over the grill and turned it off, "Okay, let's eat!"

He and Aaron went back into the house, and the old man dished the steaks out as Aaron grabbed the baked potatoes out of the oven along with the French bread. The old man dumped the plate in the sink and carried the salad bowl to the table, then banished the puppies into the hall behind a puppy gate. He finally sat down and looked at Aaron. "You want to say a prayer?"

"I'll try," Aaron said and reached for Jesse's hand, then stumbled through a short prayer. After passing the salad around, and the bread, butter, and salt and pepper everybody dug in. The old man remembered Jesse sitting in a booster chair at the same table, and thought to himself, *Yep, little Jesse isn't little anymore. She's all grown up and married, and the last of our line. Damn, that means the Cronin name ends with me. Over a hundred years, and I'm it. Okay, stop being maudlin you stupid old bastard, you should be happy. Now shut up and eat!*

After dinner, the old man and Aaron picked up the dishes, put them in the dishwasher, and the old man brought out an apple pie. "Anybody got room for pie and ice cream?"

Jesse groaned. "Oh, *now* you tell me! Damn you, Papa, you're going to force me to eat Blue Bell aren't you? And you know damn well I can't get it in California! No fair!"

Chuckling, the old man said, "So, you don't want any? Aaron?"

Aaron laughed. "Yes, sir, I'll take some."

The old man dished up three bowls of pie and ice cream, and set them on the table as he started another pot of coffee.

Jesse and Aaron ate with the vigor of the young and mostly healthy, while the old man enjoyed what he was now coming to consider a treat. Aaron picked up the bowls, dealt out the coffee cups and put dog food down for the pups before he took down the baby gate. Boo-Boo charged toward the food, but Yogi came over and laid his head on the old man's thigh, looking up at him.

The old man petted him for a minute then said, "Go eat, boy." Yogi went over to his bowl and started eating, growling occasionally when Boo-Boo tried to eat some food out of his bowl. Finally the old man said, "Well, tomorrow the adventure starts. I figure we'll do breakfast at the normal time, Aaron can get on the road, and I'll take you in about ten to meet Billy at the airport. You got your bags packed?"

Jesse and Aaron both nodded, and Jesse said, "Papa, I feel bad going off and leaving you alone here. And I really want to ride with Aaron."

"Hon, we've talked about this, no you're not well enough to spend all day in that truck, and getting you out of here is the best thing that can happen. We still don't know enough about what is going on south of the border to say whether or not somebody is going to make another try at me, you, us. I've got Yogi to keep me company," he said, prompting Yogi to come over and slobber all over the old man's jeans. "And he'll do a good job. I've plenty of work to keep me busy, Felix and Ricky are working things out well and I don't see any problems."

Jesse played with her coffee cup. "I know, Papa, but still…"

"No, I feel a helluva lot better with you out of here, at least for a while. You're too easy a target; having to go to rehab every day, the lack of mobility, you're still having some balance issues, and…"

"But I'm getting better, Papa," Jesse said. "I am, right, Aaron?"

Aaron looked uncomfortable as he replied, "Yes, dear, you *are* getting better, but you've got a long way to go yet. Once we get to Pendleton, get you official on base, and get you into the system; we'll get you into the PT program at the hospital. They won't be as nice as Tina has been to you though."

Jesse punched Aaron on the arm. *"Nice? Nice! You're calling her nice? I cannot believe you said that! I think she's a closet, hell out of the closet sadist! You… You're going to pay for that later!"*

Aaron rolled his eyes, and the old man burst out laughing. "Jesse, he's right. You haven't been paying attention. Tina treats you with kid gloves 'cause Doc Truesdale is constantly over her shoulder. You're gonna find out military PT or rehab or whatever they call it today isn't nearly as nice."

"You're looking at another three months in the cast minimum, and you're going to put on weight regardless of how hard you fight it, hon," Aaron said. "I put on almost twenty pounds when I was down, and it's taken me almost a year to get all that off. And that was running and *heavy* workouts. But the all-time worst thing was the damn itching."

"Crap, you just *had* to say that didn't you? I've been sitting her trying to ignore the urge, but, dammit, now I've got to scratch," Jesse said as she reached over for the flexible nylon rod on the table. "And I don't even want to think about how hairy my leg is going to be. I'm gonna look like a damn wookie on one side. Ahhhh."

Pulling the rod out, she held it down threateningly. "I'm gonna use this on you, you mention..." Boo-Boo grabbed the end of the rod, growling enthusiastically and trying to take it away from Jesse. "Boo-Boo, *stop that*, no toy, momma needs." Boo-Boo let go, looking up at Jesse with a quizzical expression like *why did you tease me if I wasn't supposed to chase the stick?*

The old man said, "Gotta remember, they've got *strong* ball or fetch drives, and sticks are fetch toys to them. That thing is just like a red flag to a bull."

Putting the stick down Jesse pouted. "Oh *fine*, not only spoil my fun, but remind me of my responsibility too. Nice twofer there, Papa."

The old man laughed. "Sorry, now you kids need to get to bed, Aaron's got a long day tomorrow, and you're both going to be tired puppies by the time you get to Pendleton tomorrow night. Go, scoot," he said, making a shooing motion with his hands. "I'll clean up in here, and I'm not far behind you."

The old man puttered around in the kitchen for a while, set up the coffee pot and started the dishwasher before going into the office. Bringing up the computer, he quickly typed up a statement from the shooting today, including everything he remembered both of the lead up, and the actual actions of the various officers and the cartel types.

He knew he'd already done a statement for the troopers, but this one was for his own records, and in case there were any questions later. Finally finishing it to his satisfaction, he emailed it to himself at the office and leaned back. Yogi stuck his nose against the old man's wrist, and the old man sat petting Yogi for a few minutes before he sighed and said, "I gotta go, so that probably means *you* gotta go too Yogi, come on."

Walking to the front door he opened it and let Yogi out following him to the edge of the porch and saying, "Okay, go pee dog." Yogi whuffed and jumped off the porch, then started looking for *that* spot as all dogs do. The advantage the old man noted was that Yogi had also gotten within range of both automatic lights on the front of the house, and they both came on. That was a good thing. After a couple of minutes, he called Yogi in, because he *did* need to go, and even if he was out in the country, he wouldn't take a piss off his own front porch.

After a quick shower, the old man called it a night after convincing Yogi that he had a bed and the old man had a bed, and they weren't the same bed.

Epilog

The old man rolled out at 5 AM as usual, let Yogi out, and met a grumbling Aaron carrying a squirming Boo-Boo as he headed to the kitchen to start the coffee. As the coffee finished, Aaron came back in with both dogs, and Yogi came over and looked pointedly at his dog bowl. The old man rummaged around and found both dog's food and gave them each a cup full. Boo-Boo dived in with puppy abandon, but Yogi waited until the old man told him to eat.

Handing Aaron a cup of coffee the old man asked, "What do you want for breakfast?"

Aaron shrugged. "I'm happy with anything I don't have to chase too far, and that doesn't come from the chow hall."

The old man said, "Okay bacon, eggs, and toast it is. Jesse up yet?"

"Yep, she made *me* take the dog out so she could get the first call on the bathroom."

Laughing, the old man said, "Get used to it. *Her* dog but everybody and their brother gets to take care of it. Scrambled?" The old man asked, laying bacon in the bottom of the pan. Aaron nodded as he picked up a second cup of coffee and headed to Jesse's room.

The old man had the bacon done, and was waiting to start the eggs when Jesse finally came out. She sat down at the table and said, "I'm sorry I can't help, Papa. And I'm getting *fat*... And I can't fit in anything for clothes with this damn cast." Boo-Boo came over a pawed at Jesse and she picked her up, settling Boo-Boo in her lap. "At least the dog likes me."

"What's with the pity party this morning?" The old man asked as he dumped the eggs into the cast iron pan and punched the toaster down.

Jesse played with her coffee cup. "I guess I'm scared, Papa, scared of married life, scared I'm not going to heal right, and scared I've got another damn three months in this double damned cast."

The old man cocked his head. "And?"

Jesse sighed. "And I had another damn nightmare last night, about the Alton shooting of all things. And then I couldn't get back to sleep, and Aaron woke up."

"Jesse look at me," the old man said. "You're not going crazy, and those nightmares are going to come back time to time. It's alright to be a little scared. Hell, I was scared shitless when I married your grandmother. You're going to have to adapt, and a large part of that is going to be your physical recovery. Ask Aaron, he'll tell you it's not easy even for a big bad Marine."

Aaron walked in to hear the tail end and asked, "What's not easy for a big bad Marine?" He kissed the top of Jesse's head, and went to help with getting the dishes out, coming back with his hands full.

The old man said, "Recovery, especially from serious injuries. I spent four months flat on my back in a damn military hospital once, and thought I'd never come back from that."

Aaron picked up the coffee pot and refilled cups as he answered, "Yeah, I was only down for a month and I was going nuts within a week."

Jesse threw up her hands. "Okay, so I'm a wimp, I'm sorry…"

Both of them laughed and the old man said, "Nope, you're not a wimp, whiney maybe this morning, but not a wimp."

The old man dished up the eggs as Aaron brought the plate of bacon and toast over, and Jesse put Boo-Boo down, saying, "Go bite 'em on the ankles Boo, bite 'em for me." Boo-Boo just looked up at her, one ear pricked, and trotted over to lay down next to Yogi.

Over breakfast, they discussed the logistics of the day, Aaron's plans and who was going to meet Jesse in Carlsbad. As the sun came up, the old man finished the dishes, stacked them on the rack and walked out onto the front porch with Yogi. He figured Jesse and Aaron deserved a few private minutes and he sat down with his cup of coffee to enjoy the peace and quiet.

In the bedroom, Jesse turned to Aaron. "I'm sorry I'm such a grump this morning, I really want to be going with you," she said, holding up her hand. "I know I can't and I'm not going there. It's just that our lives are now changed, hopefully forever, and you've got to go back to work. I know you've been here for three weeks, and I'm afraid you're in trouble at work."

Aaron shut her up by the simple expedient of kissing her. Finally coming up for air, he said, "No, I'm not in trouble. Everybody was on board with this, and Matt's been keeping me up to speed along with the First. Yeah, things are going to have to change, but we're both adults. It's not like we didn't go into this with our eyes open, and you've got Felicia right there for you."

He picked up his bag and put it on the bed. "Actually, I need to introduce you to the First's wife. She's tied into the wives club stuff, and the morale network for the wives. She'd be the one to really help you through the minefield."

"Minefield?" Jesse asked.

"Well, dealing with the base, and the brass and everything else."

Jesse batted her eyes. "Can't I play the dumb southern girl and get away with it?"

Aaron chuckled. "Not really, since about half the wives are southern and every one of them is sharp as a damn tack…"

Jesse laughed. "Well, I could always dye my hair blonde and claim to be from California."

"Oh, *hell* no. You're not about to do that to me," Aaron replied. "Okay, I think I'm done here. I've got all my stuff and some of yours in these two bags. You've got one bag plus your computer bag, plus your purse, right?"

Jesse said, "Yep, watch, wallet, spectacles and ovaries. Everything accounted for."

Aaron shook his head. "I'm sorry we *ever* told you that one."

Jesse put her arms around Aaron's neck. "I dunno, I'm kinda glad you did, otherwise I'd never have realized you could actually be human, and we wouldn't be here now. I love you Aaron Miller, and I want to be with you now and forever."

Aaron kissed Jesse tenderly, and murmured in her ear, "I love you, Jesse, to have and to hold, for better or worse, and I see a lot of better in our future."

Jesse kissed him again, then finally pushed him away saying, "Whew, if we keep that up, we're going to be figuring a work around for this damn cast, and I'm not up for that right now. Besides Papa is probably doing his hurry up and wait pacing."

Aaron said, "Okay, I'll go hump the bags out to the trucks. Can you make it to the front door?"

"As long as I don't have to run, I'll get there eventually. Oh, and put the little kennel in Papa's truck would you? I'm not going to make Boo-Boo ride with you."

As Aaron shuffled the bags, Jesse took one slow look around her bedroom, resolutely closed the door and stumped down the hall.

She came out on the porch with Aaron's help and sat in a straight back chair next to the old man. Reaching over, she grasped the old man's hand. "Okay, Papa, we're all done with the mushy stuff."

Aaron came back on the porch and crouched next to Jesse's chair. "Okay, I'm packed, your stuff is in the Suburban, and I'm going to hit the road."

Leaning in, he kissed her again, and held her hand as he stood.

The old man got up and stuck out his hand. "Drive safe, and lemme know if you run into any problems. Otherwise I expect an email when you get there. Take care of her, Aaron."

Aaron shook the old man's hand and replied, "Yes, sir, I will on all counts."

Turning he went out to the truck as Jesse reached for the old man's hand again, Aaron turned around the drive out, waved and headed south on Highway 18. The old man looked down to see tears rolling down Jesse's face, but he kept quiet and just held her hand.

An hour later, he loaded Jesse in the back of the Suburban and drove to the sheriff's office, giving Jesse a chance to say goodbye to the folks there, and he and the sheriff got a few quiet minutes to go over the report on the shooting on I-10. After Jesse was helped back into the Suburban and Boo-Boo corralled and put back in the kennel, it was off to the airport.

The old man pulled through the fence just as Billy's jet landed, and by the time the old man had Jesse out of the Suburban and through the little FBO[31]s office and on the ramp, Billy was on the ramp with the co-pilot opening the cargo hold and Billy trotted over to help the old man with the bags. Billy, always the wise ass looked at Jesse and deadpanned, "Dog rides in the cargo hold, right?"

---

[31] Fixed Base Operator

Jesse said, "Oh, *hell* no, Uncle Billy, you can ride back there but Boo-Boo rides up front with me."

Billy laughed. "So two sets of immobile cargo in the cabin," he said, as he gave Jesse a quick hug. "Let's get this show on the road, I'm burning daylight here, and I've got people to see and bourbons to drink."

Jesse turned to the old man and hugged him. "I love you, Papa, and I'm going to miss you."

The old man returned her hug, saying gruffly, "I'll miss you too Hon. Call me when you get there, okay?"

Jesse nodded and the copilot and the old man helped her into the airplane and into a seat. One last hug, and the old man patted her shoulder and walked off the airplane.

He watched the airplane taxi out, then walked back to the Suburban. Climbing in, he ruffled Yogi's scruff as he watched the airplane takeoff and disappear into the western sky. The old man said under his breath, "It's me and you, Yogi, me and you against the world now."

Yogi barked as the old man put the Suburban in gear and drove back toward the ranch.

ABOUT THE AUTHOR

JL Curtis was born in Louisiana in 1951 and was raised in the Ark-La-Tex area. He began his education with guns at age eight with a SAA and a Grandfather that had carried one for 'work'. He began competitive shooting in the 1970s, an interest he still pursues time permitting. He is a retired Naval Flight Officer, having spent 22 years serving his country, an NRA instructor, and currently works as an engineer in the defense industry. He lives in Northern Virginia, this is his second novel.

Other authors you make like are on the facing page...
I highly recommend all of them!

You can either use the QR code, type the URL or search for them on Amazon.com under books or Kindle.

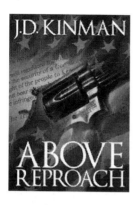

http://www.amazon.com/J.D.-
Kinman/e/B007XI8TMS/ref

http://www.amazon.com/Peter-
Grant/e/B00CS8MHJE/ref

http://www.amazon.com/Larry-Correia/e/B002D68HL8/ref

http://www.amazon.com/Marko-Kloos/e/B00BUVDP8M/ref

72709115R00208

Made in the USA
San Bernardino, CA
28 March 2018